A Warrior's Heart

by

Victoria Oliveri

Dedications

To all my adventurous gaming friends who instilled in me the love of medieval history....

To the SCA and its members who have filled my life with historic wonder, you were the catalyst for this story, no doubt...

To the many Scotsmen I have known and loved through the years, your inherent bravery and lust for life always fills my stories with the hope that there are many more of you out there...

And to the strong, independent women in my life, thank you for being my role models and guides through this illustrious drama we call life...

Chapter One

Roísíndubh Castle, Connacht, Ireland
March 1308

Keir MacLochlainn kept his body shadowed by the deep impression of the high vaulted windows as he glared at his father across the room.

"Why must I continually explain myself tae ye, Keir?" Donel MacLochlainn, his father and current chieftain of his clan, asked as he began pacing around him.

"I dinna see why it must be me tae do this," Keir said, his face hot with anger.

"Because I say it shall be ye tae do it. 'Tis no' as if ye have any pressing duties as it is, so I dinna ken why ye blather on about it."

"Blather on?" Keir faced his father's scrutinizing gaze. "'Tis no' what I want for my life! Why canna ye hear me in this?"

Keir hadn't wanted to come to Ireland, to learn the family business, or to even be a part of this future his father planned for him. And it wasn't like him to be so jaded, but the fact was, this was as good as it was going to get.

1

"'Tis no' what ye want?" Donel boomed, his deep voice resonating off the timber beams above. "'Tis no' yer decision, Keir! 'Tis my decision, as yer faither and yer Laird!"

"Weel, if ye'd act more as my faither and less as my Laird, mayhap I wouldna be so opposed tae the whole affair." Keir waved his arms about him, exasperated. The moment the words came out of his mouth, he knew he would regret them, but somehow, he didn't seem to care.

Donel stomped over to him and caught him up by his leather jerkin, holding him against the cold stone wall.

"Yer selfish, Keir," he said, "selfish and disrespectful and I willna have it. Do ye hear me? Ye do nothing but complain about yer lot in life. Ye should be so lucky tae have such a boon placed upon ye. Do ye ken how many men struggle tae find such an opportunity?"

"Give it tae them then!" Keir shouted and pushed his father away brusquely. "I dinna ask for this. I dinna ask tae be brought here, so dinna expect me tae be overjoyed with yer choices for my life." He stalked away from his father and sat himself at the large, oaken table in the center of the room.

True, his father was chieftain and no one stood against his word or his decisions, but Keir didn't feel he had anything to lose in doing so. Short of getting up and leaving, forcing his father to reject him from his home and his clan, he had little recourse in the situation.

His older brother, Bowdyn, was rightful successor to his father through the choice of his clan, and though Keir was the stronger of the two, he was younger and therefore, their second choice. He was always second choice and he was sick to death of it. For once he wanted to make his own decisions, but his father's enraged obstinacy forced him to accept what was laid out for him, regardless of his wishes. There was no way around this.

"Why do I bother with ye anymore, Keir?" Donel asked, shaking his head with more than a little regret.

"I dinna ken, why do ye?" Keir shrugged. "Why not just let me do what I feel is right? How am I tae make any of my own mistakes if ye make all my decisions for me?"

His father turned an angry face to him, obviously frustrated, when Morgunn Ó Connor, High King of Connacht, entered the chamber. For a moment Keir had forgotten where he was and why he was there.

"Good morrow, Morgunn," Donel offered to the king along with a hearty warrior's handshake, clasping forearms with the man. "You're looking well these days."

"Aye, as good as the years allow, I suppose," Morgunn returned with a smile.

"I'd like tae introduce my son tae ye," Donel said, gesturing to Keir, who nodded and did as he was bid, coming to stand by his father's side. "This is my younger son, Keir. He'll be handling the family business for me."

His father had an altogether too proud look on his face and when he threw his arm around Keir's shoulder, Keir wanted to spit. It was a gesture so hypocritical it made the bile rise in his throat.

"Well met," Morgunn said, shaking Keir's arm as well. "A strapping man as yourself will do well in this business."

Keir grimaced at that thought. He had envisioned so much more for his life.

"So, how is the family?" Morgunn asked as he took a seat at the large table. "How is Bowdyn doing with his new duties?"

"He's doing quite well actually. He has a head for politics it seems, more so than I ever did. I believe he will be a grand chieftain when his time comes." Donel smiled as he took a seat himself.

"And what of you, Keir? Are you looking forward to your duties?" Morgunn asked while handing Donel a bottle of *uisge beatha*.

"I canna say that I am," he said as he sat, noting his father's continued expression of disappointment. "I doubt I will ever see myself become chief, but I had hoped tae be of service in the guard."

"The guard?" Donel chuckled into his mug. "'Tis a service for clansmen and townsfolk, not for the son of the chieftain."

"I see no better way to show respect for the chieftain than to protect him," Morgunn said beneath furrowed brows. "Where is the harm in him doing as much?"

"If he is to handle our trade business, he will have no time to train to prepare himself for service in the guard."

"He looks to be a braw lad," Morgunn said, clasping onto one of Keir's meaty arms. "And being your son, I'm sure he knows his way around a sword. I doubt he would need much training at all."

"The decision has been made. He'll handle the family business and nothing more," Donel said, finishing off his drink.

Morgunn offered an apologetic shrug and Keir could only bow his head. Even a king couldn't change his father's mind. It was useless to try.

"I hear you have some fine cattle for me, Donel," Morgunn said, breaking the awkward silence as he refilled Donel's mug.

"Aye, the finest on the isles." Donel beamed.

Keir nodded his head at the two men and consigned himself to being idle as they spoke. He stood from the table and went to lean against the wall, peering out the window, watching the activity in the courtyard below.

"And what say you, Keir?" Morgunn asked. "Are these cattle the finest on the isles?"

Keir turned his attention to the brawny, gray haired king.

"Aye, my lord, fine enough," Keir said, noting his father's disdain at his insipid tone. "They graze upon the lush lowland greens daily and we feed them only the best grains. The beef they offer is the best I've tasted, and their hides are top quality and verra strong."

"Twould be a wonderful change from the boney cattle the English have brought us, half of them marked with disease. We can scarce feed those in our village with the meager amount of meat they proffer."

"Our cattle are free from such ailments," Donel said as he sipped his whiskey. "You'll find none finer."

Morgunn smiled and finished off his own drink as Donel pulled paperwork from a leather pouch and set a quill and ink beside it on the table.

Morgunn shuffled through the papers, reading each one thoroughly.

"Keir, will you oversee the signing?" Donel asked.

Keir grumbled under his breath and shoved away from the window, taking a seat next to the king.

"Aye," Morgunn said, clapping Keir on the back solidly. "'Tis glad I am that you will carry on with your father's ambitious venture. 'Tis a noble station for you to hold."

"Aye, my lord." Keir said and handed him the quill.

Morgunn placed his grand signature at the bottom of the document and handed the parchment back to Keir, who took up the quill himself and added his own hand to the document. When all was agreed and signed, Morgunn shook his hand and gave him a satisfied nod.

"If you do well in this business you shall truly prosper," Morgunn said with a smile, "And soon enough you will be a wealthy man with a family and keep of your own."

Keir nodded somberly, but the king's words couldn't be farther from the truth, farther from the life he wanted. Grievances aside, he put on a pleasing face and thanked the man in kind.

As the two older men chatted about what other ventures Keir might busy himself with, the king's porter entered the room and bent to Morgunn's ear, mumbling words in low tones. Morgunn's face went suddenly red, his brows furrowing angrily.

"What do ye mean, he's here?" Morgunn's voice boomed.

The porter shrugged and gave an expectant look.

"He's at the gates, my lord. He's demanding to be let in." He wrung his hands anxiously waiting for a reply.

The king stood abruptly, began pacing, and then stopped and glanced toward his steward, who had come to the door. He then turned back toward Keir and his father and offered an apologetic shake of his head.

"Should the guard let him in, my lord?" the porter asked, exchanging glances between the king and his steward.

Morgunn nodded his head, took his own mug of whiskey in hand and sat himself in the large carved chair that stood against the far wall near the hearth.

"Let him in and show him to the hall, but delay him," Morgunn answered finally.

"Delay him, My lord?" The porter furrowed his eyebrows with confusion.

"Delay him! Keep him busy. Entertain him. I shall be down shortly to deal with him."

"Aye, my lord," he said with a nod and hurriedly departed with the steward in tow.

Hunched over in his chair, Morgunn methodically rubbed his temples in his hands, grumbling curses under his breath.

"What's this about?" Donel asked, going to Morgunn's side.

"Yet another of King Edward's ploys, nothing more."

"I dinna understand, what's the problem? Is there something I can do tae help ye in any way?" Donel asked more urgently.

The king leaned back, straightened his shoulders and took a deep breath, grimacing as Donel moved to sit in the chair next to him.

"A few years back he asked me to sign a contract to betroth my daughter to his cousin, to ensure peace in the west."

"And this man at your gates, he is the man betrothed to your daughter?" Keir asked, coming to his feet, facing them both.

"No." Morgunn shook his head. "No one is betrothed to my daughter. I refused to sign the contract but instead told him I would consider it and let him know my answer at a later date."

"And you never had?" Keir asked, crouching before the king.

"No. I never answered him," Morgunn answered solemnly, "And now he sends this man to take her against my will. I will not have it."

"Nor shall we let him," Donel said, placing a comforting hand to Morgunn's shoulder.

Morgunn gave him a slow nod, then stood and paced the room in thought for a moment. "Donel, may I be so bold as to ask a favor of you?" Morgunn asked as he turned to face him.

Donel offered a reassuring smile and stood to meet the king's gaze.

"Aye, ye may, and I will do all in my power tae help ye," Donel answered.

"You can take her," Morgunn offered the large clan chief, who immediately gained a rather puzzled expression.

"Take her?"

"Aye, my brother runs an abbey at Elgin, she would be safe there and well hidden," Morgunn said pointedly.

"Elgin?" Donel questioned. "'Tis quite a journey from here, and a dangerous one at that."

"Aye, I know. I will support the journey as well as I can. I can offer horses, supplies, anything you need to get there, coin as well."

"Och, nay coin is needed tae pay us for the deed," Donel said with a grimace, then turned to look back at Keir. "What say you, Keir, are ye up for a trip tae Elgin?"

Keir balked, not sure how to respond.

"We could go as far as Lachlan Keep and from there, ye could gather some men and journey the rest of the way." Donel added.

"Aye," Keir said, nodding agreeably. "I would be willing tae do that."

"Then it is agreed," Morgunn said, clasping hands with the substantial chieftain. "I will have Anwen ready herself at once. Ye must leave immediately, so as to avoid any delays caused by our…unexpected guest."

"Aye, we shall leave presently," Donel nodded and moving to the table, gathered his paperwork, rolling it into a neat bundle. "But we only have a few men with us. Perhaps ye can request a guard tae accompany us."

"No." Morgunn shook his head vehemently. "I don't want to draw any attention to you or my daughter. Having you escorted would only make you more of a target. You can hide her in your wagon until you are out of the village. After that, you will be more than safe to travel."

Donel nodded his approval.

"Keir, go down and see that our horses are readied for departure." Donel said as he handed him the pouch carrying the documents.

"Aye, my steward will meet you there and get the order for supplies. Let him know what you will need of me." Morgunn said as he shook Keir's hand.

"Aye," Keir nodded and tucked the documents into his belt.

"Oh, and Keir," Morgunn added as they moved toward the door, "Anwen knows nothing of this discussion I had with King Edward. I would like to keep it from her until I can work this out. No need to worry the lass over a matter she has no hand in."

Keir nodded his head and gave another disgruntled glance to his father. More secrets, more deception, and yet another poor soul forced into a life they had nothing to do with. He was sickened that he had to have any part in it at all.

"'Twould be a shame tae lose yer daughter tae the enemy. I understand yer plight and I canna say I blame ye for doing what yer are about tae do," Keir offered. "We shall take good care of her, dinna ye worrit yerself overmuch."

Morgunn thanked him heartily with a great hug as they left the room, a vast journey ahead of them all.

"I don't understand why this is necessary," Anwen stated with some annoyance as her maid packed her trunk hurriedly, her father looking on from the doorway of her chambers.

"Because I said it is necessary, now I will hear no more of it, do you understand?" Morgunn said, his pointed tone relaying his meaning quite clearly.

"No," she said, turning toward her father, her hands defiantly upon her hips. "I don't understand. Why must I always be the one punished? I've done nothing wrong. I've obeyed your every command, have I not?"

"Aye, save this one," Morgunn answered beneath a furrowed brow.

"Then why must I leave? And with strangers no less, traveling across a land I know nothing about to spend my life beneath the dark, desolate roof of Uncle Peyton's abbey? What have I done to be afforded such chastisement?" she asked, her usually melodious voice now shrill and demanding.

Morgunn began rubbing his forehead once more as he sat himself upon her bed.

"They are not strangers, Anwen. 'Tis the MacLochlainn and his son, Keir."

"Keir? I know nothing of Keir," she said. "I've had the honor of meeting Bowdyn, though. Where is he?"

"You know right well Bowdyn is the MacLochlainn successor and his duties remain at their keep while his father is here. Besides, you know the MacLochlainn himself, which should be enough."

"Know him? I've met him in passing, twice perhaps. I wouldn't presume I had a relationship with the man," she said, crossing her arms in front of her.

"Why are ye being so defiant in this, Anwen? I said ye must leave and ye must leave!" Morgunn boomed and stood from the bed, making his way back to the door. "I have no time to argue this with you. Be packed and ready to leave at once. And dress in something… more appropriate," he said with a scowl, his eyes making an angry sweep of her, and left the room, slamming her door behind him.

Anwen threw herself onto her bed, her blood boiling as she stared at the canopy above her. She began pummeling the stiff mattress beneath her with balled fists.

"I cannot believe this, Máiréad," she offered to her maid, who continued to pack her trunk. "All I have ever done is obey him, every last command. I don't understand!"

Her maid nodded her head with a shrug and then closed the trunk and locked it tightly.

"Perhaps it is not meant to be understood," she offered.

"Then perhaps my only curse was not being born a son like the rest of them. Perhaps then he would have no need to send me away."

"I doubt that is the reason for his sending you off," Máiréad said.

"What other reason is there?" Anwen seethed, standing from the bed. She paced her room, her thoughts in a quandary over this disruption in her life. Nothing was making sense to her any longer and it angered her that she could not fathom what she had done wrong. It seemed to be an ongoing plight her entire life.

She pulled her tunic over her head and threw it onto the bed. Looking down at the threadbare trews that remained, she could see one reason for her father's heated mood. It had become a habit of hers to dress more like her brothers than as the lady she was. Her father did not look kindly upon the rebellious act, but after some time, he gave up trying to change her.

She removed the well-worn pants then went to her wardrobe and pulled forth one of her remaining cotehardies. It was a simple, linen dress of a faded blue. One that her father didn't particularly like, but she donned it nonetheless.

She sat at her dressing table and took up her comb and began pulling through the mass of knots in her long, unruly hair. Máiréad came up behind her, taking the comb in hand.

"This dress," her maid offered as she plaited Anwen's mass of auburn curls. "It does nothing for ye. Ye should wear the burgundy one. 'Tis more agreeable."

"Agreeable? I'll be nothing but a prisoner in a bleak abbey in a fortnight and 'tis not as if the monks will pay me any heed once I'm there."

Máiréad clicked her tongue sadly as she finished plaiting Anwen's hair. She took up the veil that Anwen handed her and centered it atop her head. Anwen then handed her a simple circlet of bronze. It had no adornments or jewels - it was simply a band of metal with a bit of carving along its circumference.

"Should I pack your other circlet, m'lady?" Máiréad asked.

"You can pack it, though I doubt I will have need of it," she said, adjusting the plain circlet that Máiréad had placed atop her head. "I'd best get myself to the stables. No doubt my father is impatiently waiting for me there."

And with that Anwen plucked her cloak from its resting place on its peg near the door, draped it over her shoulders and set out for the bailey.

Keir followed Galen, the steward, into the stables and began helping the pages already saddling horses and attaching saddlebags to them.

"We'll give you coin for the rest," Galen said quietly. "Morgunn felt it would delay you to have a full wagon in tow. We'll have foodstuffs packed for you, but you can use the coin for other goods you may need while on your travels. He's added extra for your toll to cross the North Channel." He handed Keir a small pouch, heavy with coin.

"Well," Keir said as he secured the pouch to his belt, being sure to tie it tightly. "How much could such a young lass have to bring with her?"

"You know women," Galen chuckled under his breath then turned toward the door. "Ah, there she is," he announced.

Keir turned with a start. He had no idea the lass they were to transport was no little girl, but the delicate woman that stood before him.

"Lady Anwen," Galen said, turning to Keir. "This is Keir MacLochlainn. He will be escorting you to Scotland."

Keir nodded in deference to the young woman that was introduced to him. She was a bonny lass with deep green eyes that echoed the lush verdure of her father's lands. The pale blue dress she wore did nothing but diminish the soft skin of her face, but there was a rosy glow in her cheeks that added its own adornment to her otherwise simple attire.

"M'lady," he offered with a low bow. "I will see that your journey is no' an altogether unpleasant one. Scotland is a beautiful land and ye will warm tae her quickly."

"Aye," she offered, a slight frown touching her fragile features.

"Do ye have any baggage for the horses?" he asked her, noting her gaze dropping to the ground to watch her feet kick shyly at the dirt. He felt she was a kindred spirit of sorts, forced into something she didn't agree with. He immediately understood how she was feeling without hearing another word.

15

"Nay," she said quietly. "I have a small trunk with a few of my things, that is all."

"I'll have one of the men bring it down for ye." He offered with a smile.

"If it would not be a bother, I would appreciate that very much," she said, her eyes looking up, following his every movement.

Keir smiled at her warmly. The lass would be a welcomed addition to their trip, to say the least. He watched as she went to one of the horses and ran her hand over its mane softly. The horse responded in kind, whinnying happily and shaking its head as if to laugh.

"This one is Barclay," she cooed to the horse and then turned to Keir. "He was my brother's. I helped to foal him six years past."

"Aye," he said with a smile, moving to stand beside her. He caught her scent on the air, that of honeysuckle and sweet pea, nearly intoxicating in its simplicity. "Ye did a fine job of it. 'Tis a bonny horse if ever I saw one." He put his hand upon the horse's mane as well and it nudged him with its muzzle.

"He likes you." She smiled up at him. "That's good."

"Aye," he said then moved away abruptly, his mind spiraling with the scent of her looming so near. "We should ready ourselves tae depart."

"Aye," she said. "I'll fetch the rest of my things." Then she turned and left the stables quietly, the swirl of her cloak stirring her fragrance as she passed him.

Keir ran a hand through his hair, trying to clear his mind of the odd thoughts that now ran rampant there, but it was no use.

It would be a long journey indeed.

Chapter Two

Cedric Banyon, Duke of Coventry, didn't care for Ireland. It was too damp, too cold and too bleak. How anyone could live in such a god-forsaken place was beyond him. The closest city Ireland had to the likes of London was Dubhlinn, but it was nothing more than a filthy port town. What made his trip even worse was the fact that Roísíndubh Castle lay a vast one hundred miles west of Dubhlinn, and the closest reasonably populated area was another port village called Ballinagall that lay some twenty miles yet farther southwest.

He was stuck there, through no fault of his own, save his duty. If it weren't for the fact that King Edward had a hand in his life at the moment, he would probably be enjoying the company of a handful of ladies at court instead of sitting in a damp hall waiting for a foolish old man that called himself a king to finally present himself.

And what a hall it was. For what was to be a royal keep, this place showed little sign of power or influence. Gone were the finely woven tapestries and gilded paintings that he so admired at Windsor.

Instead, the hall was drab and commonly adorned with simple furniture and a few scattered ceremonial hangings. There was a large throne toward the head of the hall he assumed was for

Morgunn, but all that set it apart from the rest of the furnishings was its rather ornate knotwork carving, and a tattered, green velvet cushion. Not much of a statement, but these were, after all, simple people. How they ever managed to run their country without England's help was anyone's guess.

Cedric wandered the expanse of the hall receiving odd glances from the servants as they went about their duties. He had dressed down a bit for his travels, but even now he felt overdressed in these meager surroundings. His claret surcoat with its gold and cream fleur-de-lis lining was considered outdated at court, but here he looked as though he were the king, and he had no quibble at all in acting as if that were the case.

He removed his fox-trimmed mantle and cloak and draped them over the back of the throne, then draped himself in the chair languidly.

Moments later, the porter returned to the hall with a nervous, but hopeful look on his weathered face. Cedric leaned his chin into his palm and rolled his eyes skyward exasperatedly, then crossed his long legs before him, steepling his fingers in agitated rhythm.

"What is it now? Is Morgunn mysteriously vanished or, let me wager, he's nowhere to be found."

"The king will be down presently," Jamison, the porter, answered unwaveringly.

"Well, if he were to be down presently, he would be here already and I would not be made to wait, would I?" Cedric retorted loudly and with no small amount of conceit.

"Would you like to refresh yourself?" Jamison asked, ignoring his pointed insults. "I assume your journey was a long and dusty one."

"Dusty? How could I be dusty if all you have in this ghastly country is mud? Besides, do I look to be filthy just now? I daresay I am probably the cleanest person in the whole of this keep." Cedric sighed arrogantly, brushing the imagined dirt from his lap.

"Amusing assumption..." Morgunn's voice echoed through the length of the hall as he entered with his trusted steward at his side.

Cedric sat up casually, but made no move to stand or make obeisance. He merely nodded to the king and shifted as if he were going to stand, but without much effort.

"Do not tire yourself, Coventry, you'll need your strength to return to England," Morgunn offered cynically and stood next to him with a self-satisfied grin, crossing his meaty arms over his chest.

"I've only just arrived. I do not intend on leaving anytime soon."

"Ah..." Morgunn nodded and glanced sideways at his steward. "What business do you have with us then?"

"Come, Morgunn. Your doors are not open for the likes of your new son?" Cedric beamed haughtily.

"How dare you address the king so?" Jamison fumed, but Morgunn silenced him with a nonchalant wave. If Coventry wanted to play this game, he was willing to play as well.

"You are not my son, Lord Coventry, and I would watch your step whilst you are on my land. Edward's reach is far, but mine runs much deeper on this soil."

"You threaten me, my lord?" Cedric mocked.

"I warn you, 'tis all. One never knows what will happen during a long journey, especially in the wilds of the west. I would take care."

"Think you the Irish are protected from Edward's grasp? You are much mistaken. He may not live within sight of your keep, but he has eyes everywhere." Cedric folded his arms behind his head and yawned in exaggerated ease. "So, where is this daughter of yours? Off wrestling in the mud or finding mischief no doubt?"

"No doubt," Morgunn grunted, shooting a wry look at his steward. "Anwen is not about at present, I'm afraid."

"Not about? Tell me, where do you suppose she is?"

"I have not seen her," Morgunn offered, glowering down at him.

"Is she here, in this keep?"

"I have not checked for her of late, but I'm sure she is about."

"I doubt that very much. If she were about, you would have brought her with you." Cedric chortled.

"Perhaps as a good and concerned suitor you should go in search of her then," Morgunn said dryly.

"And I would think as a good and concerned father you would have done the same yourself."

"If I had known ahead of time that you were calling upon her, I would have readied her for your visit. As it is, we aren't quite prepared to accept guests, you understand." Morgunn countered, clasping his hands behind his back casually.

"I am no mere guest," Cedric said, his tone touched with anger. "I am to be her husband and should be granted some privilege here, think you not?"

"Aye, I do think not. Edward should have known better than to send you here unannounced," Morgunn ground out, his jaw clenched tightly against the bile that rose at the mention of Edward's name.

"You speak boldly against my king." Cedric said.

"Your king has acted boldly against my kin!" Morgunn shouted as he slammed a fist against the solid arm of the chair.

Cedric jumped at his explosive statement and then, as he sat up a bit more attentively, put a soothing hand on Morgunn's arm.

"I pray, my lord, my intent for your daughter is only for the good of her future and her family as I have no ill-will toward either. I am just a servant to Edward and must do as he bids, you understand." Cedric's tone oozed with false compassion.

"Och," Morgunn remarked, unmoved by his dramatics. "That we should treat our cousins so poorly. Has he no respect for my family? For me?" Morgunn asked.

"She will turn up. I will find her myself if needs be," Cedric offered with some bravado.

"There will be no need. I have servants here who will go in search of her on my command if they are needed," Morgunn said.

Cedric stood, smoothed the wrinkles from his surcoat and crossed his arms commandingly as he moved a few steps away, then turned back toward Morgunn.

"And what if she is not found?" he asked.

"Then Edward shall certainly hear from me and my words will not be very pleasant!" Morgunn said angrily, taking a seat on his throne.

"You cannot be serious. As if Edward had anything to do with her disappearance."

"He had everything to do with it. He was the one who sent you here. Your presence alone certainly scared her off. She is but a young girl. What kind of fool sends a suitor to marry a noble woman without proper announcement?" Morgunn bellowed.

"Noble woman? You must be joking. Anwen is nothing more than a useless daughter to you and you know that well enough." Cedric leaned his tall, muscled frame against the cold surface of the stone wall that enclosed the hall, a sigh of tedium on his breath.

"How dare you?" Morgunn said as he stood abruptly from his throne, nearly knocking it over, and stomped toward Cedric purposefully. "And in my own hall no less. I do not know who you think to impress with your haughtiness and air of importance, but you're winning no extra points wi' me, 'tis for sure." Morgunn's lilt became more prominent as his anger grew. "I willna have my daughter, me only daughter, take up wi' a worthless bastard as yourself."

"You forget yourself, Morgunn, you risk losing much should you back out now." Cedric grinned evilly, knowingly.

"And you forget that whilst you are in my keep I am the king." Morgunn came nose to nose with him. "And I will be addressed appropriately and given due courtesy. Is that understood... Lord Coventry?" Morgunn's green eyes blazed with intensity as he huffed into his face.

"Aye, my lord." Cedric nodded indifferently and gave a brief bow.

"And wipe that ridiculous grin from your face before you go missing yourself." Morgunn shoved into him with clear intent and brusquely left the hall.

"Edward will hear of this!" Cedric shouted after him. He clenched his jaw crossly and pushed himself away from the wall. "Mark my words, he will hear of this!"

"Shall I show you to your chambers, Lord Coventry?" Jamison smiled furtively and motioned to Cedric, concealing a snigger with the back of his hand.

"I'll see myself there," Cedric grumbled and brushed past the porter. "Have my trunks brought up at once," he demanded and left the hall.

Chapter Three

Their passage to Scotland had been an arduous one, but they had made it to the rocky shores of Alba intact. Weary and now saddle sore, they approached the northern pass that led to the Lachlan keep, which sat proudly atop a craggy motte scarcely visible in the growing twilight.

Anwen yawned, her eyes barely able to remain open as she glanced over at Keir. He was stolid and silent, his eyes wary of their surroundings. He hadn't spoken to her much on the journey thus far and she couldn't help but wonder if she had said or done something to sour him to her company.

Nearing the keep, Keir prompted his mount and rode ahead of them and was soon out of sight. Anwen sighed, her gaze dropping to her saddle.

"Ye will have rest soon enough, my keep is just there," Donel patted her on the leg and then pointed to where the torchlight from the gatehouse blazed a brilliant halo of light onto the trail ahead of them. Keir had long gone inside and the men standing guard shouted a greeting to Donel as they rode through the gateway.

It was hard to determine the size of the keep in the darkness, but the foreboding shadows that loomed overhead gave the immediate and immense sensation of safety.

Anwen followed closely behind Donel as he wove his mount between the large structures and finally came to rest next to a cluster of small buildings, which she could only assume were the stables. Within moments, a young boy had dashed out to meet them and had taken hold of each of their mounts as several others unloaded their bags and removed the tack from each horse.

"Time tae get ourselves inside." He smiled, turning to Anwen. "Would you accompany a feeble old man?"

"Hardly feeble," came a voice behind her as another imposing figure moved into the glow of the torchlight that surrounded them.

"Ah, lad, there ye are. Anwen, this is Bowdyn, my eldest son. Bowdyn, this is Lady Anwen Ní Connor. She'll be staying on with us for a short time."

"Ní Connor, did ye say? I believe we met some years ago," he said, eyeing Donel questioningly, who nodded furtively in response. "Well then, Lady Anwen, I hope ye find yer stay here tae be pleasing. If ye find yerself in need of anything, just give a shout, aye?"

"Oh, aye," she said a bit confusedly, noting the strange look in his eye. "I thank you for your hospitality, my lord."

"'Tis what we do best, I suppose. What good is a keep if we dinna share it with kin and kind friends?" He smiled, throwing his arms wide in invitation.

"And it is a grand keep. I am very impressed with… well, with what I've seen so far. I hope to see it justly in the daylight." Anwen said kindly.

"I shall ask one of the boys tae give ye a tour then. Perhaps on the morrow?" Donel asked with a wink.

"Why not ask Keir tae show her about? I am sure he would be quite pleased tae do so," Bowdyn offered with a sly smile to his father, who seemed none too amused.

"Oh, nay, I'm sure he has more than enough to do without having me at his heels. A boy would be fine enough."

"Nonsense. I'll see tae it that he collects ye early on so ye have time tae see everything that ye wish." Bowdyn said.

"If you feel he can be excused from his duties, I cannot complain for his company," she said thoughtfully, then gave Donel a slow smile.

"For the now, lass, I believe we need tae find ye a bath and a private chamber where ye can rest," Donel offered, taking her hand and placing it in the crook of his arm.

"I believe Meara is in the kitchen with Christiona." Bowdyn said and stepped aside, sweeping his arm to offer passage. "Why dinna ye take her there and have them tend tae Anwen?" he offered as he followed along behind them.

"Now there's a grand idea. Och, me daughters are a spry pair and, God willing, they'll ken more about seeing tae yer comforts than I would." Donel grinned, patting her hand.

Anwen nodded in agreement and followed along as he wandered across the expanse of the courtyard, past a throng of men who gave a boisterous greeting to them.

They made their way into the great hall, and what a great hall it was. Most unlike the great hall of her father was the welcoming atmosphere that seemed to surround the entire keep.

Two huge fires with massive stone and timber hearths sat at each end of the room. In the center of the room tables and benches held scores of men socializing, playing chess and otherwise placating themselves with pitchers of ale.

As if the great hall wasn't enough to disgrace her father's keep, the kitchen shamed her more so. Rather than the dungeon-like protrusions and dark, dank feel of her own kitchen, the MacLochlainn's kitchen was spacious and well lit. One would even consider it inviting.

A handful of cherubic women tended the ovens and cauldrons at a relaxed pace, all the while chattering in the uplifting burr she was quickly growing fond of. The dogs sat eagerly watching for scraps and did not look like tethered hell beasties, but like mischievous pups ready to eat or play with whomever gave them any morsel of attention.

"If ye dinna keep yer fingers out of me pot, I'll have yer faither whack yer wee arse, Christiona," a woman warned as she tapped the back of the little girl's hand with her spoon.

Donel elbowed Anwen and gave her a devilish grin as he snuck up behind the woman and stuck his own finger in the pot, scooping up a mouthful of his own, which he poked into his mouth with a smile.

"Och, Donel! Ye too! Git yer grimy fingers out of me pot! Ye look as if ye havena washed in days. Now be off wi' ye!" she said.

"Ah, that's me lovin' wifie! Give us a kiss, Morág," Donel cooed and puckered his lips into an exaggerated kiss only to have his wife crack him solidly on the forehead with the spoon.

"I said off wi' ye!" Morág shouted.

"Bah! Now that's a fine welcome! I've a mind tae stay away next time out." Donel grimaced and rubbed his forehead.

"And I've a mind tae give ye leave tae go, aye!" Morág leered at him.

Donel chuckled and patted Morág solidly on the behind before dodging her spoon again and scampering back to where Anwen stood, mesmerized by the tomfoolery she had been observing. Not only did she find it uncomfortable to watch, but she never saw her own father act with such open mirth. Never.

"Meara, lass, come meet our new guest." Donel motioned to his daughter cheerfully.

Meara handed a pitcher to Christiona who, after looking over Anwen with much curiosity, wandered back into the great hall, watching her over her shoulder as she made her way out the door. Meara wiped her hands on her skirts and made her way across the kitchen to meet Anwen. She immediately jumped into Donel's arms and hugged him gregariously, kissing him soundly on the cheek.

"Da, I was wondering when ye would return. Bowdyn wasn't sure when tae expect ye back, I was starting tae worry."

"Ah, that's me Meara, always looking after her Da." Donel said affectionately as he snuggled her head against his chest and gave her a great squeeze, kissing the top of her head.

"I'm Meara." The girl said with a beaming smile and bobbed a quick curtsy once she was free of her father's arms.

"Anwen… Ní Connor." Anwen bobbed a quick curtsy of her own and looked back at Donel, who stood beaming at his daughter.

"Will ye take Anwen up tae the spare chamber in the north tower and see that she has a fresh, hot bath and some suitable clean clothing?" Donel asked as he gestured toward the door.

"Aye, Da. She is more than welcome tae wear anything of mine. We seem to be of a similar size." Meara grinned at Anwen and took her by the arm. "Come then. I'll see that ye are taken care of in grand style."

Anwen reluctantly left Donel's side, giving him a warm nod of thanks, and then followed Meara out of the kitchen and back through the great hall.

Anwen let out a sigh as they exited the great hall and meandered across the courtyard toward the larger of the towers that loomed overhead. Meara had been chattering animatedly, telling her of life at the keep and how wonderful her family was. She made several references to her brother, Keir, of whom she was obviously very fond.

She pointed out other siblings, and Anwen recognized names that Donel had mentioned on their journey, so she nodded in acknowledgment while Meara continued her soliloquy without taking a breath.

They passed through a heavy oaken door guarded by two men, both of whom acknowledged Meara as they went through. Up several flights of spiral stairs, they finally came to a floor noticeably well-lit and warm. Beautiful woven tapestries of zoomorphic knotwork and scenes of everyday life - of hunting, dancing and warring, lined the long hallway. Several handsome pieces of furniture lined the hallway as well, adding to the inviting atmosphere and lingering air of welcome.

"Your keep is lovely, truly lovely," Anwen offered, admiring the details and cozy touches she had never seen in her own home as Meara continued leading her. If it were left to her, she would rather prefer living in such a place as this. Given the choice, she would probably never leave.

They finally came to the chamber Donel requested for her, and Meara swung the door open, motioning for her to enter.

"'Tis rather chilly, but I will have the fire stoked mightily for ye in no time at all." A thoughtful smile came to Meara's lips as she knelt at the hearth.

"Surely I could do that in your stead." Anwen balked at her guests actions. "No need for you to tend me in your own home," she offered, gathering kindling from a bucket, which sat on the floor.

"Och, I wasna going tae set the fire for ye," Meara began to giggle and covered her mouth in good humor. "We have help tae do that for us." She sniggered again and stood, offering Anwen a hand to help her to her feet.

Embarrassed yet again, Anwen stood and brushed off her knees, shrugging in apology.

"Ye be our guest here." Meara touched her arm lightly and gave her a look of approval. "Take yer ease and rest a while. Believe me, when my faither accepts ye as kin as he has, ye'll be treated as such." Meara moved to the large bed that sat in the center of the room and yanked the heavy curtains aside.

The bed, bare as it was, still looked alluring. The thick, down mattress looked as if one could sink into its heavenly softness before ever feeling the firmness of the frame below. The mere thought of it had Anwen wanting to dive into it headlong without care, but she controlled the urge and thanked Meara gladly.

A moment later, a group of women entered the room with buckets of steaming water followed by a man carrying a large wooden tub.

"Ah, yer bath," Meara exclaimed as she pointed near the fire so the bathman could position the tub thusly. "I can only imagine how eager ye are tae get clean."

"Aye, very eager. You know not how eager." Anwen sighed, running her hand over her dirt covered face. She had forgotten just how dirty she must look to everyone. The comments and murmuring she had heard earlier hadn't been without notice.

"I'll have some clothing brought up for ye, aye. I'll also leave ye some fancier garb for the feast on the morrow and I'll be sure to have yer baggage brought up as soon as possible." Meara said.

"Feast?" Anwen asked a bit startled.

"Oh, aye. Da dinna mention it? Och, that man is losing his wits. For Ostara. We always hold a large gathering here for our clan," Meara explained. "Ye do celebrate Ostara, aye?"

"Aye, of course I do," Anwen answered blankly.

"Yer bath is ready, me lady," one of the maids announced and bobbed a quick curtsy then left the room, empty buckets in hand.

"Weel, ye need tae get tae yer bath afore it cools." Meara gestured toward the steaming tub sitting before the hearty fire.

The sight of it gave Anwen a shiver of anticipation just imagining the feel of the hot water surrounding her tired, aching body.

Meara pulled a screen from behind the large wardrobe and set it upright so the tub was blocked from view. Just as she had finished arranging the folding wall, another woman entered the chamber carrying an armload of clothing she delicately placed on the trunk at the foot of the bed.

"I see Da had the sense tae request the clothing ahead of me. Please, wear what ye like. If ye have need of anything, just ask and someone will find me for ye," Meara offered kindly.

"Thank you, Meara. This is all so thoughtful of you."

"Nay need tae thank me, 'tis my pleasure. 'Tis nice tae have someone sae close tae my age tae talk tae. Ye canna imagine how

34

boring life can become when the only conversation ye have is with a wee bairn, a handful of old women, and men who have no time for talk which doesna concern armaments of some sort." Meara chuckled.

"Believe me, I understand completely," Anwen said with a sigh and a soft chuckle of her own.

"Oh, and if ye have need of anything in the night or if I'm no' about, Keir's room is just there," Meara pointed across the hall, "So ye should be in good hands," Meara said.

"Aye, good hands." Anwen sighed, mischievous thoughts of a midnight rendezvous crossing her tired mind, taking her completely off guard.

"Please, take ease in yer bath and hie yerself tae bed. Ye look dreadful tired and I'm rambling on like an old woman."

"'Tis quite all right. I will be more than delighted to converse with you perhaps when I have rested as you said. The bath looks glorious and I will relish every moment I spend there," Anwen said with a sleepy smile.

"And remember, Keir is just there if ye have need of anything," Meara added as she moved toward the door.

"Aye, so you said." Anwen smirked.

Meara backed out of the room and shut the door soundly behind her.

Peace, quiet and a steaming hot bath. Life, so it seemed, was improving greatly. If only the thought of Keir's presence so close by didn't unnerve her as much as it was beginning to, life would indeed be perfect.

Chapter Four

Anwen woke with a smile and rolled into the voluminous bulges of the down mattress with a sigh. She opened her eyes sleepily and parted the heavy velvet curtains to the brightness of the day. Sitting up lazily, she stretched her arms overhead, yawning gleefully at how well rested she felt. It had been perhaps years since she had slept in a bed so soft, so inviting. She nearly closed the curtains and lulled herself back to sleep, but the grumbling in her stomach spoke otherwise.

It was time to join her hosts, though she grimaced at the thought of facing everyone again. It was true she was now clean and looked less like a peasant that had seen better days, but the idea of making an appearance caused her unease.

She could imagine it clearly, everyone gawking and asking questions while she tried to eat. She wanted to blend into the background and never be noticed or given a second glance, but she doubted she would get away with being a shadow here.

She threw her legs over the side of the bed and walked to the basin of water set on a small table near the window. After splashing a handful of icy water onto her face with a gasp, she turned to dry herself when a soft knock came at the door.

"Come," she answered aloud.

"I have yer garments, m'lady," came a bashful voice from

behind a shock of white-blond bangs.

She recognized Christiona from the night before. A tiny waif of a girl, she barely looked up when she addressed Anwen.

"I thought my own clothing was brought up yester eve," Anwen said perplexedly, folding the drying cloth and placing it on the bed.

Christiona carefully laid the garments on the bed and stood silent as if to await her leave.

"What is your name, little one?" she asked, a bit puzzled.

"Christiona, m'lady." The youngster gave a shy curtsy. "Christiona Nic Lochlainn."

She was a charming, bashful child. Anwen smiled at her and sat at the edge of the bed to face her.

"My name is Anwen Ní Connor and I am very pleased to meet you, Christiona." She extended a hand to her.

Young Christiona looked as if she'd faint. She glanced awkwardly at Anwen's hand and then took it briefly before blushing and pulling away.

"I am tae help ye prepare for the day," Christiona uttered softly. "And with anything else ye may need me for, m'lady."

Anwen reached over and brushed back the child's bangs, getting a glimpse of the beautiful blue eyes beneath, her face a picture of her father's.

Christiona timidly turned her head and gave Anwen a small smile, which warmed Anwen's heart to see. She ruffled Christiona's hair with a smile of her own and stood to look through the garments she brought.

"Meara suggested I bring these tae ye as the dresses that ye brought wi' ye were no' festive enough for the gather."

"I see. Well then, we can't have that. Which one shall I choose? They are all so beautiful." Anwen lifted the gowns one by one, marveling at the fabrics and trims. Meara had done a good job picking out a variety of dresses which were neither frilly nor garish. "Well?" she turned to the young girl. "What say you, Christiona?"

Christiona slowly turned to the pile of dresses and looked up at her a bit unsure.

"Are ye here tae win me brother?" Christiona asked quietly.

Anwen was taken aback by her question.

"Well, I met both of your brothers, but we do not know each other very well. I am only here for a visit." She twisted her mouth into a smirk and glanced at Christiona, who was looking at the dresses.

"Keir likes green. Green and gold." Christiona nodded assuredly.

It was too precious and Anwen's heart melted a second time. The young girl adored her brother. It was plain to see. She could only imagine how many times Christiona had been through this scenario with the countless other women he had courted. She couldn't help but wonder.

"Do you help the other women who come to see Keir, Christiona?" she asked out of curiosity.

"Nay." Christiona shook her head. "Only you."

"And why is that?" Anwen asked, now a bit confused.

"Because ye seem nice." Christiona's gaze dropped to the floor.

"And the others were not nice to you?"

"The others dinna speak tae me. They just ordered me about as if I were…"

"Were what?" Anwen nearly demanded.

"A servant. I am no' a servant," Christiona said, her small face pinched in a frown.

"Of course, you aren't." Anwen hugged the little girl and to her amazement, young Christiona threw her arms around her and hugged her in return. "Never think that. Why, if I do not watch my step, I would say that you'll be the one stealing all the men's hearts one day." Anwen grinned and Christiona's face lit up.

"Ye truly think so?"

"Aye, I do. And just to be safe, I shall let you call me by my given name." Anwen patted the girl on the back. "I could not expect a future lady of this keep to address me any other way."

Christiona's smile lit up the room and the once bashful child was suddenly a radiant and beautifully energetic little girl.

"Now, what shall I wear?" Anwen asked as her eyes went back to the dresses piled on the bed.

"This…" Christiona pulled out a beautiful brushed linen kirtle dyed in the deepest green that it nearly looked black. "And this." The sideless surcoat was made of honey gold brocade. Hand-applied pearls and offset green and gold silk embroidery enhanced the intricate designs woven into the fabric. Light golden fur trimmed the edges and was so soft she could not help but stroke it.

Agreeing upon Christiona's wonderful choices, she began to dress. The gold buttons along the length of the forearms of the kirtle would have been a problem if not for Christiona's nimble, little fingers.

Midway through their progress, Meara entered the room with a soft knock.

In comparison, Christiona would most definitely grow to match, if not surpass, her sister's beauty once she came of age. She would undeniably break a few hearts before her hand was won.

"The gown looks beautiful, m'lady," Meara cooed, smoothing the fabric with a sure hand. "I am happy that it fits ye so well."

"I thank you most kindly for the loan of them. They are very beautiful indeed." Anwen smiled.

"No need. I hardly had chance tae wear them before they were outgrown. I am just pleased that ye do them such justice," Meara said, smiling genuinely. "Now, m'lady, sit ye down and let me fix yer hair."

Meara pulled Anwen's unruly locks from their hasty bindings and began brushing the auburn mass until it practically glowed. With skilled hands, she wove ribbons of green and gold through the braids she had so neatly made around the crown of Anwen's head, letting the remaining ribbon trail with the rest of her loose hair down her back in soft waves.

As a finishing touch, Meara produced Anwen's formal circlet, which Anwen thought she'd left in Ireland. The dull brass band had been polished to a brilliant gloss, bringing out the intricate knotwork and thistle design etched along its length. The five rough emeralds dispersed evenly around its circumference shone just as brightly as the rest. She had not seen it look so stunning since the day she received it from her father, on the day of her thirteenth birthday.

Meara delicately placed the circlet about Anwen's hair and stepped back to admire her work.

"If that doesna do the trick, I fear he is hopeless." Meara smirked as she tilted her head.

"He?" Anwen asked.

"Keir, m'lady. Sometimes I wonder if his wits are about him at all."

"Why do you say that?" Anwen took up a hand mirror and adjusted the circlet just so, admiring Meara's handiwork.

"Well, being kin, I canna say that my judgment is impartial, but he's a fair looking lad. He has his share of admirers and, tae say the least, some of them are relatively attractive, but he seems opposed tae affection altogether," Meara offered.

"Opposed? How do you mean?" Anwen asked.

"He is near tae his twenty-first year now. One would think he would have long been wed and borne heirs of his own. He doesna seem tae feel it an important task and I fear it distresses my mither and faither."

"Perhaps he has yet to find his match," Anwen said a bit hopefully.

"Well, with the blessings of heaven, the sight of ye in this gown should be more than enough tae set him straight." Meara beamed as she nodded in satisfaction.

Anwen was beginning to wonder what sort of mischief Meara was up to.

"Flattered as I am to think your brother would have a mind to take note of me, and thus far he has not," she added with a grimace, "My visit here was to be a short one, that is, until we are ready to continue north to my Uncle's. I have not come with any intentions in mind."

"Mmhmm," Meara said with a nod, continuing to fuss with Anwen's hair.

Anwen furrowed her brow at Meara's obvious lack of concern and turned to continue with the assessment of her outfit. The kirtle fit her form as if it was tailored to suit her and the surcoat fell perfectly to the floor, the train adding a hint of nobility to the gown. She adjusted herself one last time before she allowed the two sisters to pull her out of the room.

They led her down the hallway, out of the tower and across the courtyard, with many an admiring eye falling favorably upon her. They stopped just outside the great hall where a large gathering had amassed in her absence. Meara gave Anwen one last inspection, then asked her to wait while she fetched her father to escort her in and with that, left her with a hug.

Christiona swallowed her up in one last hug of her own and followed her sister into the hall, leaving Anwen to stand there, alone. She could do nothing but sigh heavily as her nerves took hold of her stomach.

She didn't have long to wait. Donel's heavy footfall sounded through the open doorway, heading in her direction. As the footsteps grew louder, Anwen's heart pounded till she felt she would faint from anxiety. She stared at her feet and tried to force herself to breathe calmly, the tension easing a bit as she conjured soothing thoughts of how happy her father would be if she announced that she had finally procured a suitable husband, not that she had any intention of marrying anyone at this point. He would be overjoyed and all would be well. He would even have reason to summon her home and he would finally have a reason to love her.

The footsteps stopped short of her and she looked up to greet the MacLochlainn with an assured and confident smile, only to be greeted herself by a very handsome, very bold looking Keir. Her words stuck in her throat and she knew she would surely faint.

Keir bowed gracefully and took a step back. His eyes made a slow sweep of her from head to toe and, at last, came directly back to her eyes.

The blueness of his own eyes was of the deepest sapphire and they sparkled just as brilliantly. His hair, the color of the sweetest honey, fell in waves like a gilded frame about his face. A face she would never forget.

He was a most handsome man. Probably the most handsome man she had ever had chance to meet. And she could not imagine, considering his soft blue eyes, that he had a tense or angry bone in his body. The man she had met a fortnight before who had called himself "Keir" had to have been someone else entirely. He looked so changed.

"Anwen?" He stepped toward her slowly, the look on his face as if he had never seen her before.

Anwen looked upon him with timid approval and he gave her a warm smile in return.

"Are ye at all well, lass?" he asked with a concerned voice so silky that she feared she would surely lose her knees.

"I… why yes, I am well," she said quietly. She cleared her throat briefly, hoping the large knot she swallowed would dislodge from her throat.

"Are ye sure, lass?" he asked, catching her by the elbow. "Yer face grows pale."

"My apologies. 'Twas a long and tiresome journey and I fear the exertion of my travels has made me weary." She put a hand to his arm to steady herself.

"Let us go inside, then. We have much food to be eaten and ye can take yer ease there." He moved to hold her about the waist, but she sidestepped his grasp and took his arm instead, giving him leave to lead her.

"I shall be fine once I sit myself down." She smiled half-heartedly. Certainly, she thought, once I sit I should not be able to stand.

"If it pleases ye, we could take a turn about the grounds until ye get yer color back. 'Tis one thing tae pale with beauty, 'tis quite another tae be beauteous and pale." He said with a bold smirk.

Anwen's heart stopped.

"Ye jest, my lord." She smiled as her cheeks grew hot.

"And ye blush, m'lady. It seems yer color has returned." A smile played wickedly across his lips. "Shall we go in then?"

"Aye, I shall follow you," she said with a nod and he turned them toward the door. At the threshold of the great hall he stopped and bent to her ear.

"Ye're stunning, lass," he whispered.

Now she needed a seat.

Chapter Five

Anwen was as mesmerizing to watch as a snowflake drifting to earth, yet there was something about her Keir just couldn't understand. Why was it the mere presence of her demanded attention from everyone around her yet she seemed almost relieved when given a moment's reprieve?

He took another long pull from his tankard and leaned back into his chair, watching her from the shadows across the room. He'd never seen anyone with such a strong effect on people, including himself.

He found himself wondering what she thought… what she dreamed of. What she wished for. He'd never really cared about what a woman wanted. Truth be told, what a woman thought and cared for rarely crossed his mind. He was more concerned about the look of her and whether she would bear him strong sons. And even that wasn't altogether true. Having strong sons was what he was supposed to think of, but it was really his father who cared about heirs. A fitting worry for a chieftain, but Keir was resigned to the life he had made for himself - a life without the drama of women in it. Yet here he was, brooding in the darkness, contemplating if he should approach this incredible young woman.

He watched as handfuls of his friends and kin drew near her and chatted with her until her face came alive with laughter. Several asked her to dance and the men practically swarmed around her when she stood and walked about the room. His sister, Meara, seemed taken by the lass and quickly became her attendant, with little Christiona in tow.

Christiona spied Keir off in the corner and she jumped into his lap, prattling on about how wonderful Anwen was.

"…And she said we could go riding without the men. Isna that marvelous?" Christiona beamed as she bumped about excitedly on his knee.

"I doubt faither would allow it, *mo spideag*. Perhaps ye shouldna let a stranger's promises encourage ye so." Keir raised an eyebrow, but was met with a very cross glare.

"They were nay promises! Faither was there when she said it and he spoke nothing. In fact, he said Meara could come as well!" Christiona punctuated her statement with a stern look, jumped out of his lap and ran back to Anwen's side.

God's teeth, but the lass had everyone captivated. Why, even his father was wrapped around her finger and she hadn't even been there for one day.

He took another long pull of his ale and called out for more. One of his men came to him with a pitcher and refilled his tankard, just to watch him empty it again. That was when a friendly hand came down upon his shoulder and jostled him a bit.

"What troubles ye, Keir?" It was his cousin, Rorik, much to his dismay.

Keir's expression didn't change, but he thrust his tankard

toward him with a sneer.

"Funny, just a moon ago I bested ye on the lists, had ye practically laid out on yer back howling for mercy like a wee bairn," Rorik said with a smirk. "I pride myself as being one of the best warriors at this keep. And now I am reduced tae act as yer butler?" he asked as Keir scowled disapprovingly. "Ye realize ye will never get the courage tae speak tae her by sitting here in the dark like a bullfrog." Rorik added and refilled Keir's tankard.

Keir took another long draw, scowling over the rim of his mug.

"I dinna ask for yer council, cousin," Keir muttered into its murky depths.

"Keir, lad, what is it?" Rorik chuckled and pulled up a seat next to him. "I havena seen ye this reluctant since yer thirteenth year." He refilled Keir's tankard a second time and then his own.

"She's... different," was all that Keir said as he swallowed another pint, his eyes becoming glazed and distant as the ale began to take hold of him.

"Aye, she's different. She's of the Irish."

"Och, 'tis no' what I meant. There is something about her, something I've never seen before. 'Tis like a ghost the way she haunts this place." Keir said ominously.

Rorik nodded his head with a disbelieving chuckle.

"Perhaps she is bewitched. 'Tis possible she is no' Irish at all." Rorik offered with a laugh.

49

"She is no more bewitched than I am a king," Keir grumbled, refilling his mug once more, taking a long, slow drink.

"Better watch what ye say, Keir. Yer father has high expectations for ye as it is. All he needs do is find ye a suitable wife and then, weel…" Rorik chuckled and gave him a hearty slap on the back, but Keir was not amused. In fact, the truth of what Rorik had just said hadn't even dawned on him.

A betrothal would ensure his clan's survival by producing the heirs his father had been begging for. He could imagine how overjoyed his father would be if he were to find a wife at this gathering, which would not be a difficult task given the number of women that were in attendance. No wonder everyone was in such good spirits. He was sure he could sense them planning his wedding feast as he sat there, mulling over his ale. It was a shame that Anwen couldn't be one of them, betrothed as she was already.

Still, Keir knew it was useless to avoid getting acquainted with her, so he gritted his teeth and prepared to face his duty head-on, no matter how the thought displeased him.

With another mouthful of ale, he rose to his feet and started toward Anwen, who was speaking to his mother and her ladies. However, his body started toward her more quickly than his feet and he stumbled forward.

His face would have met abruptly with the hard stone floor had Rorik not been there to catch him.

"Whoa, cousin, it seems yer drink has gotten the best of ye." Rorik grabbed him about the jerkin and Keir clasped onto Rorik's arm as if the floor were still falling away from him.

Rorik knew it was better to save Keir's pride than make a joke of his condition, no matter how difficult it was for him to restrain his jesting, but he never saw Keir so nervous before, especially not for the fancy of a woman. They had been together numerous times before where they caroused full on and Keir was never at a loss for words when it came to women and never at odds with his drink.

Keir barely needed to open his mouth as the mere sight of him had the ladies swooning. All Keir needed to do was smile and they were at his feet praying for his attentions, which he gave gladly and without care.

Scores of women would await his arrival at local taverns if word spread that he was making his rounds that night. It was as if he were some sort of legend. And, from the gossip Rorik had overheard while the maids were busy at their chores, he had quite an enthusiastic following.

Still, as his cousin now swayed on the verge of nausea, he couldn't understand from where Keir's anxiety was coming. If he hadn't known about his previous conquests, he would have thought him to be a virgin, but he knew that wasn't remotely possible. It hadn't been a month since Rorik had the embarrassing task of rousing Keir from a maid's bed when he hadn't shown up for his duties the next morning.

Rorik sighed, puzzled, as Keir fumbled to find his chair, where he collapsed with a groan.

"Take hold of yerself, lad. What will she think that ye canna hold down a bit o' drink?" Rorik whispered gruffly into Keir's ear.

"I have hold, damn you," Keir pushed him away and cursed aloud when he found his tankard empty. Shoving the mug toward Rorik with a grunt, he was met with a firm grip on his arm and was dragged from the hall into the cold, open air of the courtyard.

"What is wrong with ye?" Rorik held him firm by his jerkin and shook him against the wall. Keir's head met solidly with the cold stone and he swore aloud a second time, swinging at Rorik with a clenched fist, connecting solidly with his jaw.

Rorik was in no mood to scrap with his drunken cousin, so he returned the blow in kind, knocking Keir out cold. Several men rushed outside when they heard Keir's bellows and Rorik stopped them before they had chance to jump to the wrong conclusions.

"He's drunk. Take him tae his chambers tae sleep it off." The group of men hurriedly gathered up their young charge and dragged him off to his room.

A few moments later, Caedmon, Keir's grandsire, rushed out into the courtyard with Donel following closely behind him.

"What's all the commotion?" Donel grasped Rorik by the arm with a concerned look in his eyes as he watched men from his guard dragging his limp son across the courtyard.

"Why not ask Keir yerself?" Rorik pulled away from him with a harsh look.

"What has he done now?" Caedmon groaned, assuming Keir had gotten himself into some sort of trouble again. Crossing his arms in front of him, he prepared to listen to a long list of appalling deeds as he had done so often before in similar situations. Keir habitually found himself at the mercy of his kin when his nights of self-indulgence were over, and Caedmon was always the first to hear of it.

Keir was a good man, but his temperament of late left little to be desired. Ejected from a handful of local taverns for starting brawls, showing up late for his duties at the keep or not at all, he had all but tried his father's patience.

Donel had more than enough to worry about without having to deal with the escapades of a son that had gone feral. It was always Caedmon who took hold of the boy and shook some sense into him, though the sense only lasted as long as his attention allowed, which was not very long at all.

Now, though he steeled himself to hear what his grandson had done, Caedmon was pleasantly surprised to see Rorik suddenly grow a smile.

"I believe, m'lord," Rorik grinned and then began to chuckle, "that young Keir has fallen in love."

"In love? With whom?" Donel asked, choking back his alarm. Lord only knew it could be one of a thousand women Keir bedded. He wasn't the most discreet young man.

"What do ye mean, who? The young Irish lass. Since she arrived he has been acting as though his head is nay attached tae his

53

body. I hae never seen him so bewildered in all my years," Rorik said with a laugh.

"How is that possible?" Donel asked, a bit perplexed.

"How is it no'?" Rorik chuckled as he patted him on the arm.

"God's blood, Caedmon, the lad truly does fancy the lass," Donel announced, bewildered.

"Aye, but does she fancy him?" Rorik asked quite genuinely as he leaned himself against the wall. "They seemed cordial at feast, but she barely said two words tae him this eve and I daresay that was what brought about his latest... mood."

"Och, it doesna matter one way or another. The lass is all but betrothed," Donel said exasperatedly.

"Och no..." Caedmon grimaced, shaking his head. He pulled out a pipe and filled it with a rough mixture that he withdrew from a pouch.

Donel shook his head disconcertedly and dug for a flask he hid in his plaid earlier that evening. After a few sips of the strong liquor, he passed it to Rorik, who choked down a few swallows of his own.

"What should we do about this, my laird?" Rorik gasped as the drink made its way down his throat.

"Nothing," he said blandly. "I daresay we should get them on good terms regardless. Rorik, ye can arrange the meeting. I shall leave it in yer capable hands tae see that Keir is on his best behavior on the morrow so he may face the lass with a tad more propriety than he showed her this eve," Donel stated.

"My laird?" Rorik balked.

"Come now, Rorik, 'tis no' as if this task is one ye have no' dealt with before," Donel said.

"Nay, my laird, although I've never had tae prepare him tae face a woman before. 'Tis a bit awkward tae tackle such a task knowing the state he'll be in on the morrow," Rorik said, accepting a second sip of the MacLochlainn's flask.

"Ah, but as his kin, ye ken the responsibility of such a task, do ye no'? We canna have her believing my son tae be some unmannered fool, ye ken," Donel added.

"Aye." Rorik groused.

"Och, he'll respond in kind… if he kens what's good for his clan." Caedmon puffed heartily on his pipe and the smoke wafted around him lazily.

"One can only hope." Donel said, eyeing his empty flask sadly, stowing it back beneath his plaid. "I'm going back inside."

Rorik nodded and followed him into the hall leaving Caedmon alone in the courtyard to enjoy his pipe.

"One can only hope…" Caedmon repeated with a sigh as he continued to savor his smoke, slipping into the darkness.

Chapter Six

Keir rolled over into the agony of blinding sunlight. His bed curtains were closed, but an errant ray of light found its way through the only break in the canopy. He grumbled a curse and rolled himself into his pillows, burrowing his face back into darkness. After a few moments, he realized his head was still pounding and he hadn't remembered returning to his chambers the night before.

Damn it to hell and back, he thought painfully, not again.

He pushed himself onto his side with some effort and wiped his face in his hands. When his mind began to break the surface of a normal consciousness, he opened his eyes with a start. *The lass.* Bloody hell. What had he done?

He caught his breath in his throat and looked slowly across the bed to check for additional occupants, then let out a breath of relief. At least he had the presence of whatever mind he had left to sleep alone.

It was one thing to revel beyond remorse at a tavern and end up in a strange lass's bed, it was quite another to do so in your own home and in the presence of noble guests.

His father would be furious, no doubt, and he'd have to do more than explain in the face of his wrath. Cursing himself a second time, he sat up and pushed the curtains aside, dropping his legs over the side of the bed.

"Good morrow." Rorik's voice startled him and he reflexively covered his nakedness with the bed curtain.

"Come right in and make yerself comfortable," Keir said, then relaxed with a deep exhale. He flung the curtain aside once more and reached for his breeches. His voice was hoarse, but he felt worse than he sounded. Running a hand through his hair, he made his way to the table where Rorik was sitting, enjoying a plate of smoked meats.

"Want some?" Rorik held a chunk of mutton inches from Keir's nose.

Keir choked, shoving his hand away.

"Cease!" he gulped back his nausea. "Why are ye here?" Keir slumped into the chair opposite Rorik and rubbed his forehead wearily.

"And a fine day tae ye, too." Rorik chuckled to himself and popped the meat into his mouth. "I've a mind tae leave ye here tae suffer alone as ye so deserve."

"And miss yer chance tae lecture me yet again about the joys of moderation? How kind of ye," Keir said blandly.

"'Tis my one true source of entertainment these days." Rorik tossed another chunk of meat into his mouth and chewed through the grin that spread across his face.

Keir's sigh of resignation seemed to please him, but Keir knew this wasn't the last time they would have this conversation. It was becoming a habit between them and Rorik's concern was nothing more than futile now. His little forays into drunken debauchery were amusing enough, but he knew his episode the prior evening went a step too far.

"Ye need tae stop this, Keir." Rorik gave him a terse look. "There is only so much I can do tae protect ye from yer faither…or yerself."

"Ye do this for yer own satisfaction, no' mine, so dinna try tae make it sound like I asked ye tae come here."

Keir reached for an empty mug and filled it with water from a pitcher that sat before him. He took a healthy drink and glared at Rorik across the table.

"Ye can believe what ye like, cousin. I'm just yer friend in this matter, no' yer accuser."

"Ye could have fooled me." Keir inspected the plate on the table and decided it was far safer to avoid eating, at least until his stomach had settled. He took another sip of water and moved the plate farther away so the smell of the meat would stop assaulting him.

"So…" Rorik propped his feet up on a spare chair and crossed his arms before him. "Are ye going tae tell me what happened last night?"

"There is nay tae tell." Keir's reply was weak. Even he knew he didn't sound convincing. He shrugged and pushed away from the table, making his way back to his bed.

"Ye havena been yerself of late," Rorik said.

"What is that supposed tae mean?" Keir lay back in his bed and threw his arm over his face. He was curious to hear what Rorik had to say, but the throbbing in his temples didn't offer much energy to listen.

"Ye ken exactly what I mean. Ye've been distracted for months. Yer temper has been foul and yer attitude is trying everyone's patience, including mine," Rorik said angrily. "I want tae know what troubles ye, aye?"

"My temper has no' been foul," Keir grunted from beneath his arm.

"Ye nearly struck young Gavin last week for no' cleaning yer swords!" Rorik stood abruptly and moved to the side of the bed, glaring down at him.

"He is my squire! That is his job!" Keir fumed, pushing himself up onto his elbows, squinting up at Rorik through the brightness of the room.

"He's eight years old!"

"And when I was eight, I cleaned swords!" Keir clenched his jaw, stood from the bed and shoved his way past Rorik. After fumbling through the clothing in the trunk at the foot of his bed, he pulled out a linen shirt and yanked it over his head.

"Fine. And what about last night?" Rorik wasn't about to let the matter go. Keir would have to explain himself before Rorik would let him leave. Judging the expression on Rorik's face, they might be there all day.

"I dinna ken," Keir finally said after a long silence.

"I'll wager I do." Rorik stood over him, his hands on his hips.

"Care tae enlighten me so I can get on wi' my day?" Keir pulled on his boots and then fastened his belt about his waist.

"'Tis the Irish lass."

"Dinna be daft. She arrived long after I yelled at Gavin."

"Dinna change the subject," Rorik retorted.

"Ye said I've been in a mood for months. I've only just met her a sen'night ago. How could she have anything tae do with this?" Keir asked.

"I'm talking about last night. 'Tis not like ye tae shy away from a bonny lass."

"I dinna shy away," Keir said under his breath.

"I disagree."

"I barely had a chance tae speak tae the girl," Keir said as he adjusted his belt and smoothed out his shirt.

"Well, maybe if ye would have been sober, that wouldna been a problem," Rorik said smartly.

"Verra funny."

"I'm no' jesting with ye. Ye need tae slow down on the drink, Keir."

"I can drink as I please," Keir said plainly, then took a strip of leather from his pouch and pulled his hair into a queue. The bound hair fell loose and he tied it several times, to no avail. He finally gave up, letting his hair fall loose to his shoulders, flinging the cord onto his bed in frustration.

"Ye need tae start taking responsibility for yer actions," Rorik stated blandly, trying to get back to the matter at hand.

"I have."

"Ye havena," Rorik said. If his tone wasn't convincing, his posture surely was. He was only two years older than Keir, but he was a good three inches taller and much broader.

Keir straightened himself in comparison, but he knew his father had made Rorik his warder for a reason. He was probably the only man in the keep who could best him.

Keir grimaced as he passed Rorik, knowing full well he was at his wits end with him and he had done nothing but fuel the fire.

"All right." Keir gave a defeated sigh and sat again at the table. "What did I do yester eve? Is the lass unharmed?" he asked as he pulled a dirk from his boot and poked at the meats carefully, discerning which slice would be the least harmful to his churning stomach.

"The lass is fine. She wasna involved in yer fit of temper, at least no' directly."

"I wish ye would stop talking in circles, Rorik, 'tis making my head ache more than it already is." Keir eyed the lump of meat that was skewered on the end of his dirk and decidedly bit into it.

Rorik sat next to him and watched as Keir fought back his nausea to nourish himself as best he could.

"Ye escorted Anwen in tae the hall, and the next thing I knew ye were sitting in a corner like a lad who had lost his pony," Rorik said a bit painfully as he watched Keir choke down his rising bile.

"What else was I tae do? As soon as the feasting ended, I turned around and she was gone."

"Ye could have gone after her," Rorik suggested.

"And look like a fawning courtier? I should say no'."

"Why no'? If ye werena so smitten with her, she would have been on yer lap all night."

"Smitten? Ye are daft! She is nothing but a child." The thought was laughable and Keir did so with very little believability.

"Keir…"

"Aye?"

"Come now, I saw the way ye looked at her last night. I saw the way ye acted. Ye're falling for her, admit it." Rorik finished the last piece of meat and pushed the plate away.

"Ye saw nothing." Keir took another drink of water to clear the sickening taste from his mouth. After a few moments, the sickness subsided, but the bile was still strong in his throat.

"I saw ye sitting in the corner, yer mood dark wi' drink, and yer eyes never left her. No' once."

"I think ye were in yer cups as well," Keir said with a grimace.

"If I were, ye wouldna have made it tae yer chamber in one piece as ye did," Rorik admitted.

"What is that supposed tae mean?"

"Ye only got in one good punch before I knocked ye out, no' that yer ale wouldna have done it for ye eventually anyway," Rorik said with a sigh as he stood and walked toward the window.

"Ye hit me?" Keir asked incredulously rubbing his sore jaw with some small remembrance.

"'Twas a sympathy punch." Rorik crossed his meaty arms over his chest and snorted angrily at his cousin. "I dinna want tae see ye embarrass yerself in front of her."

"She saw all this take place?" Keir balked.

"Lucky for ye, nay. I removed ye from the hall before yer temper got the best of ye."

Keir sat silently for a moment, then looked at his cousin with embarrassment.

"I thank ye, Rorik. Yer too good to me."

"No need tae thank me." He looked into Keir's eyes earnestly. "Just see tae yerself, aye?"

"I will try tae control my carousing until she leaves."

"'Tis no' what I meant, Keir. And if yer faither has any say, ye'll be locked in your chamber until ye decide to settle yerself."

"'Tis exactly the reason for my mood." Keir grimaced and slouched down into his chair.

"I dinna understand."

"Ye asked what troubles me. Weel, ye've just discovered my plight." Keir refilled the mug, stood and left the table, making his way into the light of the oriel on the far side of his bed.

He stood at the window watching the activities below, marking the men who were already on the lists busy at their training, wishing he were on of them. He scanned the courtyard for a glimpse of the pretty lass, but he did not see her, nor did he see his sisters, which meant they were almost certainly with her.

It was probably good he hadn't seen her. Rorik would have noticed his distraction and would have started in with harassing him about being such a coward. But he was no coward. He never had been. He was a cautious man unwilling to allow the fancy in his heart to draw him to a woman that was already promised to another. That thought alone was enough to break his heart before the fancy could even take hold.

Rorik didn't follow him into the oriel, but took a seat on his bed, facing him.

"I have nae purpose in this household. I am merely here to pick up what duties fall from Bowdyn." Keir said finally, his voice tight with resentment.

"Ye are the son of a laird, Keir. No' only will ye make a good husband someday, but ye will make a good faither, and a powerful warrior."

"A powerful warrior . . ." Keir clenched his jaw and threw his mug down with disgust.

"Aye, a powerful warrior. 'Tis what ye were born tae, Keir. I've seen ye with a sword and have been at its other end. It comes naturally tae ye."

"How can I be a powerful warrior if my faither keeps me like a useless bairn within these wretched walls?" he said, giving a look of absolute disgust that he had mentioned it at all. "Who will ever ken my skill or my strategy if they are nay seen outside the lists?"

"He keeps ye here for yer own safety."

"He keeps me here for his own futility," Keir shouted. "The men in the guard dinna respect me because I have yet tae shed blood for my clan."

"Ye think poorly of yer men, Keir. They respect ye well."

"I've heard them speak of me when they dinna realize I was listening. They think me a puppet tae my faither."

"Idle chatter," Rorik offered as he stood to fetch Keir's mug from the floor and handed it back to him. "Most of the men in our ranks fear the day ye are loosed on the battlefields. Ye have more than proven yerself on the lists. Ye've bested every man in our guard."

"Besting men on the lists is far different than facing hundreds at war, Rorik, and ye ken that well."

"'Tis only different in number, not in skill, and ye have that in abundance."

"I have nothing but a merchant's duty and no way tae defend my name," Keir said blandly.

"I think ye are overreacting. When yer time comes, ye will honor yer faither and yer clan admirably. As for defending yerself, I believe yer energies will more than compensate for yer lack of experience. God help the first man that faces ye at war, for ye will surely hack him tae bits."

Keir moved away from the window and gave Rorik an appreciative smile.

"I would, wouldn't I?" Keir chuckled despite his mood.

"Aye. And I will be right beside ye should ye need of me."
Rorik clapped Keir on the shoulder and shook a smile onto his face.

Keir nodded and clasped Rorik's arm with much amity.

"Maybe ye could clean my swords, then!" Keir joked and
ducked playfully as Rorik took a half-hearted swing at him.

"Think ye? Yer best mate?"

"Aye, what better man for the task?" Keir laughed.

"And what will yer squire do? Laze about in yer chamber
until ye return from yer warring?"

"Gavin will stay behind and tend the sheep whilst we are
away doing our duties as fighting men. 'Tis the least he could do tae
take over my previous obligations once I am declared able tae give
battle," Keir joked and then his face turned sour again.

"Ye do yerself little justice in yer words. 'Tis no' a matter of
yer ability, for it speaks enough for itself. Yer faither has his reasons
for keeping ye here during wartime. Just resign yerself tae accept that
fact and let it lie."

"Aye, let it lie." Keir's face changed suddenly and his anger
surfaced like a roaring fire. "Curse Bowdyn for burdening me with
this uselessness I feel!" he bellowed, nearly choking on his words.

"Hold yer tongue!" Rorik hissed. "How can ye say such a
thing of yer brother?" Rorik blessed himself quickly and Keir rolled
his eyes at the superstitious nature of his cousin. "Ye are more selfish
than I imagined. How could ye think that Bowdyn was chosen tae
spite ye?"

"I dinna blame him. I'm just sick tae death of everything falling in his favor. When will my time come? Why am I cursed to be little more than a lap dog tae my faither?" Keir raged. "Damn ye, Rorik!" He shoved past him and slammed the door loudly as he left.

"Good morrow, Anwen. Did ye sleep well?" Christiona's angelic voice woke Anwen from a deep sleep. The girl was opening all the shutters and Anwen pulled up her blankets as the drafts found their way to the bed. She should have had the mind to pull her bed curtains closed the night before, but she was so exhausted she was lucky to have found her way to her chambers at all.

"What is the hour?" Anwen could only imagine it was only moments past dawn and she averted her eyes as the sunlight streamed across her pillows.

"'Tis nearing noon, m'lady. I thought ye would be better prepared tae face the day if ye broke yer fast before the kitchen put away the noon meals."

Noon? How could it be noon? It was as if she had just fallen asleep moments ago.

Perhaps young Christiona didn't quite know how to properly tell the time.

"Are you sure it is noon?" Anwen rolled over and wiped her eyes, yawning deeply.

"Aye, mightily sure. The terce bells rang hours ago." Christiona nodded and made her way to the side of the bed, which was nearly as tall as she. She propped her elbow upon the mattress and smiled at Anwen kindly.

Anwen sighed and rolled down the blankets, pushing herself up on her pillows.

"And what is on our schedule today, Christiona?" Anwen asked as she patted the bed next to her. Christiona gleefully jumped up beside her with all the giddiness her age allowed and smiled warmly at Anwen's attentiveness.

"Whatever ye wish, m'lady."

"Anwen." She corrected her.

Christiona smiled sheepishly and blushed at the correction.

"Anwen." Christiona repeated with a shy smile.

"Is there no plan for my visit? I was quite sure that every waking moment would be filled with one activity or another. What, no clothing to mend? No important guests to entertain?" Anwen teased as she poked at Christiona.

"Nay!" Christiona giggled and squirmed away from her poking fingers. "I was told tae fetch ye, tae break yer fast and tae entertain ye as ye pleased. The day is yours tae do with as ye will."

"And what say you? Do you have any ideas of how we may spend our day?" Anwen asked sleepily, a deep yawn escaping as she spoke.

"We could go riding. Or we could go tae the fields and pick wild flowers. I could show ye the rest of the keep now that it is daylight." Christiona bubbled.

The thought of riding after spending so many days on a horse didn't thrill Anwen at all. And picking flowers was something she hadn't even done as a child. As much as it hurt her to admit it, she was hoping to spend the day alone, maybe watching at the lists or delving into the huge library she heard so much about the night before.

"Do you know where the library is?" Anwen asked cautiously, noting Christiona's expression.

"Of course! I ken every room in our keep. 'Tis down the hall tae the right. Would ye like to see it?"

Anwen was relieved the notion hadn't dampened Christiona's spirits.

"Aye, I would love to. I love to read and perhaps I could find something for my bedside while I am there."

Anwen hopped out of bed and stretched herself thoroughly. Her hair had been plaited for the night, so she was sure it would unravel into a huge, frizzy mess once it was undone. She was also happy to see that her own outfits were brought in the prior evening so she wouldn't have to continue to dress so extravagantly while she was visiting.

Christiona continued to insist she wear green for her brother's sake and Anwen happily donned a pleasant cotehardie of moss green wool.

Christiona hopped down off the bed and fished an elegant yet simple gold placard belt out of the trunk and a pair of boots made of soft leather.

"I shall fetch Meara tae do yer hair." Christiona offered over her shoulder as she ran out the door without waiting for a response.

Anwen adjusted the gown and took a seat in the large window that overlooked the bailey below. She could see the activity there and she fought back the urge to rush down and find the lists.

What a joy it would be to use the techniques that she had learned from her brothers. Scotsmen weren't as opposed to their women finding interest in warfare as her father was, but showing she harbored such dubious knowledge would surely embarrass her hosts and she was sure her father would learn of it eventually.

A few moments later Meara arrived with the ever boisterous Christiona at her side and Anwen sat at the window while her hair was combed out.

"Ye have such beautiful hair," Meara said as she unraveled the braids.

"Thank you," Anwen said with another yawn.

"'Tis an odd color, really," Meara mused. "No' the flaming red of the Celts, and no' quite brown either. The only color I can compare it tae is the brewer's harvest ale."

"Then harvest ale it is," Anwen announced with a smile. "I think I like that comparison as much as I like harvest ale!"

"Keir likes harvest ale, too," Christiona said cheerfully and was immediately elbowed away by Meara, who gave her a sharp look.

"He seems very nice, your brother," Anwen offered kindly. For all she knew he was a dolt. The man hadn't said two words to her all evening. He was gallant enough when he escorted her to the great hall, but once the feast was cleared, he was gone. They had chatted briefly during the removes, but their words were trite at best.

He was most certainly pleasing to the eye and Anwen caught herself staring at him many times. She watched his lips as he spoke, marveled at their fullness and wondered if they were as soft as they looked. She watched his eyes, their blueness deeper than any loch she had ever seen. And his hair was the color of summer wheat. Not like her hair, whose color couldn't be poetically described by even the cleverest of bards.

"He has his moments," Meara offered with a hint of aggravation.

"Do ye like him?" Christiona blurted out and Meara gave her another harsh look.

"I hardly had chance to speak to him, but I'm sure he's a fine young man," Anwen offered and the heat suddenly rose in her cheeks.

"Mayhap ye can visit with him this afternoon," Meara said off-handedly.

"Oh no, no... I'm sure he has more pressing duties to tend to than to have to spend time with me."

"Well, I believe there is no better duty for him this day than tae tend tae his guest," Meara said. "And I am sure he would feel the same. Christiona, go fetch Keir and tell him tae meet us in the hall."

Before Anwen could refuse, Christiona was out the door yelling his name. She had the sinking feeling that she wasn't going to be able to leave anytime soon and if Christiona had anything to do with it, she'd be in her brother's arms before the day was done. The thought of it brought a warm smile to her face and she was embarrassed when Meara noticed.

"She is a handful, that one there," Meara said as she continued to brush out her locks.

"She is very sweet," Anwen said. Thoughts of Keir were swarming around her head and she couldn't think of a thing to say to break the awkward silence. "Do you have any other siblings?"

"Aye," Meara said. "The eldest is my sister, Fina. She has been married these five years and stays at Castle MacEoghainn with her husband and children. Next is Bowdyn, then Keir and then myself... and then Christiona."

"She is much younger than you," Anwen said and then realized why there was such a large gap in their ages. "Donel tells me you have lost siblings."

It was a common occurrence, for she had lost a brother herself not twelve years earlier to the sickness, but she sensed uneasiness in Meara and knew that her loss had been more recent. She wished she hadn't brought up the subject as Meara's sunny mood turned sullen.

"Aye. My brother Desmond died a few years ago. He was two years younger than I," Meara said as she continued to brush Anwen's hair methodically as if she were trying to keep her mind from the thought of him.

"I am sorry for your loss, Meara, truly. I lost a younger brother to the sickness as well."

"He had always been a weak child. The physician dinna think he would see his second year."

"Were you here when he passed on?"

Nay, I wasna at the keep that day. We had gone tae visit my sister who had a babe a few months earlier." Meara gave a brief smile. "'Tis the only comfort we have knowing we may have lost Desmond but part of the void he left was filled with the wee Ronan."

"How old was Desmond?"

"He was just about to see his thirteenth year. 'Tis truly a shame." Meara blotted her cheeks with her sleeve and went back to her brushing duties.

"Aye, truly."

"There were two others, Connor and Kennis," Meara continued. "They were babes of six and five when the sickness took them from us. I was young when they passed on, born the same year Kennis left us, so I dinna quite grasp the loss of them."

"Aye. I was just Christiona's age when my wee brother, Bran, was taken by the sickness, so I understand."

"Aye. I suppose everyone has lost loved ones tae the sickness... and tae wars." Meara finished with Anwen's hair, opting to roll back the sides and leave its luxurious mass fall loose down her back.

The room grew silent with thoughts of the loved ones that had passed on. The winters had proven long and harsh the past few years, leaving many struggling to survive through numerous illnesses and lack of food. They survived by pulling their resources together and providing comfort for one another, but once the sickness took hold there was little anyone could do. The strong survived, but many children and elders were lost to it. Having made it through yet another harsh winter, all they could do was pray they would survive another year.

"I suppose with spring upon us, 'tis good to know we've made it through another season," Anwen offered as a consolation.

"Aye. I suppose it is," Meara said solemnly.

"Aye and I thank you for having me at your table yester eve. It meant quite a lot to me."

"We were most honored by yer presence there." Meara smiled warmly and patted Anwen on the shoulder. "I pray ye are able tae stay with us a while longer, aye. I enjoy yer company verra much."

"And I yours," Anwen said with a smile, sure that the genuine affection she felt for Meara was evident on her face.

Meara grinned, gave Anwen's hair one last look and offered her a polished brass mirror.

Anwen beamed at her reflection, pleased with Meara's work.

"I wonder what keeps Christiona?" Meara wondered aloud, and with that, Christiona came bounding back into the room.

"Keir is not about," she told Meara quietly.

Meara curtsied quickly to Anwen and pulled Christiona aside. She crouched in front of her, noting her saddened state.

"What is the matter?" she asked of Christiona, who seemed quite shaken.

"Rorik had words with Keir earlier. He said Keir's mood was dark... again." Christiona sniffled as tears began to trickle down her cheek. Meara hugged her young sister and looked up to see Anwen's concerned look.

"Is all well?"

"Aye. It seems Keir is no' about. He may have gone off with his men. I apologize."

"No need," Anwen said. "As I've said, I'm sure his duties are more pressing than trying to busy a guest. I shall be happy to find my repose in your library." She smiled kindly and patted Christiona on the head.

"I shall come with ye!" Christiona sniffed, wiping her face against her sleeve.

"No, no, I think I shall like to visit there myself, if that is all right." Anwen gave her a sad smile. "I tend to lose myself in my reading and I would not want to seem as though I were neglecting you there."

"As ye wish, Anwen," Christiona answered a bit forlornly. "Are ye sure ye dinna want my company?"

"I would love your company, but perhaps later this evening after I have read my fill." Christiona smiled at that.

"Let us leave Anwen tae her whims, shall we?" Meara offered as she winked at Anwen and coaxed her reluctant sister out of the room.

As they left, Anwen followed them to the door and could hear Christiona discussing what activities she planned to busy her with while she was at hand. Anwen smiled, watching as they turned the corner, then she left her room and headed to the tower where the MacLochlainn library awaited her attention.

Chapter Seven

The familiar smell of the library brought an instant flood of memories back to Anwen. Life at her father's keep was lonely, but she had always found peace and solitude while inside the hallowed walls of his treasured store of books.

She roamed the musty chamber, running her fingertips along the weathered spines of the tomes that lined the shelves there. She recognized several books she had read before and pulled a few forward to skim through their contents. Many were written in Latin and Greek, which surprised her, and even more were written in the familiar Gaelic that she loved so dearly. The Scots Gaelic was a bit broader than her native Irish tongue, but she could read it without much difficulty having learned a bit of it from Galen.

She noticed a familiar title and pulled it into her hands, the worn pages like an old friend. The words brought a calm to her face and she continued to read as she made her way to a small nook across the room where light streamed into the dusty chamber.

She looked up briefly to find a seat at the window only to be startled by the sight of Keir, who had already found a comfortable spot there.

His long, powerfully built legs stretched out before him, his breeches clinging tightly to his well-muscled thighs. He had a pensive look about him as his eyes traveled across the pages and she couldn't help but sense a sudden kinship to him.

She hadn't known many men who read for pleasure, especially brawny, rugged men like Keir. The look of him cradling the book in the sunlight seemed so out of character and she couldn't help but wonder what he read so intently.

As he moved to turn the page he noticed her there and suddenly looked mortified, as though he'd been caught doing something sinful. He quickly closed the book, stashing it beside him. She nodded to him as he leapt to his feet.

"A good day tae ye, my lady." He gave a low, graceful bow.

"And to you, my lord. You have a lovely library."

"'Tis satisfactory at best. I daresay we need some new books."

"I find it very agreeable." She said as she gazed across the expanse of the shelves. "You should be proud to house such a collection."

"Oh, aye." He offered her a seat at the window and she sat happily in the sunshine, the morning rays shining pleasantly down upon her, warming her shoulders.

Keir cleared his throat awkwardly, his eyes wandering out the window as if he did not wish to look upon her. Her heart sunk with that thought.

"What were you reading?" She glanced at the small book and Keir retrieved it with some hesitation.

"I was just looking for something for my faither... a passage he mentioned." He quickly reshelved the book then took a seat next to her.

"Which passage? Perhaps I could help you find it." She stood, walked to the shelf and took down the book he had just placed there. Scanning the first page, a smile came quickly to her lips.

"Boethius," Anwen said. "'Tis a marvelous text."

"Aye," he said and looked away from her, pretending to find interest out the window.

"You read Italian?" A second surprise. The stalwart Scotsman was intriguing her more with every bit of information she uncovered.

His face suddenly took on a look of resentment, as though her words struck his pride. "Aye, I do."

"Do you enjoy his philosophy?" she asked with genuine interest. "Whose?"

"Boethius. I have read his work, but I daresay the text was in a more passable English." "You dinna read Italian?" Keir asked, a touch of smugness in his tone.

"Not willingly," she laughed softly and took a seat at the window next to him. "Which passage were you looking for?" She asked as she flipped through the pages.

He looked away from her again, disdain furrowing his brow. "None," he said a bit insolently.

"None?"

"'Tis my book," he said and took the book from her hands rather harshly. With a sigh, he tossed it onto the seat next to him.

"You are ashamed to admit you read?" She didn't quite understand his reluctance.

Literature was a treasure in her household and her father made sure even the soldiers at their keep could read some form of text. Some of them could even write.

"Nay," he admitted. "No' ashamed. 'Tis just a diversion, nothing more."

"A diversion?" she remarked quite curiously. "I wish it were the same with me. Reading is one of my passions."

Anwen hugged her book to her breast and her honesty touched him. The woman barely knew him and yet she chose to reveal a small part of herself to him. He could do nothing but

feel shameful that he had been so dishonest with her about a passion they obviously shared. A passion he was still ashamed to admit to her.

"What is it that ye read?" He motioned to the book she so lovingly clasped and she smiled. Her smile, radiating of the passion she had admitted so freely, was his ruination. He was blatantly aware of the heat rising in his face… and elsewhere.

Anwen blushed herself and handed him the small tattered book.

"'The Destruction of Da Derga's Hostel,'" he read aloud. "'Tis a noble tale." Keir fingered the title printed in gold across the cover in bold letters.

"You've read it?" She took the book as he handed it back to her.

Keir paused for a moment, carefully choosing his words before speaking.

"I've read nearly all that this library holds," he finally admitted, looking over at her with a dubious smirk.

"I must say 'tis more than a diversion if your appetite for literature is so voracious." She smiled coyly.

"Aye," he said with a sigh. "'Tis a passion for me as well."
"Why did you find that so difficult to admit?"

"I dinna ken, m'lady."

"If it pleases you, you may call me by name."

"As you wish, Anwen." Her name rolled off his tongue as if he had uttered it a thousand times before and he liked the way it sounded, the way it felt on his lips. "And you may call me by name as well." He bowed his head in a gracious gesture.

"Very well, Keir," she uttered softly.

The sound of his name on her lips sent a thrill through the very core of his soul and he could do nothing but think of a thousand other things he would love to do with her luscious lips.

He tried to quell the desire rising so quickly in his blood by thinking of something other than the way her eyes sparkled or the way her breast rose and fell as she breathed, but it was no use. All his thoughts were of her and only her and he was in a desperate state sitting so near to her.

She was watching him warily and he could only imagine how she thought him a buffoon for acting so daft in her presence each time they met. He needed to steer his thoughts away from the dangerous road they were traveling before he did something truly foolish in her presence.

"Are ye enjoying your stay here?" he finally said, turning in the seat to face her, drawing his leg up in front of him.

Anwen did the same, adjusting her gown so that it flowed over the side of the window seat, draping across her leg to the floor.

"Oh, aye. Your family has a beautiful keep, at least from what I've seen."

"Ye havena seen the entire keep?" he asked with a questioning quirk of his head. "Nay," she answered. "Christiona had hoped to give me a tour of the grounds, but she

had not had the chance as of yet. I have only seen the great hall and my chambers. We arrived fairly late and I've only had time to prepare for the feast yester eve."

"Then we shall remedy that. Would ye like tae go now?"

"You do not have other business to tend to?" she asked. "I do not wish to be a hindrance to your duties."

Duties? He thought insolently. What duties could I possibly have? How could he tell her that he was nothing more than a tenant in his father's care? His duties to tend to the merchanting aspect of their family were nothing more than a façade to cover the fact that he had nothing better to do with his time.

"Nonsense," he said, biting back his resentment to show a cheerful face. "My faither will understand if I am not at hand." What foolish talk it was. He felt ridiculous saying what he had.

"I would love to see your keep," she said.

Keir stood, smoothed out his breeches and extended his arm to her. "It would be my honor tae show you," he said.

Anwen took his arm and followed him out of the library.

"We could stop at your chambers first so you can drop off your book," he offered as he looked down at her.

"That would be fine." Anwen smiled and felt the heat of a blush rise in her cheeks. It was not truly her chambers, for her own personal quarters were hundreds of miles from where they stood, but the thought of having a man she found so attractive enter her private chamber sent a chill through her. A sensation she had never known.

They reached her room and he opened the heavy oaken door, allowing her to enter before him. Surprisingly, he stood in the doorway as she moved inside.

"You may come in," she offered, but Keir had disappeared. She set the book on her bedside table and reached for the cloak that lay across the foot of the bed, draping it over her arm as she left the room. She found Keir in the hallway leaning against the wall, his face dark and sullen.

"Are you well?" she asked quietly.

"Aye." His voice cracked and he cleared his throat purposefully. "Shall we go?" He raised his chin to meet her gaze.

His eyes had a lost look, so mournful and wanting, she had an immediate urge to throw her arms about him and console him. What was it that troubled him so suddenly?

She had noted a similar look in his eyes the night before as he sat in the corner and sulked. She stole many glances at him while he sat presumably unnoticed in the darkness of the hall, and she wondered if she had done something to make him angry again. But seeing his face and the look in his eyes even then had claimed her attention. His comeliness was immediately evident, as was the charm and boldness of his words and manner, but his hesitancy confused her. A man so attractive would certainly have a bevy of beautiful young women at his command, so what would he need of her?

Anwen swallowed a heavy heart and walked ahead of Keir. They made their way down the corridor past the other chambers to the staircase that led into the bailey. Keir walked slowly so she could take her time and gather her skirts about her.

She did not want to fall. It had been months since she had worn such garments and, truth be told, she rather liked wearing breeches for their ease of use. Had it not been improper for her to continue doing so, she would have happily donned breeches this day, but all of her questionable garb had been left at home as per her father's request. She was sure she could hear her father commenting on her clothing as they carried it away the night they left Ireland and she was embarrassed now that it had been so long since she had dressed as a lady.

She continued down the stairway as demurely as possible and gave a sigh of relief when they arrived at the landing to the great hall. She dropped the handful of skirt she had been clutching and smiled nervously up at Keir, who seemed to be amused at her complete concentration at the task.

"Have ye eaten?" he asked with a smile as she continued to smooth the skirt of her cotehardie.

"Nay, I haven't, have you?" she asked.

"No' as much as I should have. I wasna feeling well this morn."

"I am sorry to hear of it," she said, placing a kind hand on his arm. "Are you feeling well now?"

"Aye, I am," he said, matter of factly. "Come tae the kitchens and we'll see what is left."

Anwen followed him across the expanse of the hall, noting the looks of the men nodding to Keir when they passed by. As they were approaching the kitchen door, a young boy came rushing to his side.

"My lord," he said in a dutiful voice. "Lady Alicia has been inquiring as tae yer whereabouts."

Keir spun on his heels and faced the boy with a grimace. "Where is she, Gavin?"

"She's in the gardens with your sister."

Keir tightened his lips and glanced over at Anwen, who stopped just short of him.

"Lady Alicia?" she asked with a cocked eyebrow. "Is she not betrothed to your brother, Bowdyn?"

"Aye," Keir stated blandly.

"Perhaps you should tend to her. She is a guest as well, after all," Anwen offered smugly. It was not as if she wanted him to leave, for she was looking forward to spending some time in his company now that they were speaking to one another.

Lady Alicia seemed nice enough when she saw her at the gathering, English or no. She was a beautiful young lady. Gracious and well spoken, if not a bit vain for her tastes, but Anwen was happy that Bowdyn had been paired with such a fine woman. She had wanted to meet her, but the men had swarmed around her like flies to a honey pot and she could scarce say two words without being drowned out by Alicia's admirers.

But something in Keir's eyes made her hesitate. It was as if he were hiding something or trying to avoid a situation that made him uncomfortable, which she found very odd considering Alicia was to be his sister-in-law soon enough.

"Gavin, tell Lady Alicia that I am no' available and that I will speak tae her during sup if she wishes it." Keir finally said, his words clipped and terse.

"Sup?" Came a voice from across the room. "Is that all that can be afforded a lady who has come so far for your attentions?"

The lady in question was Alicia, Lady Walthingham. She was more beautiful than Anwen had remembered. Her hair was as golden as sun-ripened wheat. Her skin, so pale that it looked translucent, took on a rosy glow along her high cheekbones. She had the figure of a healthy woman, with curves in all the correct places. Her low-cut, tightly strung bodice only emphasized that fact and Anwen looked down at herself with a healthy dose of self-loathing.

Alicia's gown was impeccable, made of fine fabrics, with every inch embroidered and beaded to perfection. Her skirts glided about her as she floated across the room toward them. She was graceful and her very being ebbed of importance.

It was no wonder Keir had grown uncomfortable at the mention of her name. Anwen was sure she could see the lust in his eyes as he watched Alicia approach them. It struck a chord in her, sending alarms ringing in her mind and in her heart and she immediately took a disliking to the woman, no matter how much she had liked her the night before.

"Good day, Lady Alicia." Keir gave her a gracious bow, as did his page.

"How nice it is to see you, Keir," she offered, her words peppered with flirtation. "And who is your friend?" She looked over Anwen with little regard and turned her attentions back toward Keir with a smile and a flutter of lashes.

"Lady Alicia, may I present Lady Anwen Ní Connor."

"Ní Connor?" she said almost distastefully. "You're Irish?"

"Aye, I am," Anwen returned quite proudly and then gave a look of utter detestation to the arrogant woman.

"How quaint," was all Alicia said, then she took Keir's arm and began cooing into his ear.

"Where did you go yester eve?" she whined, brushing lint from his shirt. "I looked everywhere for you, you awful man. You had promised to dance with me."

Keir, who seemed all too comfortable with Alicia about his arm, glanced over at Anwen awkwardly and then smiled down at Alicia.

"I had business with my men. I apologize for no' keeping my promise," he said with a rueful smile.

"'Tis all right, I suppose," Alicia sighed demurely. "As long as you make up for your shortcomings." She hugged his arm in hers, which Keir seemed embarrassed to receive. In fact, he began stuttering and was looking between the two of them as if he didn't know what to do next.

"Lady Alicia," he cleared his throat and a flush came to his cheeks. "I've already promised Anwen I would show her the grounds. Would it be all right if we postponed our visit until this evening?"

Alicia's cheeks reddened at his request and she turned an angered face to him as she pulled him aside.

"Keir, what is this woman to you?" she bleated. "She's not another one of your maids, is she?"

Keir ground his teeth, took a deep breath then looked over his shoulder at Anwen. He offered her a look of regret with a smile and turned back to the woman at his throat.

"I beg pardon, my lady, but my relationship with this woman is none of yer business and as my brother's betrothed, I would think that ye would carry yerself with somewhat more decorum." His voice was calm, but his meaning and tone were clear.

"You're not avoiding me, are you, my Keir?" Alicia glowered.

"I will always be your friend, Alicia, you ken that well. Soon enough I will be yer brother."

"Friend? Is that what you think I am to you, your friend?" she nearly shouted.

"Alicia, I pray you," he hushed her. "We can discuss this another time. You are no' the only guest at this keep that I must attend."

"Very well." She sighed and then gave Anwen another dismayed review. "Just make certain the seat next to you at feast this eve is left vacant for me..." She looked down on Anwen once more. "And only me." Alicia nodded, accepting an agreement he didn't freely give, and kissed him soundly on the cheek before turning with a flourish and disappearing through the door.

Anwen frowned disdainfully, giving a mocking expression of what she felt of the Lady Alicia, and then turned toward the kitchens.

Keir heaved an irritated sigh of his own and followed quickly behind her. "Anwen," he said softly, reaching out for her arm. "Wait."

"I'm hungry and would like to get some food, if that is all right with you," Anwen offered and then looked down at his hand on her arm as if it was covered in dung.

"I apologize that ye had tae see that," he said flatly, pulling his hand away with a grimace, clenching his jaw angrily. "'Twas no' my plan tae…"

"To what?" Anwen cut him off sharply. "Humiliate me in front of your… mistress?"

"Alicia isna my mistress," he huffed. "Besides, what difference would that make? Why should ye take offense if she were tae ask for my company?"

Anwen's pulse pounded in her temples. She needed to get away from this man before she saw fit to punch him square in the jaw. She knew he was right, she had no reason to be offended by Alicia's request, for they would be family soon enough. Nonetheless, her blood boiled and she had no idea why. Why did it bother her that this demeaning woman coddled him so? Odd thoughts of bludgeoning Lady Alicia with her fists flashed before her eyes.

She quickly turned and pushed through the kitchen doors to regain her composure only to find an elderly man there, bickering with an elderly woman. Anwen groaned and when she turned hastily to leave, she plowed headlong into Keir.

"Will ye listen tae me at least?" he asked at nearly a shout as he clasped her by the arms.

"All right," Anwen said blandly. "Have at it then."

"Lady Alicia and I are friends and we have been for some time," he stated and then glanced over at his grandparents, who were now listening intently. After motioning with a beseeching nod, they quickly left them to their discussion.

The elderly man patted Keir on the shoulder confidently as he passed by and left the room.

"So, you've been friends," Anwen returned sourly.

"Aye, and the fact that ye are both in this keep at the same time should prove no problem for either of ye since neither of ye have any particular claim tae me." His words were bluntly stated, but they bit hard.

"I see," she said faintly. Her heart tightened and her blood ran cold. She turned out of his grasp. So he hadn't meant what he had said the prior evening about her being beautiful. Or if he had, it was a casual compliment that he handed out freely to other women as well, and according to Alicia's rather vocal admission, there were more than a few.

She was so certain she had sensed something in him earlier, a longing or perhaps the recognition of a kindred soul. A huge misjudgment on her behalf.

She took a deep breath and tried to move past the weight she felt pressing down on her chest, but the suffocation grew stronger and her eyes began to well with tears.

"Anwen, I…" Keir paused and touched her lightly on the shoulder, marking the tension he found there. "I do enjoy yer company."

"Company?" she turned with a sob and a tear, full and wet, trickled down her cheek. "I should have assumed I was as much."

Her tears startled him and his face was suddenly awash with guilt.

"Anwen." He pulled up a stool and motioned for her to take a seat, which she did gladly. "Have I done anything tae make ye believe ye were more than a guest here?"

"No, you have not." She bowed her head and her tears dropped onto her lap. She wiped her sleeve across her cheek with a sniffle.

"Then what?" he asked, baffled. "What is it that ye are crying about?"

"I had thought we had become friends, that is all," Anwen said tearfully, looking up into his eyes.

"Och, lass," he said with a sigh and bent to touch her arm kindly, only to be pushed away.

"Don't do that," she said, her face tight with sadness and anger. "Don't make me believe I am something I am not!"

"What are ye talking about?" he asked dumbfounded, stumbling away from her.

"The way you speak so sweetly and look at me as if I were important somehow.!" she shouted. "Then you turn like a snake, full of venom, and retract any kindness you have shown me. How am I to recover from something as hurtful as that?"

"Lass." Keir lowered his tone. "I dinna ken where I had attacked ye or had been hurtful toward ye, but I apologize if it was taken as such."

"And do not speak to me as if I were a child!" she said, her words clipped and tight. "You may be able to get away with treating your sisters as children, but I assure you I am not a child."

"Weel…" He chuckled and then cleared his throat. The smile faded from his face. "My sisters are children tae me, they are younger than I am. I dinna mean tae talk down tae ye, though. I suppose 'tis a habit for me. I offer my apologies again." He placed a hand to his heart and bowed his head to her, but his gesture was not taken kindly.

"And I assume I am to accept your apology with a faint heart, curtsy modestly, and skip out of the room giggling like a foolish little girl?" Her tone mocked and she sniffed back her tears angrily, her arms crossed defiantly over her chest.

"I dinna care what ye do with yerself, as long as it doesna require me tae be polite in any form so you willna mistake it for some odd gesture and snap my head off with yer wicked tongue!" Keir's face turned angry and in defense, he took a defiant pose of his own.

"How dare you?" she said, her voice tight. "I have done all that I could to be polite to you and you have the impudence to call me wicked?" She stood abruptly and marched past him, punching through the kitchen door back into the great hall.

Keir followed behind her furiously and ignored the stunned faces surrounding them as they quarreled.

Several of the on-lookers shuffled out of the hall at Caedmon's quiet demand, though he stayed behind to witness the scene unfolding.

"When we agreed to escort ye here, we did so in good faith. We had done nothing but show ye kindness and care."

"Aye, you did," she admitted and gave Caedmon an apologetic glance, which he happily received.

93

"So why the accusations? Are ye jealous of Lady Alicia?" Keir asked.

Caedmon audibly groaned from across the room.

"Jealous? What reasons have I to be jealous of a woman like that?"

"And what is that supposed tae mean?" Keir asked incredulously.

"You know full well what I mean." She rolled her eyes and took a seat at a nearby table.

"No, I dinna ken what ye mean anymore," Keir said, taking a seat next to her on the bench. "Yer words are barbed with underlying implications that I dinna seem tae ken the meaning of."

"Lady Alicia is playing you for a fool."

"She's what?" He laughed despite his anger.

"I see the way she toys with you, and you are eating out of her hands like a starved pup."

"Pup? I see. And what could I offer her that she would want?" He leaned his chin into the palm of his hand amusedly.

"You are important to this clan with all the powers it is afforded," she stated boldly. "Do not take me for an imbecile, my lord, I am more informed than I let on."

"Oh, are ye now?" He raised his brows quizzically, regarding her formal address and its insinuation. "And what knowledge is that?"

"I, well... I," she stammered.

"I thought as much." He dismissed her with a nod. "Ye shouldna argue about something ye ken nothing about, lass. It doesna become ye at all."

"I know more than you realize, Keir MacLochlainn," she said angrily. "And if you weren't so close-minded and daft, you would see that."

"Close-minded and daft? Me?" He laughed. "Yer off yer rocker, lass, if ye think me so dim-witted, for I ken more than ye realize as weel."

"And what would you know that would be any importance to me?" she asked dubiously, brushing her hair from her face.

Keir clamped his mouth shut, noting Caedmon's angry glare from across the room. It was on the tip of his tongue. How he longed to tell her what he thought of her, how he had tormented himself these past weeks with her so close by that her scent drove him mad, but that he could not quench his thirst of her because she was betrothed to another. He wanted to tell her all this and more, but he had given his word and she was not to know of the fate that awaited her. A fate he refused to be part of.

"And I thought as much," she retorted sarcastically, marking his hesitance to answer her. "You're just as full of spit and wind as the next man."

"If I dinna think yer faither would hang me high from Saint Marnock Hill for threatening yer life, I would strangle ye wi' me own hands, though I dinna find striking ladies verra tasteful as it is."

"If you're feeling the need to strike me, have at it." Anwen said, her laughter coming in gasps. "I'm not afraid of you, Keir."

"Weel, ye should be," he said blankly, realizing he had let his anger get the best of him. "Ye should be fearful of any man that would wish tae strike ye."

"I'm not afraid of pain. I've been in many a scuffle with my brothers," she offered proudly. "I'm no frail bird that will shrivel up and die if I get bruised."

"For yer sake, I hope yer right." Keir couldn't imagine how incensed he would become if another man were to strike her. He knew she was a strong woman, but no woman was a match for a man's anger.

"May I say something?" Caedmon asked as he approached them.

Anwen nodded kindly, but Keir seemed none too pleased at the intrusion.

"I think yer quarrelling should be done at another time. 'Tis no' appropriate here. And if yer needing tae continue with it later, I think ye both need tae listen tae one another's words and no' be so damn hateful of one another."

"Grandy, no' the now," Keir dismissed him.

"Keir," Caedmon scolded. "The lass is aright. Yer tone is condescending and I willna have ye try tae brush me aside wi' it as well."

"My tone isna condescending!" Keir snapped angrily. "And since when have ye decided tae take a stranger's side o'er yer own blood?"

Anwen growled at his obvious admission of her less than welcomed aspect in his life, and stood to leave only to have Caedmon catch her by the arm.

"This girl isna a stranger, Keir," Caedmon said, turning Anwen to face him. "She has been welcomed intae this keep as kin, by yer ain faither, and should be treated as such."

"I offer my utmost apologies for treating ye otherwise, my lady," Keir scowled at them both and stood to bow to her.

"And she has a name…" Caedmon added, giving Keir a less than pleasant look.

"I beg pardon…" He paused and grimaced at Caedmon. "Lady Anwen."

"Apology accepted, Keir," she said quietly, and then offered a brief, yet comforting smile to Caedmon, though her face still bore the shock of the words they had exchanged.

"Now…" Caedmon straightened his posture and smiled to them both. "Why dinna ye both get yerselves in tae the kitchen and fetch a meal afore Morág returns and shoos ye both out empty handed."

"Aye, Grandy," Keir answered and then turned toward the kitchen, but stopped himself to allow Anwen the lead.

Anwen nodded in appreciation of his gesture and then moved past him toward the door.

"Uh, Anwen," Caedmon spoke suddenly as he turned to leave the hall. "May I have a word with ye alone for a moment, lass?"

"By all means." She turned back to him and went to his side.

Keir paused at the kitchen door and then went inside when his grandfather gave him a decisive stare.

"Lass…" Caedmon struggled to find his words and pulled Anwen aside to speak quietly.

"What is it?" she asked, wondering what his reluctance was about.

"Lass, I ken yer bewildered by all that yer facing," he said bluntly.

"Aye, I am," she said with a nod.

"Dinna fash yerself over it much. I'm sure ye will find things will turn out for the best in the end."

"It seems my father has already made his decision on my fate and did not trust me enough to tell me of it before sending me away."

"He has his reasons, lass," Caedmon gave her a hug. "All will be well, ye'll see in time."

"I pray that you are right," she said, offering him what smile she could conjure.

"I am, lass." He smiled. "Now off wi' ye tae the kitchens and get ye some food." He jostled her a bit and sent her scurrying to the kitchen where his headstrong grandson awaited her.

Caedmon wondered, as he left the hall, how soon Keir would come to know the truth in his heart. He prayed that things would fall in Anwen's favor, but there was a chance he could be wrong. If that were to happen, Anwen would be undone and it was likely she would be sent off into the hands of the enemy. He prayed Keir had the sense to see her with his heart and not through the eyes of an angry, disenchanted man.

Only time will tell, he thought humbly, and gods help us when the truth comes tae the fore.

Chapter Eight

Cedric made his way into the great hall where some of his men sat quietly talking. He caught one of the men's attention with a glare and headed for the door.

"William." Cedric motioned with a wave of his hand. "A word with you, if you please."

William went to his friend's side cautiously and jerked reflexively as Cedric threw his arm around his shoulder and drew him closer.

"I've secured some time in Morgunn's council room," Cedric shared with him in nearly a whisper as he walked him toward the stairway. "Gather the men and have them meet there as quickly as possible."

"Aye, my lord." William nodded as he pulled away. "Is something amiss?"

"Nay, nay, nothing is amiss." Cedric smiled all too composedly. "'Tis time I've met with my men to go over our duties whilst we are here."

"Aye, my lord," he said obediently, "I'll fetch the men."

Cedric went to Morgunn's council room warily, pondering what eyes and ears were prying into his current business. He glanced out the window to see who was about in the courtyard, marking anyone who looked suspicious. As his men began to arrive he questioned each of them discretely. Had they been followed? Had they noticed anyone loitering nearby? Their answers proved otherwise, but he remained uneasy with his surroundings.

"I've received word through my sources that Lady Anwen has been sent off to Scotland," he offered diligently, looking at each of his men in turn. "There is reason to believe she has been taken in by one of the southern clans."

"Do we have any connections to the clans in that area?" William asked while unrolling a map before him on the tabletop.

"There are many clans in the south…" Cedric noted as he pointed to the map with the tip of his dagger. "Campbell, Lamont, MacDonald… we would be hard pressed to pinpoint which is harboring her without some information from the clans themselves."

"The Campbell's stand with the crown, do they not?" another man asked.

"Aye, they do, and given their large numbers and spread of their people, they will be our best asset in this search. The problem lies in that if she has boarded with a rival clan, we will be faced with a veritable war."

"True enough," another stated, scanning the map spread out before them. "Perhaps we will be fortunate in our endeavors and that won't be an issue."

"As much as I would like to think that, Roberts, we cannot rely on luck here," Cedric said decisively, sheathing his dagger. "This plan must be carried out with precision and without mistakes, else we will not receive what is due us in the end."

"And what is our due, if I may ask?" Roberts asked, his voice touched with tension.

The rest of the men mumbled in unison, supporting his question.

"That depends on how well this is carried out," Cedric answered a bit crossly. "If all goes as planned, you will each receive a substantial compensation. If not, well then, you are free to return to England empty handed."

"Empty handed?" William balked. "Will we not receive compensation for carrying out what we have, regardless of the outcome?"

Cedric stared him down with a look that was obvious in its intent.

"Would you have me pay you more than you earn for doing nothing?" Cedric asked furiously.

"Nay, but we risk our necks to carry out this mission. Surely, we should receive some extra sum for that effort and risk," William said boldly, looking to his fellows for agreement. Most of them nodded, but none spoke their agreement now that Cedric's temper had been provoked.

"We all risk our lives here, William," Cedric said calmly, his words spiked with malevolence. "Will you pay me to risk my life as well?" He looked William in the eye.

"As cousin to the King and commander of this company," William said, not backing down. "I presume you earn more than enough to cover any expenses you may have, but for the rest of us, we have families and lives to tend to and no royal wage to support our kin or pay our debts if we perish."

"Aye, William speaks the truth," another soldier spoke bravely. "What do we have if we are not paid?"

"You have your health, which is more than you could say if you are dead," Cedric said, leering at the man who spoke so boldly.

"So, either way, you have the best deal of us all. Where is the fairness in that?" William said with disgust, pushing back in his seat, crossing his arms over his chest.

"I am your commander and with that responsibility, my compensation should be greater. Besides, it is I who must stay in this miserable country to marry that Irish whore. To me, that doesn't seem a bargain at all."

"Ha, no bargain you say?" Alaric, the youngest of the men, laughed aloud. "To be married to a King's daughter and stand to gain all her wealth and power, I'd say that was a decent arrangement."

"Aye, you'll be living like a veritable prince once you are married and we'll still be soldiers," another man spoke out. "There'll be no hot baths or soft beds for the likes of us. It'll be back to England where we'll be given some other dangerous task and get nothing, save a shilling and a pat on the arse."

"Aye, we're not even free to leave the kings guard, should we so desire," another stated angrily and the others shouted their agreement.

"You chose this life, not I," Cedric argued.

Still the men grumbled their disapproval.

"Nay, many of us did not have the luxury of choice." William admitted, looking to his company of brothers for support. "We were forced into service fearing poverty or extradition."

"And many of you deserved far worse than that!" Cedric stated with a laugh. "You should count yourselves lucky that you were chosen and given the opportunity to serve His Majesty."

"Aye, some opportunity." Alaric grunted. "While we're risking our lives, sleeping on the ground and eating whey bread, His Majesty is off being pampered and coddled with exotic foods and fine clothing. That's some opportunity."

"I could have you hanged for such words, Alaric!" Cedric shouted, grabbing the man by his collar. "How dare you speak of the king as if he were some peasant off the streets?"

"God forbid…" William muttered and then yawned in exaggerated boredom.

Cedric released Alaric brusquely and turned a look of disgust to the man he thought to be his friend.

"William, I am sickened by your lack of respect." Cedric looked down at him with contempt, nodding his head with disbelief. "What has happened to you?" He glanced about the room studying the faces before him. "What has happened to all of you?"

The men he had hand chosen for their honor and spirit were now turning on him like hungry wolves who hadn't eaten in days.

"What has happened to us? What has happened to you, Lord Coventry?" William asked angrily, staring back into his steel grey eyes unwaveringly.

"Nothing has happened to me, William. What are you insinuating?" Cedric questioned impertinently.

"Cedric, you are my friend and my commander, but you are far from the respected, noble knight and Duke I once knew." William sighed as he looked away. "There was once a time when honor and duty meant the world to you. Now all you care for is wealth, power and status. 'Tis not like you, not at all."

"So, I am being criticized for wanting a better life?" Cedric asked.

"A better life, but at whose expense?" William asked, turning his gaze back to Cedric, whose face began to redden in anger. "You treat everyone as if they were your subordinates when you are nothing but a soldier yourself. You have no power here, save your military rank. Still, you carry on as if you had a throne in the great hall alongside King Edward himself."

"In due time, William, in due time." Cedric chuckled.

No one at the table showed their amusement. On the contrary, Cedric's jest only proved where his heart was in the matter.

"'Twill never come to pass," William said wryly. "Your travesty will be exposed and you will be dismissed for your misdeeds and then where will you be? You've deceived all of your friends and those you couldn't deceive, you've killed."

"And yet you are still breathing. How is that, William?" Cedric asked coldly, his eyes now hollow and emotionless.

"I am... my lord..." William stammered.

Cedric began toying with the hilt of his dagger, passing behind William's chair slowly, calculatingly.

"I thought as much." Cedric nodded and then took a seat at the head of the table. "I've had enough of this quarrelling and contempt from the lot of you. We have a mission to complete and we are running out of time."

"Aye, my lord." William sighed hopelessly and sat up in his chair, dismissing the apprehensive looks of his fellow soldiers.

"Due to the importance of this task," Cedric cleared his throat and stood to go back to his pacing, "I have written a missive that you are to read and destroy. No one outside this assembly is to hear of this plan. Am I clear?" he asked as he motioned to his page.

The men all gave their nods and the page handed a small, folded parchment to William, which he was to read and pass along.

As they read the letter quietly, several of them looked up from his words to give a look of disbelief.

"What is it?" Cedric leaned on the table with his fists. "Why the disparity?"

"Lord Coventry, you cannot mean that we should..." Alaric's words faded as he reread the small piece of parchment.

"You should what?" Cedric boomed. "If any of you have a problem with this mission, I ask that you speak your minds now."

"Lord Coventry," Roberts set the note down and pushed it aside with near repulsion. "She is but an innocent. Is this at all necessary?"

"Do you have another plan?" Cedric questioned.

"No, Lord Coventry, but I am sure there is another way."

"No, there is no other way."

"Can we not even discuss this?" William implored.

Cedric turned his back to them and walked slowly toward the window. After a few moments and a chance to be sure no one was lurking nearby, he turned to face them. The madness in his eyes was all they needed to see.

"You are all a bunch of heartless women! Cowards, the lot of you!" Cedric shouted.

"Nay, Lord Coventry, you are the coward," Alaric retorted. "Why not kill her yourself?"

The room went suddenly quiet and still. Alaric's statement was made loud enough that anyone within a hundred feet of the room could have heard him.

It was possible someone had.

Cedric immediately stomped past his men to the door and opened it to peer out cautiously. The hallway was empty. He turned with a controlled breath and went immediately to Alaric and motioned him to stand.

Alaric did so without question and he didn't dare look his commander in the eye for fear of what he would find there. When he had stood to his full five feet eight inches, Cedric reeled back and punched him soundly in the stomach, doubling Alaric over, throwing him back into his seat.

"This," Cedric stated in a wicked, icy voice, "is a private meeting for a reason." He glared at Alaric, who continued to writhe in his seat.

The remaining men sat up and eyed him warily as he paced about them methodically. "If I wished for the entire keep to hear what we were about," he leaned into Alaric's chair, staring angrily into his eyes, "I would have invited the entire keep to this council."

"Aye, my lord," Alaric groaned hoarsely.

"Now, before we leave this room, I want you all to agree to this mission. Those who do not may leave," he said strongly. His men rose slowly from their seats and one by one each of them nodded, the last man placing the parchment in the brazier on the table to be burned. Cedric stooped to poke at the ashes with his dagger to determine they were sufficiently charred and then sheathed his dagger and stood to face them all once more.

"Pack only what you need and leave as quickly and quietly as possible. If you should run into any problems or hear of any news, I will be notified at once," Cedric demanded.

"Aye, my lord," his men answered in unison.

"Godspeed to you all," Cedric said blandly and turned to march out of the room.

Confident of his men's ability to carry out this task in a timely fashion, he smiled to himself with assurance and made his way to the great hall where he promised to share an evening meal with Morgunn and Galen.

In time, he imagined, this castle would be under his control. There were so many changes he longed to make here, from rebuilding the ramparts to buying new equipment for the lists. He could see the newly improved Roísíndubh in his mind with its massive towers tipped in long, fluttering pennons, to the great hall, bedecked with tapestries and finely carved furnishings. He would throw the most wonderful feasts and only those of proper breeding would attend. Tailors and seamstresses would crowd around him, vying for his gold to attire him in the latest fashions.

And he would be respected and revered, that was above all else. He would see to it those below him knew where they stood in the scheme of things.

It was a world he could envision clearly and he could almost taste the victory, as sweet as it was. Once this task was completed, his life as a royal subject would begin. And not a moment too soon.

"Lord Coventry, won't you join us?" Morgunn offered from across the great hall.

"Good eve, my lord," Cedric said with a slight bow. "I trust you've had a fair day?"

"Fair, aye. And you?"

"Fair enough, I believe." Cedric took a seat next to Morgunn and nodded to Galen with a smile.

"'Tis good then," Morgunn said as he offered Cedric a plate of candied orange peels.

Cedric took a handful and laid them out on his trencher, then placed one in his mouth and began to chew.

"These are very good," Cedric said as he swallowed and placed another in his mouth.

"Aye." Galen smiled as he chewed on one as well. "These are my favorites."

As the three men conversed, more trays were set before them; mutton and meat filled pastries, bowls of stewed vegetables, sauces and fruits. Everything that a man could want to eat and yet Cedric still cast a discerning eye over the feast before them.

Rather than berate the man for seeming ungrateful for their hospitality, Morgunn would simply take the opportunity to find out what Cedric was made of.

"So, tell me, Lord Coventry," Morgunn began, grabbing for a half-discarded roll as a servant moved to remove the tray. "What is the King about these days?"

"The King?" Cedric asked quite curiously.

"Aye, 'tis been a year or more since I have been in your country at all. What has been going on there?"

"The usual, I suppose," Cedric said curtly, chewing away at a fatty piece of pork he held in his fingers.

"I'm aware that you are not able to divulge certain aspects of the King's life or perhaps certain political issues, but generally speaking." Morgunn left it at that, giving Cedric an opening to accept his challenge or back down.

Cedric finished chewing the gristle of the pork in his hand, tossed it onto his greasy trencher then wiped his fingers on the tablecloth.

"Well," Cedric began carefully. "You are already aware of our dealings with the Scots, I assume."

"Aye, that I am," Morgunn said modestly. His family had begun in Scotland centuries before and though he himself was of Ireland, he still held ties to his kin there, many which were lost to the English. "Were you involved at all in the wars?"

"Oh aye, my lord, of course." Cedric nodded. "My first was in the battle at Falkirk. What a bloody awful scene that was." Cedric shook his head with a grimace.

"Aye, Falkirk was quite a loss for the Scots if I'm not mistaken." Morgunn passed a plate of biscuits to Cedric and then handed him a crock of honeyed butter.

"No, you are correct." Thanking him with a smile, Cedric smothered one of the biscuits with the butter. He took a bite of the biscuit and chased it with a sip of his ale. "That bastard, Wallace, thought he could do again what he had done to the English forces at Stirling, but he was sorely mistaken. Edward routed the Scots cleanly with his archers and soon the battle turned in his favor. I hear we lost more horses than men that day."

"Aye, I remember," Morgunn answered, taking a bite of his own buttered biscuit, grimacing at the visions of his own experiences

111

on the other side of that war. "Quite the brush of luck you had that day, eh?"

"I know not what to call it. The Scots have never been the great threat that they wish us to believe they are."

"Aye, I suppose," Morgunn said blandly, handing Cedric another piece of bread to cool his burning mouth, trying hard to hold his tongue and keep from throttling the man.

"After Falkirk, my regiment was called back to York where I was posted at Clifford's Tower as a member of the King's personal vanguard," Cedric said, and then took another sip of his ale. "Edward's son and I, having been in one another's company throughout our lives, gained a trust which allowed me to fall into a more secure position in his service."

"Very impressive." Morgunn nodded smugly.

Cedric moved his stew aside for the time being and reached for a plate of mutton, stacking a few meaty pieces on his trencher before returning the tray to the table.

"Have you traveled elsewhere, Lord Coventry?" Galen finally piped in after having eaten his fill of fowl and game, and he sat back from the table, loosening his belt to ease his growing belly.

"Aye, I have, though not as extensively as I would have hoped to." Cedric poured a spoonful of rapeye onto his trencher, and after a few mouthfuls, the sauce was gone.

"I hear Italy is beautiful. France as well." Galen nodded as he picked his teeth with the tip of his dagger.

"Aye, they both are," Cedric answered with a smile. "I have been to the north of France many times as my father's family hails from there. And Italy is brilliant if you do not mind the heat."

"Aye, I found Italy remarkable in history and culture. Did you not as well, Cedric?" Morgunn asked him inquisitively.

"Aye," Cedric nodded as he, too, pushed his trencher away and sat back in his chair, sated. "I wasn't aware you had been there. Where did you visit while you were there?"

"I've been to both Genoa and to Rome. Genoa is a magnificent port city. In comparison, our humble harbors look miniscule. It is no wonder they lead in the seafaring trades."

"Nay, larger than Dubhlinn?" Galen questioned his liege.

"Aye, nearly thrice the size."

"He is aright," Cedric added. "In France as well, ports there grow quickly with the amount of trade they take in."

"Thrice the size," Galen surmised. "I can't even begin to imagine."

"Aye." Cedric nodded. "It does astound the mind at times. Before I had the opportunity to travel, I had no idea what lie beyond the shores of England. Even Scotland to me was foreign, all crags and mountains. Now that I have gone elsewhere, I can only imagine what new and exciting adventures await us all."

"Och, to be young again." Morgunn sighed humbly. "I once had that fire in my belly to traverse the world far and wide, but now that I am older and settled in my life, I find those adventures I had sought so eagerly were only a diversion for what my life was lacking."

"And what is that, my lord?" Galen asked.

"Family and tradition. 'Tis what holds our lives together, think you not, Lord Coventry?"

"On the contrary, my lord, I find neither to be particularly alluring," Cedric admitted freely as he picked at his teeth.

"Well, you're English, I suppose you wouldn't." Morgunn chuckled despite himself, and Galen chuckled along with the jest.

"Am I to take offense to that?" Cedric asked with a tinge of resentment in his voice.

"Nay, not at all," Morgunn assured him, patting him on the leg solidly. "What I imply is that family and tradition are the keystones of the Gaelic peoples. They are never one without the other."

"I find tradition to be stifling myself. 'Tis quaint in its meaning and uses, but when a man adheres to tradition year after year, when is he to learn anything new to pass on if not given that chance?" Cedric asked.

"The point to tradition is learning," Galen offered. "We pass our traditions down from generation to generation in hopes that those who come after us will not forget who we were or what we have done."

The conversation between the men continued for some time, skipping from topic to topic as Morgunn continued to pick Cedric's mind for clues to who he was and what he was about. Once the men were sated and relaxed, they retired to the far end of the hall where they shared drinks near the fire.

114

"So, tell me about your daughter." Cedric asked, breaking the relaxed silence.

"What would you like to know?"

"Well, I find myself in your company awaiting her arrival for our marriage and yet I know nothing of her," Cedric stated and then chuckled. "She could be a rotund, toothless spinster for all I know."

"Bite your tongue!" Morgunn said and then turned an angry eye toward Galen, who had chuckled at the statement Cedric had made.

"Och, Anwen is a fine lass, she is," Galen offered in her defense.

"Fine in what way?" Cedric asked as he leaned back in his chair and spread his long legs out before him.

"I cannot say that my opinion, or the King's for that matter, is impartial at all, given the fact we've known her since her birth," Galen offered as he stretched himself out as well. "But I will say she is a special girl, that one. She's got a quick mind and a kind heart."

"And what of her appearance?" Cedric asked flatly.

"She's the look of her mother," Morgunn said with a sincere smile. "Fair skinned and frail boned. Her hair is the color of the leaves in autumn and her eyes echo of soft Irish moss."

"She sounds absolutely lovely," Cedric remarked with a nod to the King. "'Tis a wonder there wasn't a line of men wishing to take her hand before me."

"Anwen is an... uncommon girl," Morgunn added cautiously. "She tends to be a bit idealistic and a bit unconventional in her thoughts. I blame myself for not being stricter with her upbringing."

"She is young yet," Cedric said with a comforting smile. "In time, I will teach her the ways a wife shall behave and conduct herself. Youthful ideals can only last so long without action to bring them to fruition."

"And so I thought as well," Morgunn added. "But she is stubborn and willful. More as a son would act than a daughter, I'm afraid."

"Not for long," Cedric scoffed. "Once she is in my keeping, she will learn her place quickly."

"Think you now?" Morgunn grinned and rubbed his chin furtively in his fingers, scratching at the growth of beard appearing since his morning shave.

"'Tis a husband's place to teach his wife her duties. Some women need a bit more coaxing than others." Cedric offered with a wry smile.

"If you mean to lay a hand on her, Lord Coventry, you best change your plans. I will not stand for any abuse of my daughter," Morgunn warned him.

"If I am not mistaken, my lord, once she is in my care I have the right to do with her as I see fit. If that means punishments to make her change her ways, then so be it."

"You'll be lucky if you find yourself leaving with her at all," Galen shouted, standing from his seat.

"Sit down, Galen." Angered at the vision Cedric had placed in his mind, Morgunn rubbed his eyes to clear his head.

Galen growled and then took his seat with a grumble.

"Cedric is correct. 'Tis a husband's right, though I do not condone such punishments."

"I will keep that in mind, my lord," Cedric offered coldly. "But if your daughter provokes me, I cannot promise I will keep my temper in check."

"If you wed…" Morgunn stated through clenched teeth. There was nothing he could do in this matter since the law gave all rights to the husband to treat his wife as he would. It was not something he agreed with, but law was law.

"You realize you will have no recourse in this matter, my lord," Cedric stated bluntly. "Once she is under my roof and in my bed, I will do with her as I please."

The thought of this man touching his daughter in any way struck a nerve and his fury was coming to a boil. If he didn't act quickly, he'd have much more to explain to King Edward than he cared to.

"I believe this discussion is over, Lord Coventry," Morgunn growled, then handing his goblet to Galen, stood to leave. "If you wish to continue to take your ease until the claret is gone, feel free. I, on the other hand, have duties to attend."

"As you wish, my lord." Cedric stood to acknowledge his departure.

"I do." Morgunn grimaced.

"Good eve, my lord," Cedric offered and then took his seat once more.

"Good eve, Lord Coventry," Morgunn replied as he left the room and was out the door before more words could be spoken.

Chapter Nine

"Why have you brought me here?" Anwen asked as she wandered into the expanse of the overgrown garden.

"'Tis full of flowers," Keir smiled. "I thought lasses liked flowers and such."

"I like flowers well enough," she said, plucking a stalk of wild lavender from its stem, twirling it in her fingers.

"I wanted ye tae enjoy the tour of my keep afore ye have tae leave and I thought perhaps ye would find this place peaceful."

"Oh, I do," she said as she tromped along the weed covered stone path. "Why doesn't anyone care for this place?"

"My mither usually tends the gardens," he said as he pulled at some weeds to clear away a small stone bench built into the wall. "She had been away visiting my sister and her bairns and hasna had the chance to tend it since she returned."

"And you do not find any joy in clearing this place?"

"Me?" he asked with a chuckle, his laugh deep and hearty. "Nay. I have never been good with plants except in the filtering of them tae make ale and tea."

"Nor I," Anwen grinned in return and sat next to him on the bench, picking nettles from her skirt. "I've never been good at any of the things my father tried to interest me in."

"What things?" he asked, leaning back against the wall to take in the sun.

"All those womanly activities…" She chortled. "Sewing, needlepoint, music, none of it interests me."

"What does interest you?" he asked, waving the bugs from his face.

"Oh, well…" She paused, twisting her mouth in thought. "I know not. I love to read, but that is not useful to women unless it entails reading recipes."

"There must be other things you are interested in," he suggested, blocking the sun from his eyes with his hand.

The sun glinted off his eyes and they sparkled with the brightest blueness that Anwen had ever seen. The sun was kind to him as it touched his hair. It seemed to glow with the richness of fine jewelry, spun into thousands of strands of gold, all varying in color slight enough that the true color could not be defined. It also caressed his skin, which was a deep tan from so much time spent out of doors. The sun that showered him with its rich glow highlighted the chiseled features of his face and the masculine curve of his shoulders and arms.

A knot suddenly lodged in her throat and she picked nervously at the bracken that grew next to the bench as her heartbeat quickened. If only he knew. Her mind wandered into the corridors of her deepest thoughts, visions of Keir's bold face softened by a dreamy haze. His linen shirt clinging to his well-defined body. His breeches snuggly forming to every endowment God had gifted him with.

"Anwen?" His voice pulled her thoughts back to the bench. "There isna anything else that interests ye?"

She cleared her throat awkwardly.

"None that come to mind." She smiled at him. "What of you?"

Keir lulled his head against the wall then turned his focus back to her, looking at her with such great intent that she thought for sure he was thinking of her in the exact same way. It sent a nervous tickle through her stomach that fanned through her body.

He was quiet for a moment, looking deep into her eyes, searching for something there, though what it was she did not know.

"I like tae read, too," he said with a genuine smile, then brushed the hair from his eyes. "Isna that odd?"

"Odd? Why?" she asked, pulling her legs up, folding them against the bench as she turned toward him.

"Odd that, weel, here we are, two people from two different parts of the world and yet we seem tae have the same interests."

"I don't find that odd," she said, tucking a stray hair behind her ear. "Reading is a common pleasure throughout the world. 'Tis just coincidence."

"Coincidence?" He smiled, tucking the same stray strand behind her ear that had freed itself in the breeze once more. "That we both have enjoyed the same books, the same writers, the same topics?"

Anwen stalled at his touch, her mind spiraling at the warmth of his strong hand against her face and she couldn't help but lean her cheek into it.

"What?" Her mind was out of focus. All she could see was his face. All she could think of was his lips.

"Ye are an amazing woman, Anwen," Keir said on a sigh.

"Me? Amazing?" she choked out. He had called her a woman. No one had ever called her a woman.

"Aye," he said. "Ye're smart and well-spoken and ye've got more than poetry and music in that head of yours. Tae me, that makes ye an amazing woman."

There was a spark there. She could feel it. Like a small, slow burning ember in her belly. And at that moment, there was nothing but poetry and music in her mind.

"I know not what to say, Keir. I do not truly believe that I am anything extraordinary, but I thank you for saying as much."

"Ye're quite welcome," he said and slowly, ever so slowly, he leaned toward her.

She knew what was coming. She wanted it to happen with every part of her being, but her mind scrambled and she turned away at the most inopportune moment.

His gentle kiss landed on her ear.

"I'm sorry." She fumbled with the hem of her skirt and looked away.

"'Tis all right, lass. 'Tis me who should apologize, it was disrespectful tae make such advances on ye. I should have kent better than tae jeopardize yer honor in such a way." His words were sincere, but the look on his face revealed his disappointment. She hadn't meant to give him the wrong idea, though her mind thought otherwise.

With every nerve in her body tense and on fire, she took a bold, deep breath, leaned forward and kissed him full on the mouth.

He pulled back momentarily and looked at her peculiarly before his face relaxed and he pulled her into his strong, warm arms.

The kiss was innocent, gentle and inviting. Little tingles of energy fluttered in her stomach. Unable to pull away, she was stunned when her arms moved of their own accord to encircle his neck. It was then the kiss deepened. His hands found her hair and his fingers, tangling in its voluminous length, were sending icy shivers of heat through her scalp. A moan, soft and profound, escaped from somewhere deep inside her throat when she felt his tongue dance tenderly inside her mouth. Breathless and light-headed, she finally pulled away.

"I'm sorry," she said, a bit embarrassed as she wiped her lips with her hand and stood to leave.

He caught her by the hand.

"Dinna be," he said softly as he stood and looked down at her. "I thought it was amazing, like ye." He smiled and lifted her chin to kiss her once more, this time urgently. Hungrily.

Her mind was awash with an explosion of colors. His lips were so soft, so pleasing.

Every thought in her mind wanted to end the kiss, but her heart sang of beautiful meadows and long, lazy days with Keir beside her. She could do nothing but dive into the depths of what she felt for him at that moment and, warily, she gave in to her heart. She could feel the heat of his body through the tight confinement of her cotehardie and it broke her.

The wanting inside her as he held her tighter and tighter was undeniable. He nipped at her lips, at the flesh of her jaw and down the tender length of her neck. He left a trail of cool, wet kisses along her collarbone and when his tongue found the warm cleft of her cleavage, her back arched to meet his touch instinctively.

"Och, Anwen…" he moaned softly against her skin. "What are ye doin' tae me, lass?"

Her knees went weak then and the earth fell away beneath her as they tumbled onto the ground where he covered her with his body. The urgent hardness of him pressed against her, the eagerness of his hands unmistakable as he grasped at the fabric at her shoulder to pull it away.

She sat up with a start.

"No," she said breathlessly, pulling the fabric back into place. "No, we cannot do this."

He rolled away from her, rubbing his face in his hands as he let out an exasperated breath.

"Aye, ye are right," he said, blinking away the fog that had befallen him. "I'm sorry, I shouldna have overstepped myself." He stood and brushed the dirt from his breeches, then held out a hand to help her to her feet.

"'Tis all right, Keir," she said, brushing the mass of hair from her face. "It was as much my fault as it was yours and I am not sorry for what we have done."

"Are ye sure, lass?" he asked, tucking her wild hair behind her shoulder, lingering to feel her skin there.

"Aye, I'm sure," she said as a blush bloomed across her cheeks. "I quite enjoyed that actually."

Keir smiled and nodded his head. "Aye, weel, I canna say that it wasna the most fun I've had while giving a tour of my keep."

"Oh?" she asked, smiling demurely. "Do you give many tours then?" The thought of Lady Alicia suddenly crept into her mind and for an instant she became angry that she had let the woman intrude into her lovely thoughts.

"Nay," he chuckled, the light in his eyes sparkling. "Ye are the first woman I have taken for a tour."

"And what of Lady Alicia?" she asked, wary of her feelings.

Keir's face stiffened at the mention of her name, and she could almost sense a panic in him.

"Lady Alicia has nothing tae do with this," he said flatly.

"Are you sure?" She raised her eyebrows and turned to follow the path along the east side of the keep.

"Ye think she does?"

"I think there is something more than friendship going on between the two of you, and so yes, it does have something to do with this."

"In what way?" he asked.

So, he didn't deny that there was something going on between them. It was just as she thought. How could she have been so foolish? How could she have opened her heart so easily to a man that did not care for her truthfully?

"I don't want to be a second thought, someone for you to run off with when Alicia is not about to cavort with."

"Cavort with?" he said angrily. "Weel, I'm glad tae see ye think so highly of me tae think I merely cavort with women and have no other need of them."

"I'm sure you have other needs for women," she said haughtily, glancing down at the apparent need that had swollen beneath his breeches.

Unashamed of his current state of arousal, he stood defiantly in her path with his hands on his hips.

It was fascinating to her, this obvious show of masculinity, and amusedly she stopped, hands on her own hips as she glanced down at him again with interest.

"Doesn't that hurt?" she asked.

"What?"

"Your…?" Embarrassed, she motioned her head toward the growing bulge in his breeches.

"My…?" He waggled his head mockingly. "Nay, I'll manage." He shook out his legs and ruffled the fabric to loosen the area a bit.

She giggled.

"Won't it go away?" she asked childishly.

"What?"

"Does it go away on its own, or do you have to do something… to set things to rights?"

Shocked by her innocence, he chuckled aloud.

"Ye really have nay idea, do ye?"

"Idea?" she asked.

"Of what goes on… with this." He grabbed his groin unabashedly.

The sight of his action stunned her and she turned away shamefully, not sure how to react.

"And how would I know?" she yelped through the knot in her throat as she turned to looked back at him.

"Weel, ye do read quite a lot, and I thought perhaps…" He tilted his head and gave her a questioning look.

"Perhaps what? That I had been with a man before?" she balked at this unconceivable thought.

"Aye."

"Nay, never." She bowed her head, a bit humiliated. "I'd never even kissed a man before, well, before you."

"Are ye jesting? That was yer first kiss?" he asked, stunned once more.

"Aye, that was the first for me."

"Weel," he said with a grin. "For a novice, ye sure know yer way about a man's mouth."

"Well, I do read quite a lot." She smiled as the heat of her blush spread through her body.

"I see," he said, moving closer to her so that her lips were only a breath away from his. "And what else have ye read about in those books of yours?"

"Well," she smiled devilishly, and with sudden boldness pulled him against her and found that the area he had managed to loosen earlier was now getting tighter by the second. "I know what kisses lead to."

"And what's that, lass?" he said in nearly a whisper.

She leaned into him and fearlessly took his mouth once more. The kiss was powerful and eager, their tongues entwining passionately, each vying for space in the others territory. It was she that found his hair this time and she pulled his face closer, almost crushingly against her own as though she starved for his breath. And this time, the moan came from his lips and it rumbled from deep inside his chest like the purr of a great cat. She was losing control, and by the feel of the impatient fumbling of his hands against her body, he was as well.

She pulled her lips from his and nestled breathlessly into his throat.

"I know it leads to something we cannot do." She sighed and hugged him to her.

"Aye, we canna…" He let out a sigh of his own and smoothed her hair with his hand and then gently kissed the top of her head.

"Not that I wouldn't want to," she added, looking up at him.

"Aye?" he managed as he caught his own breath. "Sure enough, then?"

"Aye," she said awkwardly, stepping back from him as she noted the desire in his eyes, in the way they wandered over the expanse of her bodice and beyond.

"I see what yer about." He grinned smugly. "Getting me all worked intae a lather and then goin' about yer business tae let me suffer."

"No, no…" she said with her brows furrowed innocently. "That was not my intent, Keir."

"Weel, intention or no', 'tis what ye've done, ye wee evil vixen," he said, grimacing as he looked down to find himself in a full state of arousal once more.

She gasped at the engorged sight of him and then covered her mouth to conceal her giggle.

"Ye think it tae be amusing, do ye?" he asked, hands on his hips.

Anwen could do nothing but laugh aloud.

"I do beg pardon, Keir." She choked back her mirth. "It's just… I've never seen anything like it, is all."

"I should hope not," he grimaced, but then smiled at the hilarity of the situation. "Would ye like tae see it then?" he asked as he reached down for the tie of his breeches.

"No! No, that's all right." She stopped his hands from revealing what lay beneath and then turned embarrassedly away. "We should probably get back."

"Aye, we probably should," he said.

Anwen made her way through the nettles and bracken and back to the entrance of the garden where she turned to face him.

"Just out of curiosity, would you have?" she asked, squinting up at him through the sunlight.

"Would I have what?" he asked oddly.

"Would you have shown it to me?"

He began to laugh aloud, a sound so hearty and infectious that she couldn't help herself from doing the same.

"Lass, ye do indeed amaze me." He smiled broadly and, placing his arm about her shoulder, walked her back to the courtyard.

Once they came into full view of everyone mingling in the courtyard, Keir seemed to recoil and shy away from her, removing his arm from her shoulder to clasp his hands behind him.

Anwen turned to question him and he looked away.

"I beg pardon, Anwen," he said as he stepped away. "Would ye mind much if I left ye for a time so that I could tend tae some business before the evening meal?"

"No, Keir, that's fine," she said. "I do not expect you to spend all of your time with me. I'm sure you have a very busy day without me interfering."

With a nod of thanks, he sprinted off to the main tower, his strong legs taking him quickly away from her.

It wasn't but a moment later that her heart sank to depths unfathomable as she witnessed Lady Alicia making a quick step toward the tower, her shrill voice calling out to him.

In the stairwell window above, she caught sight of the two of them as they met. Keir had turned and greeted Alicia with a smile. They talked for a moment and, before she could look away from the scene that was unfolding before her, she saw them kiss. Alicia had thrown her arms about Keir's neck and was clinging to him just as she had in the garden not moments before.

With her heart now in shattered ruins at her feet, Anwen lost all sense of hope and wavered for a moment as she stood there, alone and deceived. How foolish she had been to believe him, to think he actually had feelings for her. It was obvious all he wanted from her was a momentary flight of passion, an interlude to satisfy his carnal urges, nothing more. And it was obvious at the sight of them kissing on the stairway he would indeed find a way to relieve his tension after all.

When she looked up again, they were gone. He had probably swept Alicia off her feet right then and there and was bedding her as she stood there pining for him like a fool.

It was then she vowed her foolish days were done. Determined and with much purpose, she entered the tower, anger pounding in her temples and tears blurring her vision. Swiftly she made her way up the flights of stairs to her room and stood, frozen, in the hallway. Keir's chamber door was closed and Alicia's mellifluous voice issued from the other side. Visions of Keir, naked and aroused atop Alicia, flashed through her mind. She could imagine his hands grasping at Alicia's exposed flesh, tasting her, sampling her.

Distraught with the maddening image, she turned and stumbled through her chamber door. She closed it with trembling hands, then fell to her knees and wept.

She wept for what seemed like hours. She didn't even remember hearing Alicia leave Keir's room, if she had at all. The sun was beginning to set and the springtide sky, painted with hues of purple and red, spilled into her chambers, giving the room and everything in it an odd indigo tone.

Dazed and without hope, she made her way to the wardrobe across the room. Quietly, mechanically, she took off her dress, folded it neatly and laid it on the bed. She pulled a pair of breeches and an over-sized tunic from the trunk at the foot of the bed and put them on. She belted the tunic, which nearly reached the floor, and pulled on her leather boots. Facing the wardrobe mindlessly, she plucked out a few items of her clothing and wrapped them into a bundle. At the table of her bedside she emptied a small silver box, which held what coin she had brought with her. She placed the coin in her pouch, along with a few trinkets she had with her on her journey and, as though she were moving through a fog, gathered up what she had packed and made her way, quietly and unnoticed, to the stables.

The pages did not question her as she stuffed her saddlebags with her belongings and mumbled something to them about being called away.

"I'll have the horse returned to you shortly," she offered dazedly as she turned the reins and coaxed the horse out of the stables. The pages nodded and watched her go.

With knowledge of her own keep and after seeing how tasks were carried out during her tour that afternoon, she was aware that the gate guards swapped duties at sundown. She waited in the shadows as the men exchanged pleasantries and, when she saw her opening, she gave her mount a swift kick and bolted for freedom. The men, caught off guard, followed on foot momentarily, shouting after her to stop.

She was well out of reach by the time their voices had died away and she was enveloped by the vast stillness of the twilight. She rode hard and when she finally came to her senses and slowed her mount, she stopped and turned to face where she had been.

The silhouette of Castle Lachlan loomed on the horizon, more than a mile out of reach. She could not turn back now, nor did she want to. She was on her way to a new life. Where, she did not know, but if it was far from Keir, she would be content.

Keir grasped Alicia by the shoulders and managed to pry her from his lips with some effort.

"Alicia, stop this! What are ye doin'?" he asked angrily, bodily holding her away from him as if she were a poisonous snake.

"Oh Keir," she whispered breathily, "You know it is you and not Bowdyn that I love. Why is that so hard for you to understand? Look at you, how strong and virile you are, how handsome and powerful…" her hand went to his chest where her fingers traced the lines of his muscles there. "How could I even think of another man with you in my presence? The mere scent of you sets my blood on fire and I know you feel the same. I know you do." Her voice was silky smooth as she leaned toward him.

He was nearly fooled, allowing his grip on her to ease when he felt her hand travel down and grasp him firmly.

"I can feel how you want me, Keir," she sighed.

The feel of her hand grasping him so intimately sent a shockwave through his system. The immediate sensation was not an unpleasant one, but in the same instance, the astonishment of her touch brought his mind back into focus and he seized her more firmly and held her away from him.

"Nay! This willna happen between us, Alicia," he said coldly. "It will never happen, do ye understand? Ye are betrothed tae my brother and that makes ye untouchable tae me. I dinna care if ye are the Goddess Áine sent to earth, I couldna lay a hand on ye even if I wished it so, and I dinna."

"Keir," her voice cooed. "You know you are lying to yourself. I've known how much you've wanted me. I've seen the way you look at me, how your hands long to touch me... how your tongue yearns to taste me." She leaned toward him again, but his grip was strong and her advances thwarted.

"I could never touch ye, Alicia," he said stolidly, though the thought had crossed his mind many times in the past. "My brother has given ye his vow and I canna break that trust he has in ye, and ye of all people shouldna misuse his trust as ye are."

Alicia furrowed her brow, her mouth now set in a sultry pout, but Keir was having none of it. He loosened his grip and set her away from him, crossing his massive arms before him angrily.

"Why are you being so stubborn?" she asked girlishly, batting her lashes at him seductively. "No one would ever have to know, it would be our little secret." She moved toward him alluringly.

"Your charms are no' going tae change my mind on this, I can promise ye that," he said flatly, then turned and made his way up the stairs and down the hallway to his chambers, but she had followed him and boldly entered his chamber, closing the door behind her.

"I beg to differ," she said softly as she came up behind him, running her hands over the expanse of his well-muscled back.

Keir's mind spun out of control. His thoughts flew immediately to Anwen and the mere thought of hurting her tortured him, but she was to be betrothed and just as he could never have Alicia, he could never have Anwen for the same reasons.

The feel of Anwen in his hands was more than enough to set his own body on fire, but he could never extinguish the flame she ignited and suddenly the thought of letting Alicia have her way didn't seem like such a terrible alternative. He could smother this insatiable need he had building painfully inside him and finally have something before his brother, for once in his life. Suddenly it didn't seem like a bad idea, but he just couldn't get past the repugnance of the whole situation. As much as he despised his brother at times, he couldn't get himself to break that trust between them. There was too much honor at stake.

"Beg all ye like, Alicia," he said plainly, "but I canna disrespect my brother by taking his betrothed…" He turned to face her, expecting her to be pouting or putting on some other dramatic expression. Instead he turned to find that she had unlaced the front of her gown and fully exposed herself to him. The sight of her bare body caught him off guard and his logic nearly failed, but the act somehow touched a nerve inside him and his blood began to rage. He moved toward her, his air calm and deliberate.

"Ye are a beautiful woman, Alicia," he offered, his eyes moving over her licentiously. "But had I known ye were a whore, I would have warned my brother against marrying ye if only tae save him the shame of being yer husband. Save yerself the time and effort," he said sarcastically, brushing past her deliberately to offer her the door, "I doubt I could ever afford ye anyway."

Incensed, she hurriedly laced her bodice and stomped out the door and he happily shut it behind her.

Relieved, Keir sat on the edge of his bed and lay back, letting out a huge sigh of frustration. Had Alicia pushed him any further with the current state of his need, he was not sure that he would have been able to stop himself. He lay on his bed for several moments, then went to his washing table to splash cold water on himself several times before his blood cooled to a normal temperature. After some time, he was finally able to leave his room and go in search of Anwen.

Bowdyn was coming up the stairway just as he was making his way down and Keir smiled awkwardly and kept walking past him.

"Have ye talked tae faither about Anwen's departure?" Bowdyn asked, turning to follow him as he made his way to the great hall.

"Nay, I havena. Why?"

"I saw him earlier and he mentioned wanting tae get her tae the abbey as soon as ye could get her ready tae leave."

"Why the rush?" Keir asked. "She only just arrived."

"He's received word from the Douglas chief that there is trouble afoot. English troops have been spotted as far north as Dumfries and their numbers seem tae be increasing as they continue tae move inland."

Keir stopped on the stairway and spun to face his brother. News of English troops so near could only mean one thing; Edward was meaning to attack again.

"Does faither mean tae go tae Dumfries?" Keir asked eagerly.

"Aye, he's calling council tae his side now tae discuss his plan of action and the other clans will head south as soon as they can."

Keir continued down the stairs and turned down the path that led to the courtyard instead of entering the great hall. Soon it would be alive with activity as the men in the clan gathered and prepared to head into the skirmish. And as always, Keir would not be going along.

"Faither wants ye tae prepare for yer ain departure and leave in the morn. Yer tae take Rorik and Caedmon with ye and take the lass tae Elgin as quickly as ye can manage."

"There is nay getting out of this, is there?"

"Why would you want tae get out of it? You'll be safe in the north while the rest of us are facing those bastards in the south."

"I'd rather be facing my foe than carting Anwen to an abbey," Keir grumbled. "Are ye sure I must take her? Canna someone else do it?"

"Nay, faither requested that ye do it," Bowdyn said, going to his brother's side. "Besides, we'll need someone here for when we return and I canna think of anyone's face I'd rather see than yours when we do." He punched Keir on the arm jovially, but Keir was none too pleased with their decision.

The thought of spending so much time in the company of the charming Anwen pleased him, but that charm was far outweighed by his urgency to join his clan in the struggles that faced

138

them. He had never known the gratification of standing shoulder to shoulder with his kin on the battlefield, to feel the winds of change on his face as the enemy charged them head on. His bones fairly ached for the thrill of such a spectacle, but they also ached for something more. They ached for the touch of a woman as fiery and strong as the one he was charged to transport halfway across his country, and the indecision of it made his head spin.

"Tell faither I will be ready," he said insipidly, turning to go back to his chambers. "Has anyone informed Anwen that we are leaving?"

"Nay," Bowdyn said as he followed behind him. "Faither thought he would leave that task tae you," he said with a smirk.

Keir grimaced and took to the stairs and growled as he entered his chamber. Making his way across the room, he opened his wardrobe and stuffed some of his clothing into a satchel.

Anwen would not go quietly and he couldn't blame her. He didn't want to go either. He was fairly sure he would have to fight her on this and would have to keep a close eye on her while they traveled. Not that he minded watching her, the way her body moved when she walked, or the way her russet hair caught the sun in its web and lit up like strands of burnt gold.

The mere thought of her made his groin ache. To hold her body once more, to feel her soft skin in his hands would be heavenly. The urge of it made him fair itch with hunger.

Pushing the thoughts aside, he stuffed the last of his belongings into his bag angrily. He could never have her completely and he knew that well. Why he bothered to even think about her and continue to torment himself, he didn't know, so he consigned himself to the task at hand and readied himself to leave in the morn, intent on removing her from his mind.

Chapter Ten

"What do ye mean she's gone?" Keir balked as Gavin stood before him fidgeting.

"Aye, the night guard saw her leave not an hour ago. They said she was in quite a hurry," the small boy said.

"Did she say where she was going?" Keir asked impatiently.

"Nay, just that she looked mighty upset and that she dinna stop when they called after her."

Upset? Why would she be upset? His mind scrambled, trying to think of reasons why she would leave so abruptly, and then it came to him. She must have seen Alicia kissing him on the stairway. How could he have been so imprudent? And if he knew any better, he would wager Alicia knew she was watching and that made his blood boil even more than it already was.

"Find Rorik and me Grandy and tell them tae meet me at the stables. Tell them tae be ready tae ride. Go, as quickly as ye can," he commanded the small boy, who was out the door with a nod, his footfall quickly fading down the hallway.

Keir went back to his bed and dumped his satchel there and then purposely strode to his wardrobe and threw open the doors. He roughly moved his clothing aside and reached into the depths of the cabinet where he grasped a sturdy item and pulled it forth. He hadn't had need of the claymore since the day it was gifted him on his thirteenth birthday. It sat, unused, in the darkness of his wardrobe for eleven long years, but now, there was a need.

Anwen was a smart girl, there was no doubt there, but wandering out into the unforgiving expanse of their surrounding lands, there was no telling was dangers would befall her and he wanted to be prepared, no matter what the cost. The outlands were crawling with thieves, reivers and all types of ruthless brigands, including the growing number of English troops making their way north. The thought of her falling into any of their hands made his stomach twist into a sickening knot, but he fought back his panic and set his mind to the task at hand.

He laid his claymore on his bed and went to his trunk where he pulled forth a thick, well-weathered cloak and threw it onto his bed. Then he closed the trunk and reached for his claymore, strapping the scabbard of the six foot blade across his chest so that the weight of the blade hung comfortably across his back. Then he quickly grabbed his satchel and cloak and headed down to the stables where he hoped Rorik and Caedmon were ready and waiting for him.

He took to the stairs two and three at a time and burst through the door leading out into the courtyard. Sprinting toward the stable, he saw Rorik was waiting with his reins in hand.

"Where's Grandy?" Keir asked as he dropped his bag onto the ground.

"He's gathering some things for the trip. What's happened?"

Keir went into the stable and began checking the tack on his horse and Rorik followed him inside.

"Anwen's run off," he said as he pulled the girth tight and secured the strap.

"Run off? Why?" Rorik asked as he handed Keir his saddlebags.

"I dinna want tae get intae the reasons why just now, but she's verra upset and we must find her before she gets herself intae trouble."

"Aye," Rorik said with a nod. "There's been reports of English troops scattered about the harbors. There's no telling how far inland they've come."

The knot in Keir's stomach clenched at that thought. He knew the English had been spotted, but he hadn't known they'd made their way this far north. If they found and captured her, they would not be sympathetic. He blinked against the visions in his mind and impatiently finished fitting his horse and then took the reins in hand and walked the beast outside.

"We must ride out at once," he said as he stuffed his belongings into his saddlebags, then mounted.

"Aye," Rorik said and got on his own horse.

Caedmon arrived moments later with a bag full of supplies. He took the horse given to him and followed behind as Keir aggressively coaxed his mount through the gatehouse and into the darkened braes before them.

Anwen should have known better than to stray from the heavily trodden path leading to the road, but she needed time to think about what was currently going on in her head, and in her heart.

She caught sight of Loch Fyne and had decided that taking a walk there would help her clear her mind and help her focus. She dismounted, tied the reins to a nearby tree and wandered numbly toward the shimmering waters that sparkled as the moon rose overhead.

She sat for a moment, longing to turn back time so she could feel that invulnerability that once ebbed through her veins, but looking down at the simple tunic and breeches she now wore only reminded her where she had been and what she had done...and what she was running from. It wasn't just Keir, it was her entire life.

The tears came easily this time and they were full of sadness now more than anger.

Regardless of what had occurred and what she had witnessed, she still felt a deep longing to be back in Keir's unyielding arms, but could she ever forgive him? More to the point, would he ever love her?

No, she told herself defiantly, wiping her nose against the coarse blue linen of her sleeve. He had deceived her. He had toyed with her heart with no sign of remorse or concern. Keir was a man, pure and simple. He was a slave to the urges that drove him and nothing was going to change that. In all actuality, Alicia may be only one of many on a long list of women who warmed his bed. He was a chieftain's son, handsome and strong. What woman wouldn't want such a man as a lover?

She thought back to the day they had met at her father's keep. He was indifferent then and seemingly out of his element. She conjured the time they had spent together on their journey to Scotland and did not remember him being interested in her. In fact, from what she recalled, he seemed to demand to be alone. He had been angry about something, but what? She would never know because he had never opened up to her, not even after they had become friendly.

She closed her eyes and tried to focus, to bring that time back so she could see what had truly taken place, but she could find no fault in him or his actions, save his reticent manner.

Had she misjudged him so effortlessly or was it simply an act on his part? Her heart was pounding in her chest now, her mind reeling with doubt and yet pulsing with hope.

She could not deny what she felt for him, even after what she had thought him to be. And perhaps he still was that man she despised. She had nothing to base her judgments upon for she did not know any other man so intimately. All she could do was talk to him and pray he would speak the truth in his heart. In turn, she would reveal the truth in her own heart... that she loved him.

He had called her a woman once... an amazing woman. Amazing women did not run away, they stood in the face of adversity and strove to find the truth in all matters. They did not snivel and run off like children when situations were insurmountable. Her father had told her that once. Now she would listen. She needed to stop running.

Wiping her face on her sleeve once more and taking a deep, cleansing breath, she rose to her feet and cast a glance across the loch to find the strength inside her. As the night air trailed in a ghostly path across the rippling waters, she let the coolness of it touch her face, and comb through her hair. She felt the tension slowly ease from her body and mind.

She turned her back to the loch and started up the footpath toward her mount when she heard the clamor beyond the braes. Had Keir come in search of her after all? No one aside from the pages and guards had seen her leave, though commonly they would have felt it their duty to inform the chieftain of such an incident. She was certain that was what all the noise was about. No reivers or cunning thieves would make such a racket on such a still night as this. It had to be Keir.

With a hopeful heart and a cheerful smile, she quickened her pace toward the noise and came upon them almost by accident.

Vaguely noticing the faint glow of the campfire, her senses didn't register the warning until she stepped into plain view of the company of English soldiers that were having dinner around the small fire. Her first instinct was to run, but her body had frozen, locked and unwilling to budge despite her mind's panicked demands. She had forgotten to breathe and nearly caught her tongue in her throat when she finally gasped aloud, which ultimately betrayed her to the enemy.

"What have we got here?" One of the men stood from his seat near the fire and immediately rushed to catch her by the arm. "A pretty wee plaything?" He snorted and drooled as he sniffed at her neck.

"How dare you?" she said angrily, shoving away from him and wiping her neck with her sleeve. "Get your hands off me!"

"Lively too, eh? Even better," the soldier said as he caught her again and flung her towards his comrades, who stood to catch her.

Many of them seemed to be menial men, soldiers and horsemen, probably enlisted troops. The only man looking to be of any significant rank sat alone, across from the fire, under the gnarled branches of a rowan tree reading a small book. He looked up to watch the commotion, but did not move from his spot or show any signs of interest.

"Where ye goin', miss, all dressed up an lookin' fancy?" The soldier picked at her tunic, lifting the fabric to get a closer look.

Anwen would have no part of it. Yanking the tunic from his grasp, she stepped back, and in a hasty decision, slapped the soldier across the face. Her hand connected with a clear and resounding smack.

His campmates laughed heartily.

"You're going to pay for that, ye bitch!" the man hissed and turned on her immediately, landing a blow that sent her reeling through the fire, sprawling at the feet of the officer sitting against the rowan.

Her mind was swimming with violent words that blurred into incomprehension. She came to her hands and knees, still dazed from the punch. Her blood, warm and wet, trickled down the length of her cheek. When the first drop appeared in the dirt in front of her, she began to falter and she looked up into the eyes of the man pleadingly.

"Please, sir… please stop them," she said, her voice cracking.

The man briefly looked in her direction, their eyes making contact for only an instant, and then he went back to his book, nonchalantly turning the page as if she were merely a figment of his imagination.

"Jameson, will you please do something about this mewling baggage." He sniffed and turned another page.

"Aye, as ye wish, my lord." The soldier who had struck her kicked his way through the fire and grasped her by the arm, yanking her to her feet.

"You can't do this to me," she announced in a demanding voice. "There are men looking for me at this very moment. If you harm me, you will not live to see another day," she shouted.

The men continued to laugh and Jameson, who had a firm grip on her arm, began to yank her in the direction of the small cluster of tents that were set up near the fire.

"Oh, your men are lookin' for ye, are they? So where are they then?" He put a hand to his mouth mockingly. "Hullo! Hullo, you big lads! I got your lassie here, so come an' get us," he shouted, to the amusement of his men, whose laughter had grown even louder.

He stopped for a second to pretend to listen for their arrival, giving a comical show of fear and then he waved a hand to dismiss the thought.

"No one's coming. Now stop fussin'." He jerked her arm to get her attention.

Anwen's head suddenly cleared. He was taking her to his tent to violate her and when he was done, there was no telling how many of the others would spoil her in turn. The blood drained from her body and she suddenly felt faint, but something inside her pushed her to fight.

"They are coming... and you will unhand me!" She shoved against him with every fiber of her body and could break loose momentarily.

He lurched at her in an instant, grabbing her by the shoulders and throwing her bodily into his tent where she landed on the hard ground with a jolt. Before she could even get her wits about her, he had hoisted her to her feet by her collar and threw her onto what she could only assume was a hastily thrown together sleeping area, where she landed, startled and gasping for air.

"You bitch! How dare you command me, and in front of the men no less!"

His backhand threw her off balance. As she hazily tried to crawl away from the man, he caught her up again by the shoulder, this time tearing the fabric nearly clean off, revealing more of her than she was willing to reveal. She hastily drew a hand up to hold the fabric in place.

"I beg you, please… don't," she stuttered, her pleading coming involuntarily and only one thought came to mind. "Money! I can get you money," she cried.

With crazed eyes, the man looked her over. The glimpse of her body was all he needed.

"'Tis not your money I'll be wanting from you," he said with an evil, drooling grin. "I think I'll be getting me some of that ripe fruit of yours, how 'bout it?" He grabbed her by the arm and threw her onto the floor in front of him and started to fumble for the tie on his breeches.

Anwen shook her head absently, mouthing silent, pleading words. She began to crawl away again when she found herself backed against the tent wall. In her desperate attempt to flee, she found the bottom of the tent loose and in the next moment hoisted it over her head and scrambled out into the darkness.

Not knowing where she was going, she just ran as fast as her feet could carry her. Her tunic tripped her and caught on brambles. She was desperately trying to cover herself with the fabric left at her shoulder. The shouts and whistles of the soldiers who had taken to chasing her were growing louder behind her, but she continued up the steep, rocky embankment toward the clearing ahead of her.

On hands and knees, she clambered to the top of the hill to search for her horse. When she came to the rise and saw the dimly lit silhouette of the MacLochlainn keep so far out of reach, her heart sank. Out of breath and energy, she pulled herself to her feet and stumbled toward the castle, this time losing all ability to run. Jagged edges of rocks dug into her joints as she fell haphazardly down the steep embankment into a thicket below.

The voices were closer now, and Jameson was the first to crest the hill behind her and his wicked smiled glistened in the darkness as he strode purposefully toward her.

"You're not a smart bird, are ye?" He kicked the brambles aside with a booted foot and dragged her to her feet.

"'Twas not wise of you to run like that. Now we'll have to punish you," another man sneered.

Her mind was screaming now, but her mouth was silent. Her body, limp. The soldier drew back and punched her full in the stomach, doubling her over so that she thought she would die from the loss of breath. It left her completely and she lost all ability to refill her lungs. She gasped convulsively, her eyes wide with terror as she groped at her throat searching for air. Her tormentors stood over her like spiraling crows.

"Enough already! Stop with yer belly achin'," Jameson demanded as he kicked at her.

When her beaten body finally gave in, she sank into a world so dark and quiet that it seemed a nicer place to be. In a haze of voices and blurred visions, she felt her heavy, limp body hoisted onto a shoulder, her head bobbing like a dead chicken's as the soldier walked back to camp. Conversations buzzed dully in her head and the unmistakable scent of the men surrounding her, a mixture of smoke and sweat, numbed her mind further. She was dumped again onto bedding and she lay there, lifeless.

"So, what do we do with her?" A voice asked and there was a silence. Fingers poked at her, trying to jostle her into consciousness. Suddenly, there was a murmur of voices and the air seemed to change.

"Bind her, Jameson, but leave her be. I believe I know this girl," another voice said. "I'll deal with her on the morrow."

Chapter Eleven

"This is madness!' Keir said as he threw his hands in the air and kicked at the rocky ground beneath his feet. "We've absolutely no idea which direction tae go, aye?"

Caedmon and Rorik looked at him sympathetically but said nothing in response.

Caedmon struggled ahead a bit more, giving the impression that he hadn't given up hope of finding Anwen, but Rorik's face told a different story. The hopelessness was apparent in his eyes. Rorik ran his dirty hands through his hair and sat on one of the boulders that surrounded them, jutting up from the earth like blockades to their search.

"Keir," Rorik said through his fingers as he rubbed his face in his hands exasperatedly. "We've got tae head back, aye? We're nearly out of sight of yer land and those clouds are starting tae look angry." He stood again and climbed the boulder he had sat on, looking out over the landscape, watching as the clouds gathered intensity.

"'Tis all yer good for, aye, Rorik? Always thinking of yerself. Go then! Run home!" Keir stomped over to where Rorik was perched and shoved him from the rock.

Rorik took a tumble and immediately came to his haunches, seething.

"Yer a madman, do ye ken?" Rorik shouted. "We're trying tae help ye here, but this is dangerous!"

"Do ye think I dinna ken that? I'd rather be back at the hall with my feet up on the hearth as well, no' traipsing about the countryside without any idea of where the bloody hell we're going," Keir yelled.

"We ken, lad," Caedmon said as he touched Keir's arm. "We both ken how important this is tae ye, but there comes a time when ye have tae take hold of yerself and accept that there's nothing more ye can do."

"Important?" Keir jerked away and turned on him. "Ye think this is important tae me? 'Tis no' important, 'tis my life on the line! If we leave now, if we turn and run home, I will be tae blame. I gave my word tae her faither that she wouldna be harmed. I canna go back and tell him she is gone. I just canna, can ye?" he pounded a fingertip into Caedmon's chest, then gave the same, dark, questioning look to Rorik.

Rorik made no move to come to his feet; rather he pulled up his knees and laid his forehead down atop them.

"Keir, be reasonable. What will we accomplish here, now? 'Tis dark and Rorik's right, those clouds look tae be bringing a mighty storm our way. If we're no' tae head home, we should at least put off our search and take cover for the night. We could start fresh on the morrow." Caedmon patted Rorik on the shoulder and offered a hand to get him to his feet, but he nodded and went back to his meditations.

Keir stood defiantly away from them. His arms crossed against his chest as the gathering wind whipped his hair angrily behind him.

He had to find her. There was no other choice. He wouldn't rest until he knew she was safe. But he knew Rorik was right. It had been too long and the chances of them finding her in the darkness were very slim. Deep down, he had confidence they would find her and she'd be alert and unharmed when they finally stumbled upon her. Then their trip home would be a joyous one. She was a fighter, he told himself over and over… a fighter.

"Aye," Keir said quietly, dropping his arms coolly to his sides, turning to Caedmon. "We'll stop here for the night, but ken that I plan tae rise afore the sun and God help us if she is no' found on the morrow."

"Good lad." Caedmon patted him on the shoulder and gave him a sincere, comforting smile.

Rorik finally rose to his feet and Keir offered him a mumbled apology and a handshake. Rorik remained grim, but he accepted his hand and shook firmly, agreeing to remain civil until they returned to the keep. As it started to rain, softly at first and then in a downpour with droplets the size of agates, the men rushed to search for shelter.

"Over here!" Rorik shouted above the booming thunder. "There's a cairn on the other side where we can be dry."

"A cairn? Are ye mad?" Keir roared through the din of the storm.

"'Twill be dry, Keir. We've no other choice," Caedmon shouted as he followed behind Rorik, who ducked beneath the huge stone structure. Keir stopped short of the cairn, said a silent prayer and then ducked his head beneath the bolstered stones.

It was an uneasy feeling. The three of them crouched around the small compartment of the ancient burial place barely glancing at one another for fear their movement might wake the dead beneath them. The steam from their breath formed an eerie fog that enveloped them and flashes of lightning set off the stones, creating shadows of sinister figures around them.

"I dinna like this at all," Keir grumbled. He pulled his knees into his chest and wrapped his cloak around himself as tightly as he could to brace against the chill. Caedmon did the same. Rorik opted to wear his plaid on this journey and the extra length of it was now drawn up over his head like a hood.

"Do ye ken a better idea? We're in the middle of bloody nowhere," Rorik shouted, but Keir nodded and peered out through the opening nearest him toward the darkened sky. Anwen was caught up in this terrible squall with little or no provision for herself. He hoped to God she'd found her way off the rocks where tree cover was significant enough to shelter her for the night. His throat tightened at the thought of her, small and helpless, shivering and wet in the darkness. The nausea came later when he realized she may not be alone. British troops were everywhere and they wouldn't take kindly to a young, Irish runaway… especially if she were female.

"Hae ye heard any more about the English up this way?" Keir asked aloud, breaking the awkward silence beneath the cairn.

"Aye," Caedmon acknowledged. "Edward is convinced we've sent for mercenaries from Ireland so they've been searching the inlets tae threaten any incoming vessels. We've lost plenty of trade tae those bastards already."

"Do ye no' think it odd that we havena seen any troops this whole night? If they're everywhere, why haven't we seen any?"

"Aye, 'tis odd. Maybe they've given up and headed back tae England," Caedmon offered and Keir shrugged at the suggestion.

"We should be so lucky," Rorik chuckled. "Maybe they've just given up on the lowlands and gone tae where the trouble truly is, up in the hills."

"You canna be serious." Keir balked at Rorik's statement.

"'Twas never the lowlanders that gave them any trouble. We mind our own business and keep tae ourselves," Rorik added as he wiped his face on his sleeve.

"Ye are serious. How can ye say that?" Keir shouted as another clap of thunder boomed overhead.

"'Tis the bloody Highlanders, and ye ken I tell the truth in this. If it werena for their damn arrogance we would have never gone tae war with the English in the first place." Rorik said, pulling his hood closer to his face.

"If it werena for their damn arrogance, we'd be serving Edward as the cowering slaves he wanted us tae be, scraping by on a peasant's meal with no land of our own tae call home." Keir shouted angrily.

"Lads, lads," Caedmon scolded, "'tis neither here nor there now. Come, leave yer arguments for another day."

"Nay, I willna," Keir grumbled. "God's teeth, Rorik, ye of all people. Ye ken well enough our clan hails from Highland blood. How can ye say such a thing?" Keir asked, shaking his head at him incredulously.

"I can say it as 'tis true," Rorik answered. "Besides, ye are no more a Highlander than I am."

"Lest ye forget, lads," Caedmon added, his brow wrinkled in agitation. "That Hieland blood of yers began on Irish soil, in the hearts of the O'Neill Kings."

"Dinna be ridiculous." Keir laughed.

"Ask yer faither if ye dinna believe me then," Caedmon said. "He'll tell ye the truth of where his family began. How do ye think he kens the Connacht king as weel as he does?"

"If he kens him as weel as ye say he does, why dinna he ken about Anwen's betrothal all those years ago?" Keir asked.

"I canna tell ye what I dinna ken. I assume King Morgunn dinna tell much of anyone as he dinna ken what tae do about the situation at hand." Caedmon offered with a shrug.

"Situation?" Keir asked, now more confused than ever.

Caedmon held his breath a second and then looked back to Keir with a clenched jaw.

"From what yer faither tells me, Morgunn feels that signing the contract to wed her tae the King's cousin is his only choice now. Edward has given him no quarter."

"How could Morgunn sell her off so easily, and tae the enemy no less?" Keir questioned.

"I dinna ken, but I do ken how ye feel about the lass and I'm much tae blame for it," Caedmon said, patting Keir on the leg.

"Tae blame, for how I feel about her?" Keir chuckled. "Ye are a strong presence in my life, Grandy, but I daresay ye dinna control my feelings for any woman."

"But in this one, I feel I do, Keir," Caedmon offered with a repentant smile. "I kent she had feelings for ye all along and I was so happy tae have met someone who was so much like ye… I kent I had tae do all I could tae get ye together."

"How is that?" Keir asked, puzzled.

"I kent she was tae be betrothed, but I felt that there was something between ye, something that needed to be brought out. When she came tae us, she was not so keen on getting tae ken ye better." He shrugged dismissively.

"And what made her change her mind?" Keir asked.

"Ye did, Keir." Caedmon smiled. "When I had spoken tae her after ye had that argument in the hall, I kent right away the two of ye were put on this earth for one another."

"And?" Keir coaxed.

"And after ye finally talked tae one another and truly listened with yer hearts, I could see it in her eyes."

"See what?" Keir argued. "All the lass did was complain and fight with me."

"A woman is a strange creature, Keir," Caedmon started and Keir rolled his eyes with a nod. "Being on this earth as long as I have, ye learn tae ken when a woman's heart speaks tae her in soft voices. When Anwen looked intae yer eyes and saw beyond the angry man ye were, I could see a spark there."

"The old man has gone off." Keir laughed, glancing over at Rorik.

"Aye, I ken he has." Rorik chuckled, wiping the rain from his face with his plaid.

"Am I wrong?" Caedmon asked.

Keir laughed aloud.

"I think ye have soft voices in yer own heid, 'tis what I think. How could ye see a spark in her eye if ye dinna even ken the lass?"

"A woman is a woman, no matter who she is." Caedmon said knowingly. "Dinna ye notice the way her face softened when she looked at ye, the way she breathed a bit quicker when ye spoke?"

"I noticed the way she tried tae bludgeon me when I tried tae help her, 'tis what I noticed," Keir said and Rorik laughed aloud, shaking his head.

"Och," Caedmon grumbled. "Regardless, dinna ye at least see it in her eyes before she left?"

Keir took a deep, shaky breath and turned to look out beyond the cairn. He saw more than a spark not a day before, feeling the warmth of her in his arms. He saw the way she opened to him, unwaveringly. He saw her give herself to him freely and without question, and he felt a want and a need in her touch that matched his own. He saw a love in her eyes the likes of which he had never seen in any other woman's eyes before in his life. Not even Alicia's, who protested she loved him. Why, then, hadn't Anwen told him the truth of how she felt? Did she think so poorly of him that a mention of her heart's desire would send him running or make him feel apprehensive somehow? She could have trusted him with that much.

She was the first woman he opened his heart to. She was the first woman he truly let himself feel for, and now she was gone and the possibility of her ever returning was growing dimmer with the passing of the moon. He choked back the tears stinging his eyes and he turned to Caedmon.

"Aye, I saw it," he said softly. "And I felt it as weel."

"Aye, ye see, I was right." Caedmon beamed. "Did she tell ye as much? How did ye ken?"

"I felt it in her kiss," was all Keir said before he grimaced and dashed out into the rain.

Anwen woke to the sound of harried movement. She could not see what was going on around her, for her eyes were blindfolded. When she moved to remove it, she found her hands were bound tightly behind her and her legs were tied at the knees. She was lying on a mattress of sorts like the night before; the rough wool of the blanket scratched her cheek as she strained to see beneath the blindfold. Her mouth was gagged with a torn cloth and it tasted as though it had been recently used to oil weapons.

Every inch of her body was in pain. Her jaw throbbed. Every bone in her body ached. Her ribs hurt so fiercely she had to breathe in gasps as the movement of her lungs seemed to set her body on fire. Her knees were tied so tightly she had lost all sensation below them. From what she could feel, she was still clothed. In fact, a faint weight on her legs implied she had been covered with a blanket of sorts.

Anwen wondered for a moment if they had violated her. She was unconscious the entire night and everything hurt. There was no way for her to know for sure and that thought alone frightened her. She laid there for a long while listening to everything going on around her in hopes that she could find some clue as to who her captors were. Most of the men, it seemed, were simple soldiers, their lowborn English accents giving away their apparent lack of education. But there was one voice that caught her attention immediately. It was the officer from the rowan tree - the one they called William. He was giving orders for the men to dismantle the camp…and he was the one who had ordered her to be bound.

"Those Scots are a keen bunch. They'll track us if we leave any sign of our being here. I want that fire pit buried and covered over with leaf and I want our tracks raked," he commanded.

162

"What about the girl?" It was the evil man that had started the whole episode the prior evening. She would remember his voice for the rest of her life.

"I'll take care of her," William said flatly. "'Tis none of your concern. Now tend to your duties." His footsteps approached the tent and the sharp, cold air slapped her face when he flung the door flap aside to enter.

He was not like the other men. He even had a different scent, that of leather and mint. He smelled clean, proper even, but his voice did not match the cleanliness she sensed. It was cold, shrewd and without emotion. He had a pompousness about him that she assumed was due to his rank, especially since he seemed to be the only man in charge of this motley bunch of men.

She strained again to see, just to get a glimpse so she knew where he was, but it was no use. He shuffled about and by the volume of his voice, she could only assume he had pulled up a chair to sit by her bedside.

"What is your name, girl?" he asked, removing the rag from her mouth.

She instinctively flinched away from him when he spoke.

"Don't worry. I'm not here to hurt you." He chuckled softly and leaned toward her. "God knows the boys have done a fine job of that already."

She wanted to answer the man, wanted to put him in his place. I am the Lady Anwen Ní Connor, daughter of Morgunn, High King of Connacht, she wanted to shout, but the words would not come. The only sound she made was a breathy moan that cracked and faded.

William sighed and moved his chair, scraping it across the dirt floor. His footsteps shuffled as he walked the expanse of the tent. After a few moments, the bed she laid upon shifted beneath her and she flinched again when his hand was suddenly on her shoulder.

"I'm going to sit you up," he said softly, almost with a care in his voice. "Here, take some water."

He pressed a cup to her swollen, cracked lips and she winced, but found she was suddenly wanting for the drink. She gulped at the liquid as he poured it into her mouth and she choked and sputtered as the cold of it hit the back of her throat. Then he pulled the cup away.

"There, better now, eh?" he asked.

She moved her head away from him defiantly. Better? How could a simple sip of water make everything better? As if her thoughts were suddenly audible to the man, he stood with an almost sympathetic sigh and moved back across the room.

"Now, tell me who you are."

"No one of import," she said, her voice faint and frail.

"I beg to differ," he surmised. "Tell me who you are so we may return you safely."

"A bit late for that, think you not?" she mumbled through her throbbing, swollen lips.

"What are you implying? That we would not release you?" he asked.

"I'm implying that if you had no intention of keeping me, I would not have been beaten and bound as I have."

"You were beaten and bound because you refused to follow orders," he stated, marking his words with impudence.

"And who are you that I should follow your orders?" she demanded almost haughtily.

"Like you, no one of import, but I daresay you are outnumbered and therefore 'tis only right that I give the orders to follow."

"Not for long..." Anwen managed through clenched teeth.

"I beg pardon?" he asked curiously.

"I said 'not for long.'" The words came louder this time and she clenched her jaw in anger as she uttered them.

"And may I ask what you mean by that?"

"I will not be outnumbered for long," she countered defiantly.

"Ah, yes, your clansmen, gathering and searching endlessly for you. Tell me, m'lady, who are these clansmen, and how is it they move so stealthily as to not be noticed or heard from since you have been in our company?"

"They are out there. They will find me."

"They? Who are they that you speak of?" he asked.

"MacLochlainn and his men, hundreds of them. When they find you, they will kill every one of you."

"MacLochlainn," he repeated, his tone mocking.

"Aye, MacLochlainn. If you've no knowledge of their strength, I shall be more than happy to enlighten you," she boasted.

"There will be no need, for I know them well," he said with a feigned sigh and leaned close to her ear. "Almost as well as I feel I know you, Lady Anwen," he hissed, then stood with a chuckle.

"Get her ready for departure," his voice boomed across the room and another cool wind slapped her face as he left. It was then that she began praying for her life.

Chapter Twelve

Anwen felt as if she had been walking for days, when in all actuality it had only been a few minutes.

The men had quickly packed camp and had spent some time arguing about her demise. She had no idea why they held her captive, but she could only imagine these men had some political agenda and they'd use her as a pawn. Her mind did not stop searching for an escape plan of her own. She was hoping they would come upon some of MacLochlainn's men, but as far as she could see, there was no one about this place, save a few drovers and farmers and they would not get involved with the English after what they had already endured.

"Enjoying your stroll?" William glowered down at her from atop his mount.

"'Tis lovely." She smiled insincerely, blowing the hair from her face. "Have you ever seen such a beautiful place?"

"I find it rather wet and gloomy, myself," he said. "I much rather like the countryside in England."

"You would." She laughed and then cried out as she stumbled and fell to one knee.

Tethered to William's saddle, she was dragged for a few feet before he stopped and yanked on the lead. They had lashed the bindings of her wrists behind her back and ran it to a rope tightly knotted about her neck so she could not bend over and the rope was now choking her as she struggled to stand.

"Get to your feet, you're slowing us down," William said angrily.

"You could let me ride. That would certainly speed this up a bit," she said haughtily, coughing against the restriction at her throat.

William disagreed at first and then motioned to his men.

"You will not be given the reins. There is no chance for you to escape," he growled as he fumbled with the knot of her lead attached to his saddle. When the knot would not give, he barked a command for one of the men to undo the lead from her wrists.

Anwen waited as the man fiddled with the knot behind her back. It was tied over the bindings that were already around her wrists and she was hoping he would confuse one with the other and loosen her wrists in the process, but that did not happen.

With one last bit of effort, he could undo the lead and it was at that instant she made a decision to run. Her hands were still tied behind her, but her legs were free and she moved them as quickly as she could manage.

Stumbling over the rocky terrain, she headed north on the sun's heading, back in the direction of the keep in hopes that she would soon see the faces of MacLochlainn's men, but William and the rest of the men on horseback took to quick pursuit of her and were biting at her heels only moments after her freedom was gained.

Managing the loose stony crags with no arms to steady her flight and a choking noose about her neck was difficult. Her ankles twisted and ached, but she pushed through the pain.

There was a wide clearing ahead and she ran with every ounce of energy she had to get to the thick denseness of trees on the other side. It was there she hoped she could lose them, curl up so tiny and cover over with muck that they would pass her and never find her. But as her mind jumped ahead to freedom, she was suddenly pulled back to reality when the ground fell out from beneath her feet.

The men shouted behind her, both in chase and in surprise. Her mind reeled and without her arms to brace herself, she watched, stunned, as the ground below her opened and swallowed her whole.

The large fissure, which had grown over with moss and thickets, was a hidden gateway to hell and she found it in her attempt to flee. It was as if she had fallen a mile, banging off the sharp, rocky edges of the huge crack before she hit bottom with a violent crash. Loose shale and mud spilled down around her. High above, William and his men shouted for her.

After a while, their voices died away and the last sound she heard was William announcing she was almost certainly dead and that he wasn't willing to risk the lives of his men to go down to save her.

"And if you're not dead, Godspeed you to a quick one," William offered as a parting statement and they were gone.

Moments later, her world closed in around her and her thoughts died away into blackness.

The sun beat down on the cold, bleak landscape, not that Anwen could feel its heat from where she laid. She had awakened when an errant ray of sun broke through the breach above and lit the ground about her faintly, but the cavernous area remained cold and dark, far below the opening of the fissure she'd fallen into.

Her vision was improving, though, and her eyes slowly began to adjust to the darkness surrounding her. There was not much to see in this place but layers of rock and mud.

She had been lying on her side for so long now that she had gone numb. She struggled to turn herself over to sit up if she could. There wasn't much room in the small area where she landed, but she did what she could to move and get her blood flowing again.

Her legs ached horribly and throbbed in so many places that she was sure she had broken bones. In comparison, the rest of her body ached just as painfully. She wasn't quite sure what was broken and what was not. She struggled again with the bindings on her wrists, but the moisture tightened them even more than before, along with the noose at her neck, which was slowly choking the breath from her.

But all hope was not yet lost though. In a burst of energy, she kicked her legs out and could pin her feet to the rocky wall of stone next to her. The leverage was just enough to help her sit upright, but the instant rush of blood from her head sent her reeling. Nearly fainting, she closed her eyes and breathed deeply to try to control herself. The nausea came in waves and she coughed reflexively at the rising bile in her throat.

She took a deep breath and focused, gathering all her strength to try to shout for help.

Nothing came forth but a raspy, harsh sound and the noose about her neck tightened in the effort. She could feel the darkness coming for her again, creeping into her world. Her mind swerved and seemed to take a step back. Before she could control it, the humming in her ears intensified, overpowering her and she fell again into that black chasm of hell.

Chapter Thirteen

"Are you sure we hadn't come this way?" Rorik asked as he shielded his eyes from the rising sun and searched the horizon ahead of them.

"Aye," Keir said. "I'm sure of it. See there, the crooked rowan. We turned west there yester eve. I think we should head south along the loch."

The three of them agreed and urged their horses toward the glistening waters of the lake. Caedmon had dismounted and stooped to sip from a small, trickling stream that flowed downhill toward the large body of water when he cried out.

"Lads!" he hollered. "Lads, come quick!"

Keir and Rorik broke into a gallop, jumping felled trees and boulders in their paths to get there quickly.

"What is it?" Keir asked, his breath ragged and harsh as he dismounted at his grandfather's side.

Caedmon held a scrap of fabric in his hand. He was looking at it intently, and then he turned and slowly handed it to Keir.

"This is the linen Meara used." Keir smoothed the small piece of fabric in his fingertips and glanced up at Rorik, who stopped short of them.

"Aye," Caedmon answered. "Did she no' make a tunic for Bowdyn with this fabric some years ago?"

"Aye," Keir said and reflexively held the soft blue fabric to his nose. It smelt of smoke and dirt, but beneath the unforgiving earthy smells, it was there. The scent of the woman he loved.

Caedmon reacted to the look in his eyes and began to search the ground where he found the scrap of cloth. Moments later, Rorik dove in as well, dismounting and pulling his dirk from his boot to poke at the mud.

Keir wandered the small area looking for clues. Moments later, his suspicions had been justified.

"Grandy," he said, holding a small object in his hand. "What is it, lad?"

Keir had knelt then, losing the strength in his legs to stand. He closed his eyes against the images that swam before his mind. Taking a deep breath, he found the power to come to his feet and walk to where Caedmon and Rorik had been digging.

Caedmon, fearing the worst, held out his hand to see what it was his grandson found. His heart sank when Keir dropped the small gold button into his palm. There was no mistaking the insignia on its face, that of King Edward's troops.

"We'll find her, lad," Caedmon offered as he stood and clasped Keir on the shoulder.

."Aye, they canna have gone far." Rorik stood and jammed his dirk back in his boot, kicking the ground with his foot. "There are embers here, campfire, no more than a day old…"

Keir bent to feel the ground, crumbled the charred earth in his fingers. He nodded as he stood and faced them, sullen and dire.

"Which way would they have gone from here?"

"No' north, that would be foolish," Rorik said as he turned to take in his surroundings. "I'd say either west tae the coast or south toward Rothesay."

Keir wandered the area, his mind in a fog. He noted small divots in the ground where horses and footmen had moved, though none gave away their chosen direction.

Then he saw it, as though it were a figment of his imagination. He had to stop and stare for a moment to be sure it wasn't. He took three long strides and charged up the embankment beyond the rowan to find another shorn piece of the blue linen, tattered and dangling helplessly in the brambles there. He looked out beyond the brambles, with the fabric in his hand, and he knew. Beyond the braes, in the direction she would have been running, his father's keep loomed like a proud protector. She was struggling to return to him.

A shout from him was all it took and the men headed over the embankment toward the castle. They spread out then, searching for signs of struggle, signs of movement... signs of life. Rorik noticed the hoof prints first and he ran toward Keir, in the direction they were facing.

"There!" Rorik shouted and pointed to a patch of ground where the moss was scraped away by the horses that had been there. "They were running," he added and turned to look at Keir.

"Chasing after her," Keir said as he looked off into the distance. "She was heading back tae the castle." He pointed to the keep on the horizon.

"But they were on horseback, she wouldna have gotten far." Caedmon added as he came up behind them.

"She had taken a horse from our stables," Keir said as his stride widened and he quickened his pace, searching the ground with wide eyes, looking for further evidence of her flight.

"Aye," Rorik answered. "But her tunic would no' have been torn on the brambles if she were on horseback, she would have been too high up."

"Aye." Keir nodded, clenching his jaw tightly. "Spread out a bit, but continue in this direction." He said as he mounted his horse.

Rorik raced ahead, following the faint hoof prints scattered northeast of where they were. Caedmon did the same, following a second set of tracks heading more northerly, leading his mount behind him.

Keir followed his heart and went straight toward the castle, knowing that's what Anwen would have done had she been pursued as she was. He picked up the faint scent of men and could see tracks scattered, but nothing was obvious to him. The scent could have been from anyone... reivers, crofters... soldiers on patrol. The tracks were too soft to discern if they were fresh or not. He just prayed quietly to himself as he rushed forward, hoping to catch a glimpse of Anwen somewhere in the distance.

Through crumbling layers of rock, slick moss and treacherous brambles the three men wandered, hoping beyond hope that Anwen would come into view.

Small signs of her presence were found along the way - scraps of the blue fabric littered the area. Rorik found a swatch of long, russet hair clinging to the twisted limbs of the brambles that covered the mossy ground. It could have belonged to anyone, but Keir held onto the hope that it was hers. It had to be hers.

The men, breathless, converged at the rise of the next hill and Keir gaped at what lie ahead of them - A long, flat plane of rock and on the far side, dense forest.

She would have gone there to hide from them, he thought to himself.

"She's there," he gasped through ragged breaths. "She has tae be there."

"Aye." Caedmon nodded. "She's a smart lass. She would have gone intae the woods tae hide."

"Aye," Rorik said, breathless himself. "She would have gone intae the woods."

Without another word, the three men galloped across the stony field toward the dense tree line. Keir was at least ten yards ahead of them, his heart pounding high in his throat, when the ground gave way beneath his horse's feet, throwing him into the sliding rock.

He grasped wildly at the brambles around him to stop from falling. The short, jagged thorns tore into the palms of his hands. He kicked with his feet, trying to catch an edge with a toehold before he slid completely into the crumbling cleft.

Within seconds, Rorik dove toward him, throwing him a length of his plaid as a rope to pull himself back. Caedmon grasped Rorik by his belt and hauled him back away from the massive hole that was swallowing his grandson more rapidly than they could control.

Keir clung to the lip of the crevasse desperately trying to pull himself out when he stopped moving and looked back at them, wide-eyed.

"Keir!" Caedmon cried. "Keir, lad, pull yerself out!"

Keir stopped struggling and fell below the lip of the opening while Rorik scrambled to reach his cousin. Moments later, Keir's grubby, dirt and blood-covered hands appeared and with one quick movement he hauled himself bodily out of the breach.

Lying, gasping for breath, his legs still hanging into the hole, Keir smiled and held out his hand to them, a ragged piece of blue linen clenched in his fingers. In an instant, he scrambled to his hands and knees and, peering over the edge, shouted for her, once... twice.

There was no answer.

"She's down there." He gasped. "I would wager any amount on it. She must have fallen in as they chased her."

Rorik moved cautiously to the edge of the chasm on his hands and knees and peered into its depths.

"How will we get tae her?" Rorik questioned, looking back at them. "'Tis verra deep, I canna even see the bottom."

"I'll go," Keir said as he sat up on his haunches and wiped his bloody palms on his tunic. "We need supplies from the keep, though. Caedmon, go back. Get men and a litter… as much rope as you can find and some torches."

"Aye." Caedmon nodded as he went to his horse, mounted and bolted toward the keep, which sat no more than a mile from their location.

"And what about me?" Rorik asked, taking a seat next to his cousin.

"Ye will be my anchor." Keir smiled. "All that weight will finally be put tae good use." He chuckled as he pat Rorik on the stomach.

Rorik let out a guffaw and then quieted as he bowed his head.

"I hope she's alive, Keir," he said as he turned to his cousin with a sincere look.

"Aye," Keir answered, "She's a strong lass. She'll be well."

Chapter Fourteen

It seemed like hours before Caedmon returned with supplies. Keir continued to try to work his way down into the chasm, but struggled with the sliding shale and uneasy footing and decided not to risk himself further. Anwen would be much better off if he found her safely and didn't land on top of her after falling the same distance she had.

He and Rorik quickly tied the massive lengths of rope together and formed a harness from the hand-braided cord.

"God be wi' ye," Caedmon said solemnly as they lowered Keir down into the dark cleft.

"I will see ye all in a wee while." Keir nodded, a blazing torch in one hand

The light from the torch faded as they lowered him down and Rorik slowly let out slack as Keir descended into the hell below them.

Little by little, the coils of rope let out until there was but a short length of it left. Rorik offered a questioning glance to Caedmon, who, clasping the rope with all his might, nodded in deference to the situation.

"It canna be much farther tae the bottom," Rorik said, edging the rope lower and lower as the end of the length neared. "Surely the earth canna be sae deep."

Caedmon nodded his head remorsefully.

"The earth, she is a vast and wondrous place." He grimaced. "She is far deeper and stranger than we will ever ken her tae be."

And with that said, Rorik braced himself with the last bit of rope tightly bound in his hands.

"'Tis all we have," he said, looking over at the fissure.

"Then 'tis all he gets, I suppose." Caedmon shrugged, glancing over at the opening himself.

They stood, holding the weight of Keir on the rope, feeling the jolts of his movements from the other end as Keir struggled to reach Anwen. After a few moments, the weight shifted, and loosened. The men stood silent, holding their breath, glancing at one another solemnly for long moments and then suddenly the rope became weighted once more and they felt a tug at the other end, Keir's signal to begin retrieving him from the chasm.

They looped the end of the rope onto one of the horses and began pulling up its length.

The other men Caedmon brought with him helped in the struggle to pull them to the surface.

"Keir!" Caedmon cried out as he ran to the opening and knelt there, peering into the blackness below. He heard faint shouts, but nothing discernable in the echoing depths below him. "Keir, lad, we'll get ye out as quick as we can!"

He stood and rushed to the rope, taking a length of it in his now blistering hands, pulling with all of his strength. Slowly, the rope came up; sections of it covered in muck and rotted roots. The rope continued to sway and jerk as they ascended from the pit and soon the top of Keir's head became visible at the edge of the fissure.

"Grab her," Keir shouted, fumbling with the weight of her in his arms. "Someone grab her!"

Rorik planted his feet firmly where he stood and Caedmon and one of the other men scrambled to Keir's aid, pulling a limp Anwen from his grasp. Just as quickly, Keir was up and out of the crevice, hurriedly untying the rope from his waist, rushing to kneel beside her as he lay lifeless on the rocky ground where she laid.

Panic stricken, he rushed to cut her bindings free, grimacing angrily at the bloody scores across her neck beneath the tight rope and then he crouched to her chest, placing an ear over her heart. He listened, eyes wide and full of fear, trying to find a pulse.

"I dinna hear anything!" Keir cried out and then bent down to listen again. "Grandy, I dinna hear a heartbeat!"

Caedmon took Anwen's wrist in his hands. Her frail, pale fingers lifeless and cold. Her tiny, delicate fingernails muddy, broken and tinged with a purple hue. He squeezed her wrist in his hand, rubbed her forearm briskly to get the blood flowing, but she showed no signs of life. Not even a twitch.

"Grandy," Keir bellowed, his eyes pleading, "Do something!"

"I'm no' a healer, lad." Caedmon sighed mournfully, glancing up at Rorik, whose brawny face was now touched with grief. "I dinna have the knowledge needed tae help her. The best we can do is rush her back tae the keep where Somhairle can tend tae her proper."

181

"Aye," Keir said as he stood and gathered the litter and went back to Anwen. With the help of the other men, they quickly secured her to the makeshift stretcher and lash the leads onto the strongest horse they had with them. Keir stuffed furs around her face and neck so the rough ride would not jostle her further. Reflexively, he bent and kissed her as they began to pull away.

She was so cold, her lips swollen and stained a deathly blue as her breath died within her. Her hair, its lush mass of russet fire which he once savored in his hands was now caked in blood and grime. Her striking eyes of the deepest green were now concealed beneath her swollen eyelids. Her beautiful face, the one he had grown to admire, was bruised and unrecognizable.

His heart clenched in his chest and he fell to his knees, letting out a wretched roar as if his soul had been torn bodily from him. It was as if someone had punched him violently in the stomach and he wanted to die with her. He wanted to do something, anything, to bring her back to him, but her life was in the Almighty's hands now. There was no interfering with fate, no matter how tempting, and God didn't take kindly to mortals meddling in his business.

Keir leapt onto the back of Rorik's horse and the group of them set out as quickly as they could without jostling the litter overmuch. As they rode swiftly over the terrain ahead of them, Keir kept watch on Anwen hoping to see some sign of life in her; a flicker of lashes, a twitch of her fingers.

It destroyed him to see her this way and have no power of his own to help her. She was lifeless. She seemed surreal to him, as if she were a doll and not a person at all. He could still hear her lilting laughter in his mind, see the way her emerald eyes sparkled in the lazy afternoon sunshine. He remembered how she felt, warm and alive beneath his hands as she responded to his touch.

Those moments were gone now. He could not even begin to imagine they had ever occurred, looking upon her defeated and fragile body now. He surely couldn't begin to believe they would ever share those moments again.

As they pulled through the castle gates, everyone rushed into the courtyard to aid them.

Keir pushed them aside as he worked to free the leads from the litter and helped bear the weight of the precious cargo as the men whisked her up the stairs of the tower to her chambers.

He was forced out of her room momentarily while the women unclothed her and washed away what grime they could without hurting her further. He shouted to be let in, pounding his fists in angst against the hard-oaken door separating them, brusquely casting aside any sympathies offered from kin who stood in the darkened hallway with him.

When the women had finished and the healer appeared at Anwen's chamber, Keir escorted him into her room and slammed the door firmly behind them, closing out anyone else who would keep him from her.

Somhairle, the healer, leaned over the bed and pressed his ear to her chest. The look on his face concerned Keir, and he moved closer to the bed hoping his presence would somehow bring her back to him.

"There is a faint beat," Somhairle said finally as he moved to the bedside table to open his satchel. "'Tis verra weak, but 'tis there."

Keir gave a sigh of relief that brought tears to his eyes and he nearly collapsed with the shock of elation the news gave him, but he knew her condition was still dire. He sat at the edge of the bed and brushed the damp hair from her swollen face, biting his lip knowing how much pain she must be feeling. For that reason alone he was quite thankful she was unconscious.

Somhairle pulled out a vial and a pouch and placed them on the bed.

"Help me sit her up," he said as he motioned to Keir. They leaned her forward a bit and Keir hastily pushed her pillows up behind her to make her more comfortable. The healer opened the vial and took a quick smell to check its potency. He held the vial to her lips and tilted her head back to pour the tincture down her throat. She coughed weakly, which made Keir smile, as it was the first sign of life he had seen since he had dragged her out of that hell.

"What is that?" he asked the healer, who had recorked the vial and placed it back in his satchel.

"*Ruideal*," Somhairle said, matter of factly, then reached for the pouch.

"Red Robin?"

"Aye," the healer said, bemused. "Ye ken yer herbs."

"Aye, weel." Keir nodded humbly. "Havin' Morág as me

Mum nearly insures I'll learn all that needs tae be learned about herbs."

"There is that." Somhairle smiled and opened the pouch. "And what of this?" He offered the opened pouch to Keir, who stuck in his nose, sniffed and gasped at the smell. After poking at the mixture and pulling out a sample to rub between his fingers, he smiled.

"Weel, I canna be certain, but I would say it's felonwort and tree mallow."

"Verra good again," the healer said, taking back the pouch and after dipping his own fingers in, spread the lumpy poultice over Anwen's eyes and lips. "But you missed the ragwort." He smiled.

"What will that do?" Keir asked as Somhairle smoothed out the poultice and covered her face with a cool, damp linen.

"It will aid in the healing process, reduce the swelling and bruising. I canna yet ken whether any bones in her face are broken since she is so swollen, but this will help ease some of the pressure until I can determine her condition." While he spoke, he pulled out a small jar that was swarming with leeches and he placed a few on the more swollen parts of her face to ease the pressure further.

Keir watched in dazed silence.

"Will she be well, do ye think?" Keir asked, his voice soft, bitter.

"I canna say." Somhairle nodded, putting the jar to the side. "She is verra badly injured." He continued to check every inch of her for damage. At the exposure of her, flesh Keir longed to see and

185

touch, he now felt repulsion and turned away. There wasn't an inch of her that wasn't bruised and he couldn't control his emotions at the sight of it.

He moved away from the bed and wandered aimlessly to the oriel where he stumbled, weak-kneed and sat to gaze out the window, his sight glazed over and hazy.

"Do ye think she'll live?" he asked softly, desperately, not turning to face the healer. Afraid to hear the truth.

"I canna say, Keir, I wish I could," Somhairle answered. "She seems tae be of sturdy stock and was healthy prior tae this incident, so I can say she has at least a fighting chance of it."

"That's good." Keir said, his thoughts trailing off to happier times, happier thoughts.

"Her arms are severely scraped but unbroken," Somhairle said as he continued to survey her limbs. "She may have a fractured leg. I canna tell through the swelling, though. I will bind it and we will have tae check it later."

The healer went about his duties, wrapping and binding wounds, splinting limbs, changing damp cloths to keep her head cool.

Keir gradually regained his senses and returned to her bedside and sat again, stroking her hair as he had done before.

"We'll have tae watch her closely for the next few days," the healer said as he packed the items back into his satchel. "If she shows any signs of fever, weel…"

Keir nodded as he looked down at her. "I'll no' leave her side," he offered.

"I ken ye willna," Somhairle said and smiled warmly, patting Keir on the shoulder. "Dinna let yerself get worn out by this, Keir. Ye need rest and nourishment yerself now and again. Dinna let yerself go."

"Thank ye, Somhairle," he said and clasped the healer's hand. "Thank ye for all ye've done."

"I've done nothing miraculous. 'Tis up tae the lass tae do the rest herself." Somhairle smiled and left them alone, closing the door behind him as he left.

Keir spent the next several hours watching Anwen as she slept peacefully and without a sound. He replaced her cool head linen every half hour and reapplied the poultice Somhairle had left for him.

Meara had come to Anwen's chambers, offering to care for her fallen friend in his stead. After some coaxing, Keir unbolted the door and let her in. She had gently combed the length of Anwen's damp hair until it was free of knots and debris and she tenderly braided it into a thick tail, which she draped down the side of the pillow.

"Will ye no' come down tae the hall tae take your ease, Keir?" Meara asked as she hovered near the door.

"I willna leave her side," he said, not taking his gaze from Anwen.

"Ye need tae let her rest now," she said plainly, "and ye havena eaten a thing in hours. Ye'll need yer strength if ye hope tae help her through this."

Keir didn't respond to her. He barely noticed she was in the room. All he could see or think of was Anwen. That wouldn't change until she opened her beautiful eyes and smiled up at him. And then, he was sure, he would think of no one else.

Meara nodded ruefully and with a sigh, left the room, closing the door softly behind her.

Sometime later she would find it in her heart to fix up a plate of food and bring it to Anwen's room so Keir could fill his stomach, though he wouldn't take a bite. He could not think of food or sleep while she lay there. All he could think of was his life without her and he knew he would surely die of a broken heart if she were to slip away.

The early morning sun broke through the thickening clouds with a startling shock, casting an intense slash of light through the oriel windows, across the floor to the bed where Anwen lay.

The force of it hit her like a fist and the pain behind her eyelids was deafening in its brilliance. As if she were in a dream, she opened her eyes and the world around her was hazy, distant and distorted. Though alert, she felt as though she hadn't slept in weeks.

Slowly, urgently, as each of her limbs began to reawaken from their slumber, the pain began to trickle like a slow-moving stream through her blood. Sharp aching jolts set off like fiery sparks in every part of her body, but dazedly, she seemed unable to move past them. A sound, harsh and ragged, escaped from her lips as the brunt of the pain shot through her and she flinched convulsively to retreat.

"Anwen," Keir said urgently, "Anwen, can ye hear me, lass?"

At the frantic sound of his voice, Meara rushed in from down the hallway to Anwen's bedside.

"She had awakened," he said, stroking her forehead with a damp cloth. "I saw her lashes flutter and for a moment, I thought I heard her speak."

Meara looked down at Anwen, who lay just as peaceful as she had for the past three days.

"Her face looks much better today," she said softly, touching it lightly.

"Aye, her neck as well." Keir sighed as he gently touched the bruised scabs left from the rope he had cut from her. He straightened the sheets around her with a nod. "She is a swift healer, as Somhairle said she was. Soon she will be on her feet."

"Aye," Meara said softly. "Soon enough." She wandered to the bedside table, lifted the tray she had brought earlier and turned to leave.

"Thank you, Meara," he said, looking up at her.

"Ye need tae eat, Keir." Meara said a bit angrily. "Look at ye. Ye havena slept for days, ye've barely eaten. What good will ye be tae her if ye willna have the strength tae go on yerself?"

"I'll be fine," he said despondently. "She needs me here."

"She doesna need ye, Keir," Meara said. "She hasna moved in days and having ye hovering about her will hardly bring her back. Now get yerself tae the hall, eat a full meal and then get tae yer own chamber and get some sleep."

"I canna!" he shouted, standing from the bed. "I canna leave her in this condition."

"She doesna have a condition," Meara said exasperatedly. "She's asleep, neither here nor there. There's nothing ye can do tae speed her return tae us."

"I never thought ye tae be a pitiless lass," he offered crassly as he moved past her to tuck in the other side of the bed.

"Keir," Meara said, setting the tray at the foot of the bed. "I'm no' trying tae be mean tae ye. I love ye, but I canna stand tae see ye in a state yerself."

"I am in no state," he growled.

"Ye're in more of a state than she is," she said with a grimace as he shot her an angry look. "There's nothing more for ye tae do here but wait, so why no' get some food and rest for a while." Meara offered, her plea touching her eyes.

"Aye, perhaps I should," Keir said despondently.

"Aye. Now get yerself tae the kitchen," she said with a coaxing smile.

Keir, downcast and somber, pulled himself away from Anwen's bedside and after a last glance at her face from across the room, he quietly closed the door to let her sleep in peace.

Chapter Fifteen

The food had done him good. He hadn't realized just how hungry he was until his mother began filling plate after plate with fish, mutton and fowl, with large helpings of bread, cheese and mugs of ale to boot. By the time he finished, at least four plates and three mugs later, he could barely stand from his seat, his stomach was so swollen and heavy.

"Now take yerself, wi' all yer pith, and hie yerself tae bed afore yer wits are chasin' mice," she said, shoeing him out of the kitchen with a gentle nudge.

"Aye, Mum." He smiled and gave her a great hug. "I should be grateful for the kin I have that dinna let me walk myself off a cliff."

"Och, 'tis what kin are for," she said with a smile. "And dinna be worrit overmuch about the wee lassie. Nay need tae be fearin' for the days ye've never seen. She'll come about when she's good and ready for it."

"Thanks Mum." He hugged her again, tearfully, and then took his full belly back to the tower.

Without hesitation, he went to his own chambers where he undressed, pulled back the thick coverlet and for hours, slept fitfully.

Meara's voice came to him like a bolt of lightning. His dreams disturbed him, visions of death and chaos swimming around his clouded mind. He woke instantly and sat bolt-upright in his bed as Meara grasped his arm.

"'Tis Anwen," she said, a tinge of fear and excitement in her voice that he could not fail to notice. "She awoke just moments ago."

Meara hurried out of his room and he hastily threw on his breeches and shirt then scrambled across the hallway bare-footed, stumbling through her doorway with little grace.

Anwen was lying in a half-seated position, her back propped up on the mass of pillows at her head. Her face was pale, her eyes wide and glazed as she looked about the room in fear, yet she spoke not a word, not until he entered the room.

"Keir!" Anwen bellowed, clutching her coverlet so tightly her knuckles turned white. Then she began to mumble, moaning and whimpering incoherently as she backed away from everyone, cowering against the headboard.

"Anwen," he offered gently, nearly whispering her name. "Hush now, lass, yer safe now," he said as he sat at the edge of the bed. The touch of his hand on her leg made her jerk, nearly leaping from the bed. It was agonizing to watch, her complete inability to recognize she was safe and away from the hell that had befallen her earlier.

"Fetch Somhairle," Keir ordered and Meara rushed out of the room without a word. Christiona, who had fallen asleep in the window seat, woke when Anwen's voice pierced the silence of the room. She jumped down and hurried to the side of the bed.

"Is she all right?" she asked in a sleepy, sheepish voice, noting Anwen's harried state.

"No' the now, Christiona," Keir said with some frustration. "Ye dinna need tae be here tae see this. Now off wi' ye." The look he gave halted any retort she had and the little girl backed out of the room without a word, her footfall scurrying down the hallway and fading down the stairs.

Keir turned all his attention back to Anwen. The look in her eyes frightened him as nothing had ever frightened him before in his life. She had been through a horrifying experience, one that would no doubt haunt her for the rest of her life. Knowing this, he could not help the mounting angst that had been building in his heart like a boulder that had landed there with a violent, crushing thud.

He backed away from her a bit and sat, cross-legged at the foot of the bed so she wouldn't feel threatened by his proximity.

Her eyes continued to take in her surroundings and gradually her features softened and she loosened her grip on the coverlet. She focused on his face and shifted into a more comfortable position against the headboard, still a bit cautious of her audience.

"Where am I?" her voice cracked.

Keir stood slowly and went to her side where he poured a mug of water and held it out for her. She flinched for a moment as he neared and then warily took the mug from him and drank hungrily until it was empty.

"Yer at Lachlan Keep, lass," he said softly, edging his way to the side of the bed where he sat. Anwen marked his movements with wide eyes, but did not move away from him.

"How long have I been here?" she asked, handing back the mug.

"Near tae five days now," he said as he refilled the mug and handed it back to her. "How do ye feel, lass?"

Anwen drank the second mug more slowly and, relaxing a bit more, set it down on the bedside table herself.

"I don't rightly know," she said as she gradually stretched her legs out beneath the coverlet. At the shock of pain, she flinched and took in a sharp breath. She glanced down at her bandaged forearm and with her free hand tried to move the numb fingers dangling out of the wrappings. "Is it broken?"

"Nay, just badly cut," he said. "The healer is verra impressed with your progress."

"Impressed?"

Keir shuddered for a moment, recalling her condition when she had arrived not a week earlier.

"Ye were in a fairly bad way when we found ye," he started, carefully choosing his words as to not frighten her further. "Somhairle applied a poultice tae your wounds and wrapped what he felt was worse off, but within a day or two, you were showing signs of complete recovery. Your face is hardly bruised now and the swelling has gone down in your leg."

Anwen lifted the cover cautiously and glanced down at her leg. It was scabbed and bruised, but for all intents and purposes, looked normal.

"Is it broken?" she asked as she let the cover down.

"Nay," he said. "We thought it might have been fractured, but the swelling had been too much tae be able tae tell. Yester eve Somhairle removed the splint and was able tae determine it was just badly banged up, but no' broken at all. Ye have very strong bones, lass." He smiled.

"Aye, and a thick skull." She smiled faintly and rubbed the knots she found there.

"Aye, that too," he said with a hint of a smile. "You're lucky, I suppose, that yer a strong lass. Others would have fared far worse."

"Aye, I suppose I am lucky," she said, shifting again on the bed.

"Are ye comfortable?" he asked, standing from the bed, looking down at her with concern.

"I, um..." she squirmed on the bed, looking away. "I need to use the...." She looked up at him with embarrassment.

"Oh, aye!" He nodded. "I'll have tae help ye get up. I daresay ye willna be able tae walk on yer own for a few days."

"All right," she said, giving him an awkward glance. "But I don't seem to be clothed."

Keir grimaced then went to the wardrobe on the far side of the room and pulled a lightweight shift from it. Making his way back to the bed, he noted the look on Anwen's face.

"I ken it is improper for me tae see ye in this," he started, handing her the shift. "Mayhap I should go and fetch Meara tae help ye with this... matter."

"Nay," Anwen shook her head, looking down at the shift. "I daresay this cannot wait. If you would be so kind as to turn away, I will cover myself. This will be fine."

Keir went to the oriel and turned away from her. He could hear her fumbling on the bed, letting out quiet gasps and hisses as she maneuvered her aching limbs into the shift.

"I'm ready," she said behind him and he turned and went to her side.

The shift was cock-eyed and the bulky bandage on her arm prevented her from pulling the sleeve into place, thus leaving her shoulder bare for him to view. It was different from the last time he had seen her, when her body was so beaten and broken that it was as if it wasn't her at all. Now that she was nearly recovered, he could not help but feel the way he did, and it pleased him even more knowing the threat of her death no longer hovered over her like a dark cloud.

He offered her an arm to help her swing her legs over the side of the bed, but she flinched at the slightest movement and he cringed with the pain she showed.

"Here," he offered, then rolled back the coverlet and lifted her bodily off the bed.

She was so small and frail in his arms, he barely noted the weight. In the week that she had been laid up, she had lost a lot of weight, making her already trim frame even smaller and more fragile.

Anwen put her free arm about his neck and he shifted so her undergarment dropped down to cover her exposed legs. He was more concerned about her comfort now and tried not to take note of the soft, white flesh that was bared, but his body reacted on its own. Concentrating his attention on her bandaged arm, he managed to make his way down the hall to the garderobe and was able to pull the door open with his foot where he slowly lowered her to the floor.

"Put yer weight on yer good leg, aye," he said. He held her under her arms, trying to take up her weight until she could manage to stand and she smiled up at him awkwardly.

"My legs are so weak," she said, her body swaying as she caught the doorjamb with her good arm to steady herself.

"Aye, they will be for a while." He slowly removed his hands, watching her eyes to make sure she was ready to stand on her own. She wavered a bit, and then gradually hopped into the small alcove, steadying herself as she moved. "All right then?" he asked with concern.

"Yes, I should be fine," she said. "You can close the door."

"Aye," he offered. "If ye need help, just call out and I'll do what I can tae help ye."

"Thank you, Keir." She smiled and he closed the door between them.

While Anwen tended to her business, Keir paced the hallway. He could hear her struggling with her shift and when all was quiet, he panicked and went back to the door.

"Are ye all right in there?" he asked aloud, his ear pressed against the door.

"Yes, just fine," she said, her voice muffled by the door.

Keir let out a breath of relief and went back to his pacing until he noted Meara and Somhairle coming down the hallway.

"Keir, lad," Somhairle said as they came toward him. "Where is Anwen?"

At that moment, the garderobe door swung open and Anwen's head peered out. "I'm here," she said as she limped toward them. Keir moved quickly to her side and swept her back into his arms.

"Let me get ye back tae bed," he said, walking back toward her chambers.

"How are ye feeling, lass?" Somhairle asked as he followed behind Keir's substantial form.

"I'm fine," Anwen said.

"She's still in a bit of pain," Keir said blandly, making his way back to her chambers, where he placed her gently back on the bed. Somhairle stood in the doorway with Meara as Keir set her bed to rights.

"How much longer must I stay in bed?" Anwen asked, adjusting her shift, pulling the covers up to cover herself properly.

"As long as it takes ye tae heal, lass," Somhairle said entering the room.

Anwen winced again as she moved into a more comfortable position, tears coming uncontrollably to her eyes. Keir could hardly stand to see her in pain, but now as she sat there tearfully, he was fair bent with anguish and his stomach clenched into a nauseating ball, stealing his breath for a moment. He went back to her bedside and sat, taking her hand in his own.

"I think I should let the healer see tae ye now. Ye need yer rest, happy though I am tae see ye awake again." He squeezed her hand in his and then stood from the bed and motioned to Somhairle.

Somhairle looked pleased at her current condition and Keir could hear him praising her quick recovery as he left the room. He hovered outside the doorway and listened for a moment as the two of them chatted about her injuries and then he walked away.

He decided a chat with his father was necessary at this point. He wanted to offer his hand to wed Anwen, not only to try to break the horrendous contract that had been drawn up, but because he knew now that he loved her and it was high time he had done something about it.

Chapter Sixteen

"Come in, sit down," Donel offered, pulling out a chair for him, but Keir crossed his arms and paced away from him.

"I dinna want tae sit," he said coldly. "Tell me why it is that ye have been nearly round the bend trying tae get me tae wed and now that I tell ye I want tae marry Anwen, ye act as though I had just asked ye if I could kill a neighbor's sheep?"

"Keir, this is a difficult matter, one your fit of temper will no' make easier for any of us." Donel sat again at his desk, trying to convey his meaning through the stern look he gave.

"Then explain it tae me," Keir demanded as he sat before his father and leaned onto the desk to stare back. "Dinna beat around the bush about it, tell me. Why canna we get her out of this contract?"

"Because it has already been signed," his father said, and then gave a concerned look at his baffled reaction. "I received a missive from Morgunn just yester eve telling me so. She is all but wed at this point."

"How?" Keir gasped. "How could her faither pledge her tae the enemy, how could he…" Keir's mind trailed off, remembering what he and Anwen had shared, what he felt for her. He knew this was not what she would want. This news could not be worse for him to swallow. "How do we ken this contract is unbreakable?"

"As Edward is behind it, I am sure it is unbreakable." Donel shrugged.

Keir stood and paced again, his footfall heavy against the slate floor. His mind buzzed with a thousand voices at once. How could she be betrothed to an Englishman? He shook his head to erase the thought.

"I still dinna believe it. Anwen willna agree to it, no' after what we have shared."

"Shared?" His father asked. "What have ye shared with the lass, Keir? Ye havena bed her, have ye?" he asked incredulously. "If I find ye laid a hand on her I'll have ye beaten within an inch of yer life for sure."

"Nay, I dinna bed her, what do ye take me for?" Keir answered angrily, unforgiving as his sizeable form towered over his father's desk.

"Then what have ye shared with the girl that put ye on such intimate terms with her?"

"I've spent time with her," Keir growled. "We've talked and gotten tae know one another, 'tis all."

"Are ye sure, lad?"

"And I kissed her," Keir stammered, looking down into his father's livid eyes. "But nothing more, I swear tae ye."

"I dinna ken what tae tell ye then, Keir. All I ken is that as soon as she is well enough for travel, we must get her out of here."

"Aye, I agree." Keir nodded. "Has anyone told her that she must depart soon?"

"I think she would take the news better from you, Keir. She trusts you."

"Does she? With all the arguments we've been having, I beg tae have a different opinion." He scoffed.

"Ye ken well enough she would rather hear such news from you than from me or from Caedmon."

"Aye." Keir nodded. "I suppose she would, but I dinna think I could bear tae tell her."

"Ye must, Keir. For the lass's sake, ye must."

"I canna," he shouted, fighting back the anger that was boiling under his skin. He didn't want to take her away. He didn't want their time together to end.

"Ye are truly fond of the lass, are ye no'?" Donel asked, coming to stand behind his son, laying a hand upon his shoulder sympathetically.

"I regret that I am," Keir said, bowing his head, taking a deep breath to move past the emotions that were building inside his chest like a sudden storm. But it was no use. The more he thought of her the more his heart ached for her, for what they would never have. He sank into the chair before him and covered his eyes with his hand.

"Lad," Donel said as he rubbed his son's shoulders compassionately. "There will be others that will find their way intae yer heart."

"Aye," Keir mumbled and rubbed his eyes in his fingers. "Though I canna say I have ever felt this way about any other."

"Aye, but ye are young, Keir. Soon enough some other woman will come tae ye and ye will find ye are just as taken with her as ye are with Anwen."

"Nay, I doubt that." He said a bit angrier than he intended, but the thought of feeling this way about any other woman nauseated him.

"I ken, lad, I ken how ye feel about Anwen and I'm sorry for it."

"Is there nothing ye can do tae break this betrothal?" he asked, nearly pleading.

"Nay, I dinna think it possible." Donel nodded dolefully.

"Why?"

"She's betrothed to King Edward's cousin," Donel answered. "I doubt if I would be far from my mark if I guessed the match was made for political reasons and there is nothing I can do tae change things in that case. I ken Morgunn well, and he wouldna marry his only daughter off tae the enemy on a whim. There has tae be a good reason."

"Aye, I suppose ye are right, but canna we try?"

"The contract is binding, Keir. What more do ye want me tae do?" Donel asked.

"Will ye at least try for me?" he said, begging.

"Aye, I can speak tae Morgunn, but I assure ye, there is nothing he can do tae change Anwen's fate." Donel said and then pulled him into his arms. "I love ye, Keir, know that if nothing else."

"And I love ye, faither…" he said and they embraced as Keir had wished they had embraced so many times before.

Chapter Seventeen

The pain in Anwen's leg had subsided enough that she was able to get out of bed on her own a week later. She had been sleeping so much that she was beginning to lose track of the days and hours. Dawn was beginning to look like dusk and she wasn't quite sure anymore which was which.

Standing perilously at the edge of her bed, she slowly pushed away and put her full weight on her legs, then with a groan, shakily made her way to the oriel where she could sit and look at something more than her bed curtains. Christiona had left a lap blanket there from the previous evening when she had come in to read to her from her picture books.

The little girl had made up stories to go along with the pictures, telling tales of fair maidens, evil villains and handsome princes and began asking her questions only fit for a princess to answer. Humbled, Anwen giggled and did as she was bid, answered all questions offered in a regal tone and then waved a hand pompously and comically for Christiona to continue with her story. Christiona was rapt with the attention she was receiving and was thoroughly convinced by the time she had left that she was now one of Anwen's courtiers, and Anwen could not deny her that privilege.

They had named themselves "Ladies of the Enchanted Thimble" after Anwen had plucked said thimble from a basket near her bed, blessed it and kissed it before placing it on Christiona's thumb. Near beaming, Christiona had left the room, no doubt to slumber the night away dreaming of her own handsome prince as she fell off into a peaceful sleep.

The dreams Anwen had been having of late, however, were mixed with wondrous visions of cloud-suspended castles and colorful fields covered in flowers, but they were also peppered with the unsettling imagery of death, blood and rotting corpses. Many nights she was roused from a deep sleep to find herself covered with sweat, her bedclothes plastered to her body as she unconsciously struggled to free herself from their confinement. And more nights than she cared to remember, her own screams woke her without warning.

It was on those nights she was the most terrified of what she could not see in the darkness of her room, but Keir would never fail to appear at her door, candle in hand, to comfort her and settle her back into a comfortable sleep. On the nights she could not do so, he would remain there, fighting his own fatigue to sit up and talk with her until the sun rose from behind the mountains and the lark began singing his happy morning tunes. Then she would slowly drift into sleep while Keir extinguished the candles and quietly left the room.

Now, taking a comfortable position at the velvet-cushioned window seat, she draped the lap blanket over herself, pulled her shawl more tightly around her and leaned back against the hard stone to peer out the beveled glass.

She guessed it couldn't be much past dawn as the hazy sun rose above the eastern hills. The mist clung low to the braes and the grazing animals seemed to walk amongst the clouds as they ate their morning meals. No one was about in the courtyard below, but as she continued to watch, the keep woke from a long night's rest and clusters of folk started to go about their daily chores until the courtyard was humming with activity.

Horses were being washed and shod. Feed was being gathered from stockpiles and carried to store areas within the stables. The guards were attending their duties, yawning and stretching before making their way to their posts. The activity that blossomed below made her smile. It had been a long time since she felt at home with herself and here she knew she could. She wasn't alone anymore and had nothing to fear in the daylight.

A few moments later, a soft knock came at her door and Keir, his hair still tousled from sleep, leaned his head inside to see if she was awake.

"Ah, out of bed already," he said with a smile. "Are ye all right?"

"Aye, I'm fine." She nodded and pulled her shawl more closely to conceal the thin, linen shift she wore.

Keir averted his eyes for a moment and then after checking briefly down the hallway, moved into the room, closing the door behind him.

She was suddenly overwhelmed with the thought of Keir asleep. What would he look like, his face softened with slumber, his breath slow and rhythmic? The thought of something so intimate brought a sudden warmth to her cheeks and she turned away momentarily, convinced he would notice and immediately know what she was thinking, as if he could peer into her thoughts.

"Did ye sleep well enough?" he asked as he took a seat opposite her and leaned back with a yawn, ruffling his hair with his hand.

"Aye, I did. I have young Christiona to thank I suppose."

"Christiona? What on earth for?"

"She came to sit with me yester eve and told me stories from her picture book. She told great tales of fierce warriors and fair maids." She smiled and nodded at Keir's startled expression. "Oh aye, she has quite the imagination."

"Aye, that she does," he said with a smile and then his countenance changed. Sobered. He stood suddenly, and she flinched, nearly falling off the window seat. He paced the room and then turned to face her.

"Ye need tae leave." He blurted out and then bowed his head to stare at the floor, kicking at the inlaid stone with his toe.

"What?" She was dumbfounded. "What did I do?" she asked, grasping at her jumbled thoughts.

"Ye did nothing wrong, ye just need tae leave." His words were clipped, dry. "Yer tae be sent tae the abbey straight away," he finally said when he looked at her again. "Yer faither was fair adamant about it when ye left and was quite cross to find ye havena arrived there yet."

"I see," she offered, still unsure of where his heart was in the scheme of things. "So… you do fancy Alicia?"

Keir grimaced at the mention of her name.

"What? Nay, 'tis nothing like that. She's betrothed tae my brother, nothing more. I could never do anything tae break that pledge between them. She is a lovely girl, aye, but no amount of charm or beauty would force me tae betray my own blood."

It was on the tip of her tongue then. She so desperately wanted to ask him about the kiss she saw, but the words would not come.

"'Tis very noble of you, truly," she offered. Knowing how weak-kneed she became when she was in his presence, she didn't know if she would ever be able to deny him if she were tempted against her best judgment, blood or not.

Sighing, he finally took a seat next to her.

"Ye'd be surprised how clear yer convictions become when everything is at risk."

"I suppose, though I have never been put in your position."

"But ye would stand behind yer kin should ye be faced with the choice, aye?"

"Aye, I would."

"Then ye are as noble as I. Ye are no different."

Noble. The way the word fell so naturally from his lips made him seem all the more honorable. He was dressed in nothing more than a linen shirt and a pair of simple breeches, but his poise belied his clothing. He was a truly remarkable man. Beneath the terse manner and chiseled, brawny musculature was an intense, emotional soul whose carriage only enhanced the man she came to know. How he could ever think of them as being on equal footing was beyond her reason.

"But we are different." She stalled a moment and looked him over, her eyes taking in every potent inch of him. "You're so confident and your presence is so commanding. Me… I'm always so unsure of myself."

"Ye just think ye are unsure. I've seen ye be plenty confident in the time I've known ye. Ye just have tae believe in yerself and the feeling will follow."

"Ah, so that's the trick?" she asked.

"Aye. Do ye really think I'm some invulnerable, omnipotent man? 'Tis all in how ye present yerself."

"'Tis good to know," she said with a generous smile and then looked up at him skeptically. "So, who is the true Keir? Have I met him yet?"

Keir quieted at her question and his smile faded into something more vulnerable. He looked deeply into her eyes, searching for an explanation and then he nodded solemnly.

"I think ye are probably one of the only people in this world tae have seen the real me. 'Tis no' too often I let my guard down, but ye seem tae respect that I am no' always the tough, harsh warrior," he said with a grimace, touching her knee. "'Tis actually quite a relief."

His hand was so warm, so gentle and she couldn't help but place her hand over his and give him a knowing nod.

"Aye, I find it just as easy to open up to you. I don't know what it is, but I feel so protected when I am with you, so comfortable. 'Tis as if I could say anything and you would understand without question."

Keir nodded and smiled at her quietly. No words needed to be spoken. In an instant, she felt a bond with him, something so sublime and pure that it was palpable. She could feel it in the air between them as if they were linked by a chain, attached at the heart and soul. By the look on his face, she knew he could feel it as well. As his features softened, his eyes became windows into his very thoughts and it sent a rush of warm heat through her.

He pulled his hand away then and after searching the world outside the window, he stood and smoothed the fabric of his breeches.

"Ye need tae prepare tae leave." His words were tinged with remorse and tenderness. He moved away from her, his posture taking on a more defeated stance. Catching the latch of her door in his hand, he turned back toward her, but his eyes never raised to meet her gaze.

"We leave on the morrow," he said and then turned to leave the room, but faltered and finally looked back at her.

"What is it, Keir?" she asked, standing and going to his side.

"There is something I must tell ye, something I vowed I would no', but I must. I canna keep it from ye any longer." He hung his head disgracefully.

"What?" she asked, bringing her hands to his face. She lifted his chin so that his eyes moved to meet hers.

"I ken the reason yer faither sent ye away," he said, his words clenched. Tortured.

Anwen shook her head disbelievingly and could not speak. Her eyes voiced the questions that were running through her mind.

"Yer betrothed, Anwen," he started, trying to look away from her, but she held his jaw in her hand, her grip tightening as his words hit her.

"Betrothed? No, it cannot be," she laughed nervously. "If I were betrothed, why would he send me away?"

Keir reached up and removed her hands from his face, holding them tightly in his own, tears filling his eyes.

"Yer betrothed to an Englishman," he started. "Yer faither wanted tae get ye away in order tae find some way tae get ye out of the contract."

"An Englishman?" she balked. "Why would he betroth me to an Englishman? That would be madness."

"Aye, I ken," he nodded. "It was a contract drawn up by King Edward. Yer faither had been asked tae comply in order tae keep his lands free from English rule."

Anwen's mind reeled. Her father had sold her off to save his own skin. Blood be damned. She could not conceive such a heartless, selfish act, especially from her father. She thought he disliked her in the past, but not enough to discard her so entirely, sending her into the hands of the enemy without care, with not even a word to her to allow her some dignity.

Her legs buckled beneath her then and Keir caught her up in his arms. He carried her to her bed where she sat, stunned speechless. Her heart, so full of hope and love not moments before was now void as if it had stopped beating altogether. Nothing mattered. For all she had struggled through, she now wished she had died in that deep, dark pit she had fallen into for she felt as though she were back there again.

"I wish there were something I could do," Keir said softly as he knelt before her. "I've battered my head against walls these last days trying tae come up with something, anything tae get ye out of this horrible mess, but there's nothing."

Anwen nodded blankly. His words seemed to echo around her as if he spoke and said nothing. She felt faint and nauseous. She wanted to disappear.

"Anwen, please," Keir pleaded, taking her hands in his. "Say something."

Anwen looked at him then, her vision dark and void.

"Who am I to marry?" she asked, her voice coming from a place so far away that she could barely hear herself speak.

"He's a Duke, cousin of the King," he said mournfully. "I ken nothing else of him or what kind of man he is. I just pray that he strives tae deserve ye, 'tis all I can do now."

"There's nothing to be done then…" she murmured, pulling her hands away from his.

"Nay," he offered, bowing his head. "The contract has already been signed, yer faither was convinced Edward would start a war if he refused. Believe me, if I could marry ye myself, I would."

She almost did not hear his words for the blood pulsing so loudly in her ears, but what he said drifted back to her like a dream and she looked at him incredulously.

"Ye'd marry me to get me out of this contract?"

"Nay," he said, his eyes speaking volumes as tears fell almost immediately. "I'd marry ye because I loved ye."

His statement brought her to tears at once and she fell limp against her pillows, sobbing.

"Lass, please dinna cry," he whispered as he stood beside her, his hand stroking her hair comfortingly. Her sobs came more convulsively as he caressed her. "I beg of ye, hush now."

Anwen pushed herself away from her pillows and turned to face him. He had spoken the words she had longed to hear for so long and yet, she could not rejoice and shout at the top of her lungs of her love for him because his words no longer had the same meaning. He couldn't marry her. She had been betrothed to a man she did not know and knew she would never love, and there was nothing that could be done about it.

She had, for the first time in her life, found a man so endearing that their thoughts seemed to mirror one another, and yet she was being forced to deny herself even the smallest amount of

215

happiness to save her father's crown. She was being forced to surrender her bliss for her father's pride, a man that had not loved her since the day she was born. It didn't seem rational and yet she knew it was her duty, as a daughter, to do as she was bade. It was her lot in life to be a pawn.

"Had I not been betrothed, would you have felt the same need to pledge yourself to me?" she asked him between sniffles.

"Had ye no' been betrothed, I would have told ye I loved ye the first day we met," he said with sincerity. "It was all I could do tae keep my thoughts from ye and now…"

"I know," she said as she began to sob again, placing her fingers to his lips. "Please, don't say anything more. I can't bear it."

Keir backed away then and went to the door. His face drawn and grave, his eyes mere dark pools of blueness shadowed by the same heart wrenching pain that was coursing through her own veins. His eyes watched her, almost pleadingly and then, with a touch of anger, he grasped the latch in his hand, opened the door and walked out of the room, and she feared, out of her life.

Chapter Eighteen

The rage that clawed inside Keir's chest was unbearable. He entered his chambers, slamming the door behind him so that it nearly came unhinged. Stalking to his window, he braced his hands against the wall and a growl, churning deep in his stomach, erupted from his throat in a deafening, soul-shattering roar. He pummeled his fists against the hardness of the wall until his knuckles bled red against the cold, grey stone, but no pain he could cause himself would lessen what quaked inside him.

He searched the room in his fury for something to destroy, something to release this anger that seared him from within. He picked up a chair and heaved it against the wall. The wood splintered and crashed to the ground, as did he, falling to his knees in defeat.

Regardless of what his father had said, he felt cursed. He spent his life shunning the effects of love, never wanting to partake in its frivolity. He had partaken in the lusts of his body, had sampled the pleasures of what love had to offer, but he was careful to choose his partners with a wary eye. They had been women of loose morals, with nary an eye towards marriage or a lasting relationship and for many years, that suited him. He could relieve himself of his carnal urges and walk away without a care, continue with his life as he had planned.

He had never once thought to fall in love, had never found a woman who intrigued him enough to change how he felt about it… until he met Anwen. As she wandered into his life like a whisper on the wind, her scent teasing his senses. He could think of nothing else from that moment on.

The mere sight of her aroused him like no woman had ever done. Even now, as his stomach clenched at the thought of losing her, the simple thought of her set his body on edge. The longing he felt for her was beyond the sexual, beyond the urge to feel her in his arms. He wanted to delve into her mind, share life with her, become one in heart and soul. The thought that he would never be able to do so destroyed him. The thought that another man was taking that away from him sickened him.

Keir sat back on his haunches and closed his eyes, tried to calm himself, but the rage was still there. He had allowed himself to fall in love, had allowed himself to sample what small morsel he could innocently take from the woman who had stolen his heart and now he wished he had never done so. Giving in to the need he felt for her, pushing himself past that line he had drawn, he now had the indelible taste of her on his lips, the feel of her in his hands. Had he stood his ground and not gone to that place he had avoided for so long, perhaps her departure wouldn't have been so unbearably torturous. But he could not change what was already done.

He ran his hands over his face and through his hair, pulling at it to feel the pain, to make it real. He came to his feet and paced about his room, but could not quell the tension racing through him.

Moving to his bed, he sat and reached for the bottle that had been tucked in his bedside table. He uncorked the bottle and brought it to his lips, drinking deeply, choking on the harshness as it hit the back of his throat. He could feel it burn its way to his stomach and soon the burn from the amber liquid seemed to take the place of the ache that had been there before.

He left his room then and wandered the halls of the keep aimlessly, trying to divert his attention with other duties, but even the sparring on the lists could not keep his mind from her.

On several occasions Rorik tried to coax him into a hunt or a trip to Keir's once favorite tavern before their journey, but nothing seemed to remove the veil of melancholy that shrouded him. And on this day, all his anxiety had reached its breaking point.

With nowhere else to turn, he found his feet wandering toward his father's chambers, though his mind was still clouded by the aggravating voices in his mind and the spirits he had consumed. He entered the room resolutely and took a seat opposite the desk where his father sat rummaging through paperwork.

"How do ye fare this day, Keir?" his father asked as he looked up from his work.

"Has there been any word from Connacht?" he asked solemnly, ignoring his father's concern for his welfare.

"Aye," Donel nodded. "I received a missive just this morn. 'Tis no' good news at all."

"Weel, what is it?" Keir asked sullenly.

"We're tae send her back home and no' tae Elgin."

"Home? Why?"

"It seems her betrothed has uncovered Morgunn's ill-begotten plan and demands her return at once. Morgunn doesna wish tae get Edward involved, lest he find himself in more trouble than he had been in." Donel said, reaching for his mug of ale.

"So, what are my options?" Keir asked grimly, leaning back in his chair, rubbing his throbbing temples in his fingertips.

"Ye have no options, Keir. The contract has been finalized, agreed tae and signed by her father's hand and stamped with the seal of England. There is nothing more tae do."

"There have tae be options," Keir argued. "There are always options."

"No' in this case, there aren't."

"What if we were tae be married, here, before she left?"

His father was taken aback by this request and his expression suggested he was suspicious of his motives.

"I couldna allow that, Keir."

"'Tis no' a question of propriety anymore, faither. I want tae marry her."

"I ken, Keir," Donel said plainly. "And I canna allow it."

"Canna?" he asked plainly, not looking away from his father's inquisitive eyes. "Ye canna or you willna?"

"What's the difference?" Donel questioned.

"You canna because some law prohibits it or ye willna because ye'd rather send her off tae be tormented by that English bastard that's waiting for her in Ireland."

"Come now, Keir, ye ken I wouldna deliberately harm the lass," Donel said, his voice marking the shock of his implication.

"Why no'? 'Tis all politics after all. What did they offer ye tae send her tae her fate? Land? Titles of yer own?"

Donel stood from his desk, his face reddened with anger.

"Watch yer tongue, Keir," Donel warned, the unbridled resentment apparent in his words. "Ye ken damn well there's nothing that can be offered me that would force me tae do something against my will."

"Then why canna ye allow us tae marry? It would negate the contract and ye ken that well," he challenged.

"Nay, it wouldna negate anything, Keir," Donel boomed. "The contract is signed and sealed. For all intents and purposes, she is already wed tae the man, ceremony or no'. If I were tae allow ye tae marry, it would be considered a treasonous act against the crown and ye would surely hang for yer actions and so would I for allowing it."

Keir rolled his eyes heavenward and heaved a sigh heavy with exasperation.

"Since when have ye been so keen on what the crown says?"

"When they threaten my life or the life of my kin, I take heed," Donel said, more calmly, as he took his seat. "They are no' an insignificant force tae be meddled with and I dinna have the men tae stand against their armies now, no' after we have lost so many tae them already."

Keir weighed his father's words and realized he was in no better position than he was before. The situation was hopeless and it was becoming more and more apparent he had no choice but to face his bleak reality.

"So, I'm tae just let her go?" he asked.

"Aye, I'm sorry, but ye must."

There was a silence between them as Keir's mind reeled, searching for alternatives he had not thought of prior.

"What if she were with child, with my child?" he asked suddenly.

Donel glared at him across the desk and took a deep breath as the ire in his eyes began to dance once more.

"Ye havena done what I've warned ye against, have ye?" Donel asked angrily.

Keir was tired of everyone's games and questions. He wanted this to be over.

"Answer my question!" he demanded of his father, who returned a rather startled expression at his haughty attitude.

"Nay, if she carried yer child it wouldna make a damned bit of difference. In fact, ye would probably face the same treasonous charges as ye would if ye married her."

"I see," he said, stiffening as though he had been slapped across the face.

"The lass isna with child… is she?" Donel questioned, his voice anxious.

"Nay," he shook his head. "It was just a thought."

"Thank God."

"Aye," was all that Keir could say. Deep in his heart he had wished she were pregnant. Treason or no, he would take her somewhere the law couldn't touch them and they would be happy together. But happiness seemed a faint illusion to him now, a memory peppered with brief moments he shared with her.

"I am truly sorry, Keir," Donel offered quietly, his words bringing Keir back to the awful reality he faced.

"Aye, I ken…" Keir stood from his chair despondently. "Somhairle has given her leave to go. She can depart here on the morrow."

Donel was silent for a moment, noting the anguish in his son's face, the dark emptiness in his eyes.

"Do ye wish tae accompany her to Ireland?"

"Aye," he responded blandly as he made his way to the door.

"Aye, then gather some men and form a traveling party tae go with ye. I leave for Dumfries myself as soon as I am done here, so if ye need of anything before ye leave, let me ken yer wishes."

"Aye, faither, I will."

"And Keir," Donel added as Keir left the room. "Take care. Dinna do anything irrational on yer travels."

"I ken, faither. I'll take care tae watch my step."

"Do ye have everything ye came with?" Meara asked as she folded the last of her chemises and stuffed them into the pack basket.

Anwen stood motionless at the oriel, gazing out over the courtyard as she watched the men below ready the horses for her voyage. This was the end, she thought to herself.

She toyed with the circlet she held in her hands, smoothing her thumbs over each of the rough emeralds that were set into the polished brass band. She traced the knotwork with her fingertips feeling each curve and cut as it swirled about the piece. It was once a symbol of her status, the lady she was to become and now it was merely a representation of her demise. Had she not been who she was, born into a royal household as she had, she would not have found herself in this position. Powerful kingdoms would not be vying for her hand as if she were some hostage in their political affairs and she would be left to love whom she pleased, to live how she wished to live, but she was the High King's daughter after all. That fact turned her stomach so violently she wished she could denounce her name. She wished she could disappear and never be known again. Living a life of isolation and loneliness would be so much easier than living without the man she truly loved beside her.

Like Keir, she had no options. Her hand was sold to the highest bidder, her body free to be violated by a man she did not know or care for, though her heart would never waver. It would always belong to Keir.

"Anwen?" Meara's voice brought her back to where she stood, staring out the window of the closest thing to a true home she would ever know.

"Aye, I'm sorry, Meara," she smiled faintly and turned to face her. "What were you saying?"

"Are ye sure ye packed all of yer things?" Meara asked again, setting the pack basket next to the door.

"Oh, aye," she said as she moved toward Meara. "Have you seen Christiona at all today?"

"Aye," Meara nodded. "She's in her chambers. I'm afraid she's quite troubled by your departure and doesna wish tae see ye off."

"I understand." She nodded and handed Meara the circlet. "I wish her to have this. 'Tis my circlet given to me by my father. Tell her I expect to see her wearing it properly when I return for a visit."

Meara nodded remorsefully, a tear rising in her eye.

"What a beautiful gesture, m'lady," Meara said as she hugged her soundly. "I'm sure this will be her most precious possession and she will certainly cherish it."

"'Tis nothing really," she said apathetically. "It really has no meaning for me any longer and I am sure I will receive another upon my... marriage." Her words faded as she looked past Meara to see Keir standing in the hallway before her. His face was drawn. His expression was disconsolate and grim.

"'Tis time, m'lady," he said, his voice resigned.

Upon hearing the words, she broke into tears, the heat of them trickling down her cheeks in torrents. He seemed unmoved by her sobs and, inconsolably, turned and walked away.

Meara stood speechless between them, her own eyes overflowing with tears as she toyed with the circlet she held in her hands. She stooped and picked up the basket at her feet and touched Anwen's arm lightly.

"I'll walk down with ye, if ye'd like," Meara said, and Anwen nodded, her chin trembling uncontrollably as she smothered the sobs in her hand. "'Twill be fine, Anwen, truly," she offered, taking Anwen's arm to lead her down the hallway toward the stairs.

Anwen could not control the tears any longer. The sobs came strong and hard as she passed each doorway, as she took each step closer to her exodus.

In the courtyard, Keir was at his mount fiddling with his saddlebag as the rest of the men, Rorik and Caedmon included, secured packs to their horses and readied to leave.

Upon seeing Anwen's arrival, Caedmon turned and went to her, pulling her into a crushing embrace.

"Lass, lass…" he cooed. "Everything will be fine. We'll get ye home safely and I'm sure your kin will be most pleased tae see ye."

"Aye," she whimpered against his shoulder, sniffling loudly.

"And once ye are settled in and everything is back tae normal, ye can make plans tae visit us, aye?" he offered as he handed her a handkerchief.

"I fear my life will never be normal, Caedmon," she managed through her sobs, blowing her nose loudly into the linen.

"Och, lass, never fear," he smiled, hugging her again. "All will be well. The gods will see tae it."

At his words, Keir slapped his saddlebag shut loudly and mounted his horse.

"Let's go," he said blankly, urgently, making sure not to look back at Anwen's tearful face.

"Aye," Caedmon answered. "'Tis best that we leave now while the sun is still low in it's morning rise."

He took the basket Meara handed him and secured it to Anwen's mount, then kissed his granddaughter firmly on the forehead.

"Ye be good tae yer Gran while we're away, hear me?" he said with a grin.

"Aye, Grandy," she nodded and hugged him, and then she turned to Anwen and embraced her fiercely.

"I had once hoped ye would become my sister," she whispered into Anwen's ear. "Now I ken it doesna take a marriage tae make ye my sister. I feel we are sisters already, aye?"

"Aye," Anwen said through her sobs, hugging Meara again. "I wish I had something to give you to remember me by, but regrettably, I have little but the clothing I carried with me when I arrived."

"'Tis all right," Meara smiled, placing a soothing hand to Anwen's cheek. "Ye'll be back soon enough and I won't need tae remember."

"Thank you for everything you've done," she sniffled, holding Meara's hand against her cheek. "If ever you need to talk to me, please send me a letter and I will be more than happy to correspond with you. 'Tis the least I could do."

"I would like that verra much." Meara nodded and pulled Anwen into a final hug. "Goodbye, my sister," she whispered and then she turned and rushed back into the tower.

Anwen wiped her face with the handkerchief and, taking a long, cleansing breath, took up her reins and mounted her horse.

"Are we ready?" Keir asked aloud and the men answered in turn. He turned to Anwen finally and gave her a questioning look.

"Aye, I'm ready," she said solemnly, looking away as she answered.

With that, Keir spurred his mount into movement and headed out the main gates with his men following closely behind. Anwen and Caedmon were the last to depart and as they crossed the courtyard, Anwen looked up to see Christiona perched at the open window of the library.

Tearfully she was waving her thumb in the air, the enchanted thimble borne proudly there. With a weepy smile, Anwen gave a low and regal bow to her and blew her a kiss before they passed beneath the gatehouse and out of the keep.

The feeling of loss was overwhelming. Not only was she losing the man that she loved so dearly, she was losing the love and consolation of a family, something she had never known in her lifetime.

As they rode on and the castle grew smaller and smaller on the horizon, the feeling of emptiness only seemed to grow and spread through her body. It was as if she were merely a shell now, emotionless and empty, and nothing could pull her back from that threshold.

Chapter Nineteen

The journey to the outer reaches of Dunaverty on the isle of Kintyre was arduous at the very least. English troops were scattered along every path and road and the rain became more incessant as they moved south. They had only been on the road for five days, but it felt as if it were a month.

"See there," Rorik shouted over the din of the drizzle, "Dunaverty port is beyond that steeple."

The steeple of St. Michael's chapel stood like a proud sentry along the crowded façade of Kirk Street. Though the rain was falling more heavily now, the merchants did not withdraw or pack away their wares. They huddled beneath rickety shelters and makeshift canopies, still loudly plying their goods.

"We should stop for food before we depart," Caedmon said beneath his drenched woolen hood.

"Aye," Keir agreed. "We should take our rest tae prepare for the remaining journey."

There was a murmur of agreement amongst the men and they continued down the slick, muddied street until they reached the corner where Dunn Street crossed before them, the glistening wet wooden planks of the quay waiting beyond.

Caedmon dismounted and took Anwen's horse by the bit while Rorik helped her down. Keir had tethered his leads to a nearby post and hurried himself into the *Wayfarer's Rest*, a dilapidated tavern situated at the crossroads. Anwen glanced sideways at Caedmon, who threw his arm around her shoulder and nudged her playfully.

"All will be well, lass." He gave her a toothy grin. "Let's get ye inside afore ye catch yer death."

The tavern was like all the others she had chance to visit; dark, dank and musty, though this one smelt more of fish than the others. Not unexpected considering its location along the harbor.

The denizens that filled the small tavern were mostly seafarers; fishermen and sailors huddling inside awaiting duties. Fishing poles, crabbing nets and other trappings were stacked in piles near the door, adding to the rustic, working class feel of the establishment. There was a gathering of men in the corner singing drunkenly while others joined in with bladder pipes and a hurdy-gurdy. Others sat throughout playing cards and gambling with dice.

Caedmon ordered a round of warm cider and the lot of them took a seat near the door where they could at least hear themselves think. Keir was at the end of the bar talking with a grisly looking man who had a long pipe clasped in his crooked, yellowed teeth.

"Who is that man?" Anwen motioned toward Keir and Caedmon looked over his shoulder at him.

"I dinna ken," he answered as he warmed his fingers around his hot mug. "Probably a fisherman."

"Why is Keir talking to him?" she asked as she sipped her drink, the heat of it fanning through her body in a wave, sending chills up her already cold back.

"He's trying tae get information on vessels that will be leaving here so we can get ye home quickly."

"You mean we don't already have passage hired?"

"Och, no, lass," he said with a grimace. "Schedules change daily round these parts. One never kens if bad weather or troop movement will halt a vessel from leaving her moorings. 'Tis best tae book passage the day ye wish tae leave tae assure ye'll actually get what ye paid for."

Anwen rubbed her forehead. Her temples were throbbing relentlessly and she could barely think. The thought of traveling on some broken down cog or a perilous smuggler's rig frightened her, regardless if she did have six men along with her. This was not the type of journey she had imagined.

After a heated discussion with the old man, Keir made his way to their table and took a seat.

"There's a vessel tae leave on the morrow, name of *Mawdelyn Blithe*. She's heading tae Ballycastle. Trip should take two days if we're lucky with the weather."

"How much?" Rorik asked.

"He says he would talk tae the Captain, that he'd maybe charge a crown a piece."

"A crown? Is he mad?" Caedmon balked.

"'Tis that or travel as cargo for two shilling a head."

"Travel as cargo?" Anwen asked, horrid thoughts filling her head.

"Aye, lie in the hold until we arrive." Keir said blandly as if it were nothing.

"Lie in the hold?" she said in surprise. "You mean sit in the belly of the ship for two days?"

"Perhaps longer." Keir nodded.

"That's absurd! What if we need air?" she asked, setting her mug down with trembling hands.

"We wait until we reach Ballycastle," Keir answered.

"Nay, I cannot sit for two days in the belly of a ship." She nodded fiercely.

"Do ye propose we go another way, strapped to a kittiwake's back perhaps?" Keir asked sarcastically and Rorik chuckled beside her.

She was not finding this at all amusing.

"I'm not trying to sound presumptuous, Keir, 'tis just that I cannot imagine sitting in…. a dark hole for two days without air or sun. I don't know if I could bear it."

Keir searched her eyes and realized what she was saying. She'd been in a dark hole before and it nearly killed her.

"Weel, we can pay the seven crowns and go aboard, but that would only leave us with about nine pound tae last us the rest of our trip." Keir said.

"We could sell the horses." Caedmon offered hopefully.

"We could, but then we would have tae risk trying tae find new ones upon our return." Keir answered.

"No matter, my father would gladly give you more wages to see you home." Anwen offered.

"All right, then we sell the horses, that'll save us stabling fees and we could use the money tae pay for travel from Ballycastle." Caedmon agreed and smiled over at Keir, who seemed less amused than she was.

"I do have some money as well, not much, maybe five pence, but it's something I can add it to help us," she offered, reaching for her pouch. "Besides, Ballycastle isn't very far from my home, perhaps an afternoon's travel."

"Nay, keep yer money, lass," Caedmon grasped her hand and gave her a pat. "We have enough tae get us by."

"Aye, we dinna need ye emptying yer pockets on our account. We'll manage." Keir said, and Anwen wasn't sure if he was being sincere or spiteful. At this point, she didn't care.

"Then 'tis done," Caedmon said. "Give the man our decision."

Keir went back to the bar and clasped arms with the old fisherman and the man got up with a wink and left the tavern with a limp. Keir then chattered with the publican, who refilled his mug and exchanged pleasantries with him before he returned to the table.

"I've gotten us rooms above. Caedmon, Rorik and I will take one, Andrew, Cullen and Randal will take the other. I've gotten Anwen a room of her own… for obvious reasons." Keir said, trying to smile kindly, but his mouth twitched as he looked away from her.

"The rooms have washbasins for us tae use if we need them. Hot water is two pence a bucket."

"How about meals? Do we eat here?" Andrew asked, scrubbing his chin in his fingers. "We can, though the fare here is limited. The innkeeper said there is a larger tavern up the hill on Castle Street called *Captain's Keep* which serves a larger menu."

"What do they have here?" Cullen asked.

"Mostly fish, fried or boiled. The other place has a diverse menu of fish, foul and game, or so he says."

"I'm fine with fish," Rorik said with a yawn, "but it's up tae the rest of ye."

"I say we go up the street." Andrew said.

"Aye, I'm no' much of a fish lover." Caedmon added with a grimace.

"All right, we go then." Keir nodded and turned to leave. The group followed him back out into the rain, which had tapered off into a soft, steady drizzle.

The *Captain's Keep* was only two blocks away, set in the center of the street between an apothecary and a chandler's shop. It seemed to be a busy establishment and the crowd that gathered inside seemed less sordid than those at the Wayfarer.

They found a large table toward the back of the room and within moments they were attended by a young, buxom woman holding a large tray.

"Wha' can I get for ye?" she asked with a smile, her eyes falling favorably upon Keir. "Ye strappin' lads look like ye could use a good meal, aye?"

"What do ye have that's good?" Keir asked her with a bold smile.

"Och, all's good eatin' here," she said with a grin and a wink.

Anwen looked away in disgust.

"We've got venison, beef and grouse, loads of local catch and shellfish. I think we still have rabbit and mutton as well," the serving wench added.

"Aye, I'll take the venison, with skirlie and some bread," Caedmon piped in, rubbing his stomach hungrily.

"I'll have that as well," Andrew answered in turn.

"Beef, and lots of it." Keir nodded, leaning back in his seat, clapping Cullen on the shoulder.

"Same with me." Cullen smiled.

Rorik twisted his mouth as he thought for a moment. "Smokies and potatoes," he said, "and shortbread if ye have any."

The woman nodded and shifted her tray.

"Venison for me." Randal said and then looked toward Anwen, who had yet to order.

"And ye, lassie?" the woman asked, eyebrows raised inquisitively.

"Stew and some bannocks, if I could," she said softly.

"No' a big eater, aye?" she chuckled. "Butter as well?"

"Aye, butter as well." Anwen nodded and glanced to the men at her table, who were looking back at her amusedly.

"Ale all around?" the woman asked as she started to turn away.

"Aye, and a whiskey," Caedmon added and then noted the faces around him "two...three whiskies and, Anwen?"

"Hot tea is fine." She smiled.

"Three whiskies and a hot tea. I'll get yer orders tae ye right away," the serving wench said and gave another wink to Keir, who smiled after her.

Anwen was infuriated by Keir's brazenness and his smile faded as he noted her grimace across the table. He was a man, after all, and she could not keep him from acting like one.

"I'll be at the bar," Keir grumbled, then stood and left the table.

Anwen sighed and tightened her lips as she watched him stalk away and then took a deep breath to calm herself. This would be over in a few days, she thought to herself, and Keir would be gone from her life. That thought alone made her stomach churn and a sudden wave of nausea hit her like a fierce, hot slap.

"I beg pardon," she said brusquely as she stumbled from her seat and moved to rush out of the tavern.

Caedmon, shaking his head with disbelief, nudged Rorik, who sat next to him.

"I'll go after the lass," he said curtly. "See if ye can maybe pound some sense intae yer cousin so we can remain civil for the rest of the journey."

"Aye," he nodded, "I'll do what I can, but I'm no' promising a miracle."

Caedmon chuckled half-heartedly and headed out of the tavern. It was dusk, and torches were being lit along the street, setting it in a warm, glowing haze. He searched the immediate area around the tavern, but Anwen was not about. He glanced toward Kilcannon Street, where the market vendors were beginning to pull in their carts of vegetables and butchered meats for the night, but there was no sign of her there. Back toward Dunn Street, the corner grew dim and he could not make out any faces among the crowd of people who walked there, so he turned and started in that direction.

Beyond High Street, the ramparts of an old Viking fort sat above its clouded moat. On the wooden bridge leading to its entry, Anwen stood motionless, staring into the moat's black depths.

"Anwen, lass, ye shouldna run off like that, no' alone," Caedmon chided as he neared her.

Anwen did not note his approach, she merely nodded to acknowledge his scolding words.

"Do you think it's possible to love someone you have never met?" she asked softly.

Caedmon shuddered and took her by the arm.

"Lass," he sighed heavily, "ye'll come tae love yer husband in time. No' all matches are perfect, but if ye work on it together, ye'll come tae appreciate one another."

"And what if he does not fancy me?"

"What's no' tae fancy?" he smiled reluctantly.

"I mean that, truly Caedmon," she said sourly as she turned toward him. "What if he despises me? What if he discards me, locks me away in some tower to rot while he goes off with some other woman?"

Caedmon's horrified expression did not calm her nerves, nor did it answer any of her questions. And once she had affirmed her thoughts aloud, she could not help but fret over what could possibly happen to her once she wed this man… this English man.

"I dinna ken what tae tell ye, lass," he said finally with a grimace. "There have been many a marriage that have ended as such, with the wife being mightily abused and betrayed. I pray it doesna come tae pass. And I canna promise it willna," he shrugged hopelessly. "I can only hope and pray along with ye that the man is fair and just and ye come tae love one another in time."

"Aye," she murmured, and then stood, silent for a long while. "You know that I love Keir…" she said softly.

"Aye, I ken, lass," he answered.

"I don't know how I will go on without him, Caedmon."

"Ye can remain as friends," he offered with a slight smile.

"You see how friendly he is to me now? How friendly do you think he'll be once I'm wed and sleeping in another man's bed?"

Caedmon nodded and turned away for a moment, knowing.

"Keir is a difficult lad, he always has been," he started as he rubbed his grey beard in his fingers. "Ever since Bowdyn was chosen successor, he has made himself believe that some curse has befallen him and that he is never meant tae be happy in his life. This whole state of affairs with ye has only solidified that for him. He struggles with the loss just as ye do, maybe more."

"How could he be struggling more? He still has his life ahead of him, free to marry whom he chooses, to fall in love again. I don't have that choice."

"But tae him, he has nay life ahead without ye in it. He loves ye deeply, lass, more deeply than ye ken. I doubt, much tae his father's vexation, that he will ever marry now."

Anwen let out a wavering sigh as a tear trickled down her cheek.

"Do you truly think he will never marry?"

"If he does, 'twill be out of respect for the clan and no' for love. Never for love." Caedmon said.

"I can't blame him for I feel the same, though I feel much to blame for it."

"Dinna fash yerself," he said matter-of-factly. "Before ye came intae his life, he wasna much of a courtin' man at any rate."

"Truly?" she asked tearfully.

"Aye, truly," he nodded. "He has run off more than once when his faither had announced that he had found a woman for him tae wed. He had always intended tae leave the keep and travel north, tae lose himself in the hielands."

"Surely he did not think he would not be found."

"Aye, foolishly he did. We are lucky tae have kin scattered everywhere north of the keep. He wouldna gotten far regardless."

"So, he felt trapped, as I do, into marrying someone he did not love," she said sadly.

"Aye, so it would seem. And in the end, he probably will still."

Anwen shuddered and wandered a few steps away from him, then turned, her face hot and covered with tears.

"I cannot live knowing another woman will bear his children." She sobbed aloud.

"I ken, lass, but we canna change things now. Ye must go on with yer life as he must. No use in mourning the days ye've never seen."

"God help me, but I cannot go on," she sobbed and dropped to her knees. "I would rather be dead than live a day without him."

"Hush lass," he whispered and went to her side. "Dinna speak such nonsense."

"'Tis not nonsense, I've never felt this way about any other man and I can't help that I do."

"How many other men have ye kent that ye can decide that?"

"I don't want to know any others." She sobbed.

"Ye must, lass,' he said with encouragement. "Ye must go on with yer life. I ken Keir is being harsh on ye now, but he will come around and ye will be friends for a long time tae come."

"I don't know that he will, Caedmon. He is so unwavering as if this is all or nothing. I daresay he will never warm to me again."

"Aye, he will, if he kens what's good for him. Once some time has passed between ye, he will realize he misses yer company and he will pay heed."

Anwen struggled with that thought and anguished over whether she could come to terms with only being a friend to Keir. It would be agonizing to have to hold back from him, to not be able to share her life with him. How could she when he was living his own life without her?

"I will try," she said finally, looking up at him.

"Grand, lass," he smiled, taking her by the elbow to help her to her feet. "Now, let's get ourselves back tae the tavern afore our sup goes cold, aye?"

"Aye," she sniffled and brushed the dirt from her kirtle.

The walk back to the tavern was hazy, as if in a dream. Anwen could sense her own footfall, see the distance passing as they neared the door of the tavern, but life seemed to be moving around her, without her. Would she remain like this, in a fog, for the rest of her days? She took a deep shaky breath and cleared her mind of her thoughts hoping to find some distant, calm place to remain until this was over. Only then could she think of the future. A future without Keir.

They made their way back to the table where the rest of the men were seated, calmly talking amongst themselves. Keir, who had returned to the table, sat silently with a mug in his hand. His face had softened a bit and he seemed less irritated than he had been. He seemed almost at peace, which concerned Anwen. What had happened while she was gone for him to resign himself so quickly? Had his men spoken to him? Had he gone off and had a quick tumble with the serving wench? She quickly discarded that thought and smiled civilly as she took her seat at the end of the table. Caedmon sat next to her and in a gesture of compassion, took her hand beneath the table and gave it a squeeze as he smiled fondly at her. She gave him a quick squeeze in return and cleared her throat to speak.

"Do you think we'll have a fair journey on the morrow, Rorik?" she asked, trying to change the mood at the table, which was ominous at best.

"Och aye," he smiled awkwardly. "I spoke tae a fisherman at the bar and he says the rain should stop this eve and that fair weather is approaching from the west."

"Aye, that's good news," Andrew chimed in. "Since we are heading west, surely we will face intae sunnier skies."

"I surely hope we do," she smiled with a nod. "I know that if the seas are rough, I should surely become ill."

"Och, nay need tae worry, lass," Caedmon nudged her. "Morág has given me parcels of ginger root and peppermint that will ease yer stomach if the ride is rough."

"'Tis good to know," she said with a sigh of relief. "Morág has a wonderful knowledge of remedies. I only wish I could have spent more time with her to have learned from her experience."

"Keir is quite good with remedies," Caedmon added proudly as he glanced at his grandson. "He's spent much time with her over the years and has learned much himself, have ye no', lad?"

"Aye, I have," he said plainly and after receiving a coaxing nudge from Rorik, looked up from his drink and smiled briefly. "I've brought packets of my own for stomach pains… mixtures of gentian, wild garlic and dried heather. They should work as well as the other mixtures."

"I didn't realize you were so well versed with herbal remedies," she said, a mark of surprise in her voice.

"Aye, Keir's a veritable nursemaid," Rorik laughed aloud, then caught an elbow in the ribs and a sharp look from Keir.

"I've learned much from my Mum and from Somhairle, ye remember him from the keep?" Keir asked with a nod.

"Aye, I do. He was a wonderful healer," she acknowledged. "I'm sorry I did not get a chance to thank him properly before we left."

"Not tae worry," Keir offered. "I will be sure tae pass on your kind words tae him. He will be happy tae hear them."

"I thank you for that," she smiled in return and received a smile from Keir that sent a small shiver of warmth through her heart. She didn't want to end things with him sourly and if she could remain civil and even friendly with him, it would be best for her in the end knowing she could still converse with him when she needed his company, even though he would be hundreds of miles away.

While they all continued to sit and chat amicably about the trip ahead and what they expected to see on their journey, the serving wench returned with their meals. Plates heaped with meats and vegetables were placed before them as well as baskets of bread, scone and cheese and a crock of butter.

They ate quietly, the slurping and crunching intermittently peppered with small talk, but soon the plates were picked clean and they sat sated, laughing and talking. Rorik, whose appetite was as big as his stature, added an order of raisin cake, pudding and apple tart to his plate and he continued to eat, with Anwen and the men stealing mouthfuls away from him when they could, until he was sated as well.

As the tavern slowly emptied of its occupants, so did they decide to retire. It had been a long day of travel and emotion and they had another handful of long days ahead of them.

Keir had finally opened up enough to speak quietly to Anwen on the walk back and Caedmon and the other men went ahead so they could continue their conversation in peace.

"I'm sorry for being so distant," Keir offered, watching his feet as he walked.

"I am as well," Anwen offered softly, her eyes not leaving her own shoes.

"I dinna mean tae be difficult," he said as he shuffled along. "'Tis just that sometimes I dinna ken how tae handle the way I feel about things and I'd rather go off on my own than tae burden anyone with my thoughts."

"I understand. I'm much the same as you."

"We *are* the same, ye and I," he said with a sigh, kicking a stone ahead of him. "'Tis a shame things could no' work out between us."

"But things have worked out," she said hopefully. "We get on well enough. I daresay I cannot speak as openly with my brothers as I can with you. I hold that fact in the highest of respects."

"Do ye?" he asked, stopping and turning toward her.

"You know I do, I always have, and I hope things don't change between us," she smiled genuinely, then her smile faded. "Well, not that I wouldn't rather have you as more than a friend, but if that is all I am afforded in this life, then that is what I will accept."

Keir nodded his head somberly and looked away.

"Aye, I ken it will be difficult tae do, remain as only friends, as it were," he sighed, "but I will remain steadfast tae ye, I will be there always if ye need someone tae talk tae. I hope ye can at least trust me with that much."

"Aye," she said with a huge smile. "Aye, of course I can. And I hope you treat me with the same respect. I want to be a part of your life, I want to know everything."

"Everything?" he asked, gazing at her perplexedly. "Surely ye dinna mean that."

"Aye, I do," she said, touching his arm gently. "Though it will pain me to hear, I want to know how you fare in life. I want to know of your wife, of your strong, handsome sons…"

Keir turned then and walked abruptly away at her words. The street in front of the *Wayfarer's Rest* was dark, but she could still hear his choked breaths and knew that he was moved by what she had said.

"Keir," she said softly as she went to him and touched his arm.

He pulled away sharply, hiding his face from her as he tried to regain his composure.

"How can ye endure this?" he said finally, his face stricken.

"I can't," she said as she looked away, her own eyes filling with tears. "But I must, for pity sake."

"I canna even begin tae imagine ye as a mother tae another man's bairns, I can barely imagine how ye'd come by them," he growled, his voice tight with emotion.

"As I can barely imagine the same of you, but to deny it will happen is foolish, Keir. My marriage is settled, there is no changing the situation. In time, I will be expected to produce heirs for my husband, to carry on the family. 'Tis not something I am looking forward to, as many a new wife should, but I have to for my own sake."

"I dinna believe that I can."

"That you can what?" she asked.

"Marry… have children… I canna conceive of doing either without ye." He moved to the side of the tavern and leaned against its rough wall. The glow from the torch near the doorway cast a flickering shadow over his face, bringing her back to the evening in her father's stables when he had come to escort her to Scotland, how his face had been shadowed in the darkness, yet she felt something warm and sincere in his voice. She had been right all along. He was sincere and warm beyond her dreams. Fate had brought them together that night, and now fate was tearing them apart.

She considered his words, the thought of him marrying and having children with another woman nauseated her and she would be happy if he chose not to. Perhaps her husband was elderly and would die soon after marriage and then she would be free to marry as she pleased. She hadn't given it much thought until now. Would her new husband be young? Old? Would he be a comely young man or a bloated, smelly old beast? She hadn't even been told his name. Regardless, she would never see him in the same light as she did Keir.

"You should marry," she said quietly as she leaned against the wall next to him. "And have bairns of your own."

"I canna."

"You must. You need to continue your bloodline so there will be generations of MacLochlainn's to follow."

"I dinna care if I am the last," he sighed and looked heavenward, a single tear trickling down his cheek. "'Tis no matter tae me now."

"But you are the last of the MacLochlainn sons, does that

not mean something to you?"

"Nay, I ken it should, but it doesna, no' anymore."

"Why on earth not?" she asked tearfully.

"I dinna ken," he said, wiping his cheek against his sleeve. "'Tis just that in the past, I could never imagine marrying or having bairns of my own, but after I met ye and fell in love with ye, I kent there was a reason for it, that ye had been sent tae me tae change my mind… tae change my heart. And now, I canna bear tae think I will do these things without ye."

Anwen went silent. Her heart quickened with happiness knowing that he felt the same as she did, but she was also saddened that, together, they would have to cope with being apart. And she had no words to help either of them.

The bells of St. Michael's chapel tolled the midnight hour then and she glanced into the distance, where the chapel stood, and she sighed.

"We must get to our rest, 'tis a long day ahead on the morrow," she managed through her tears.

"Aye, I ken," he said.

The two of them turned and entered the tavern, its once crowded room now quiet and empty. They made their way silently up the creaky staircase and down to the rooms at the end of the scarcely lit hallway.

"This is your room," he said, lifting the latch and entering before her to make sure her room was set to rights.

It was a small room, with only enough space for a small bed

and a bedside table. He lit the candle that was set upon the table and turned to her with a faint smile. "I hope ye rest well."

"And you as well," she said, moving past him to sit on the small, creaking bed.

"If ye need of me, I'm in the room just opposite there," he pointed out the door. "Dinna hesitate tae knock if ye need anything."

"I won't," she said with a soft smile.

"Good eve tae ye, princess," he smiled, bent to kiss her cheek softly and then turned and left the room, closing the door behind him.

"Good eve to you, my prince," she whispered with a sigh, removed her kirtle and crawled into her bed to try to find peace in her dreams.

His hands were on her, tearing at her clothing, shredding them as he groped her. The room was dark, so dark she could not see but a flicker of candlelight in the corner that only diverted the shadows, making it harder for her to discern one shape from another.

He was brutal, his breath hot and rank on her face. His hands were calloused and icy cold, fondling her, caressing her in ways that revolted her and she turned away in disgust.

He tore at her shift, clenching the skin at her hips, pulling her closer.

"You will not have me," she shouted, "Never!"

His hand came down hard and quick, the slap throwing her head violently against the headboard. He demanded she obey, that she give in to his advances. She could feel his weight upon her, though she still could not see his face. The stench of him, the slickness of his sweaty nakedness repulsed her and she fought against him, kicking and scratching.

His hand covered her mouth as he entered her and the pain was excruciating, tearing her apart from the inside. She tried to call out, to scream in protest, but his hand was tightly placed.

He continued his assault, probing her, violating every inch of her body until she felt shattered and empty.

"My seed is firmly planted now," he whispered wickedly into her ear, his drool dripping repulsively down her neck. "You are mine now," he sneered. "You belong to England."

"No!" Anwen screamed aloud and sat up in the utter darkness of her room. Her heart pounding wildly in her throat, her face dripping with sweat, her chemise soaked through.

Her door flew open with a crash and she screamed, backing against her headboard. "No!' she wailed, "Don't touch me!"

"Anwen, lass," Keir's voice cooed as he rushed to her side and pulled her into his arms. She fought against him wildly, punching and pounding against his chest, sobbing uncontrollably.

"Stop!" She flailed against him. "Don't touch me!"

"Anwen, lass, 'tis me!" he cried out, grasping her face in his hands.

Her eyes were dark, empty and glazed over as if she were in a dream and then slowly, as her sobs intensified, the realization returned to her face and she went limp, weeping against his shoulder.

"Oh Keir, don't leave me," she cried, "He was horrible."

"Who was horrible?" he asked softly, stroking her hair down her back.

"I don't know," she sobbed, "he was tearing at my clothing, beating me… violating me." She shuddered violently against him.

Though he knew it was only a nightmare she spoke of, Keir could not help but become aware of the fury building inside him. He could not help but despise the man who was to be her husband for deeds he had never committed. He envisioned this evil, lecherous fiend, groping and molesting Anwen and the bile began to rise in his throat until he was choking.

"'Tis all right, lass, 'twas only a nightmare," he whispered gruffly, closing his eyes against the helplessness he felt running through his veins.

When he opened his eyes, he found Caedmon and the others standing in the hallway half dressed, weapons readied. He gave them a deliberate shake of his head as he continued to soothe Anwen, rocking her in his arms.

Caedmon, accustomed to Anwen's horrendous dreams from her nights at the keep, nodded obediently at Keir and shuffled the men away, closing the door behind him.

"Please don't leave," she whimpered. "Stay with me."

"Ye ken I canna stay here, lass," he whispered, kissing her hair softly.

"I beg of you, I cannot stay here alone."

Her words were painful to hear, her face panicked and pale. Modesty did not allow him to stay with her, but rules be damned. He could not leave her in such a state and he did not care at that moment what the others thought of him.

"Aye," he said softly, "I willna leave ye."

He pulled her tightly against his chest and in a matter of moments, they were sound asleep, safe in each other's arms.

Chapter Twenty

"The vessel's at the far end of the quay," Keir motioned, squinting down the pier. "The Captain's name is Braddock. I've paid our fee and he's awaiting our arrival. He departs on the hour."

Caedmon shuffled his baggage from one shoulder to the other, and then stooped down to pick up the basket at his feet. Rorik and the other men gathered their belongings and walked off down the quay toward the cog. Anwen stood silently across from them, peering blankly out across the harbor.

"Is she all right?" Caedmon asked looking after her pitifully.

"Aye," Keir nodded, "She'll be fine. Her nightmares are getting worse, I fear."

"'Twas no' proper for ye tae have stayed with her all night."

"Grandy, please dinna preach tae me now. I ken what is expected of me and I dinna care. I couldna have left her there tae cower in the darkness, terrified of her own shadow."

"Lad," Caedmon nodded, "I ken, and I understand completely. I couldna have left her either. I think it best that no one makes mention of this tae anyone though."

"Agreed." Keir shifted his own bag on his shoulder.

"I've already spoken tae the men and they have vowed tae keep silent," Caedmon offered. "They are aware of her state since her abduction and they understand as well."

"I am glad for it," Keir smiled and gave a thankful nod. "I beg pardon, but we are running out of time. I need tae collect the monies owed us for the horses and get tae the vessel afore she leaves without me."

"Aye, do as ye will and hurry yerself aboard. I'll be sure tae keep us at anchor until ye return." Caedmon said, patting Keir on the arm meaningfully. "And I'll take Anwen with me, make sure she is settled comfortably onboard."

"Thank ye, Grandy," Keir said with a wink and then he jogged off toward the stables to fetch the money he was owed.

Anwen was still silent as they made their way aboard. The fees they had paid, eight crowns in total, afforded them room in the steerage. Their baggage was placed in the hold with the rest of the cargo and Caedmon went with Anwen into the small area to settle her in, to make her comfortable for the journey ahead.

"'Tis very small," she said as she looked about the room, the large arm of the tiller jutting in from the stern.

The bunks were of a goodly size, a bit larger than a cot, with heavy blankets and small pillows. There was a small writing desk off to the side with a mounted inkwell and a bin for quills. The candleholder next to the desk was also mounted, but loosely hinged so it would be able to remain unwavering as the vessel rolled with the waves of the open waters.

"Will ye be comfortable here, lass?" Caedmon asked.

"Aye, this is fine enough," she smiled. "I know I've been quite a burden already, I don't need to add to it by demanding to be pampered."

"Och, ye've been nay burden tae any of us, lass." He dismissed her concerns with a wave.

"I'm sorry about last night," she said softly, averting her eyes from his consoling expression.

"'Tis all right, lass." He nodded. "These things take time. 'Tis yer minds way of healing itself."

"I don't like this form of healing," she grimaced. "I'd rather not heal at all if this is what I must endure night after night."

"All will mend itself in time, ye'll see."

She was grateful to have Caedmon with her. Though Keir was of great consolation to her, having Caedmon was a comfort on a different level. There were things she could not tell him that she could freely discuss with Keir, but in the same breath, there were things she could not discuss with Keir that she could easily discuss with Caedmon. It was a fine line, but with each she knew her boundaries and it was a relief nonetheless.

"Where is Keir?" she asked, suddenly realizing she hadn't seen him aboard. "He went off tae fetch the money for the horses. He should be back shortly." "Are you sure they won't leave without him?"

"Aye, I've spoken tae Captain Braddock and he has agreed tae stay docked until Keir is safely onboard," he said, fiddling with the inkwell.

The craft began to bob then, and shift on its moorings.

"It feels like we are moving!" Anwen exclaimed, grasping onto the bunk for leverage. "Aye," Caedmon said with concern. "I'll check tae see what's going on."

Caedmon dashed beneath the low bulkhead with Anwen following behind him and came out onto the deck, startled. The ship was moving away from the dock and Keir was still nowhere in sight.

"What are ye doin'?" he shouted across the deck at the Captain, who was standing on the forecastle with a map in his hands.

"Shoving off, what does it look like?"

"But my grandson is no' onboard yet, ye gave me yer word that ye wouldna depart without him."

"We received word that there's a storm coming in from the south, if we dinna depart now, we'll get hit head on."

"We canna just leave him here, he's needed in our travels." Caedmon argued.

"I dinna ken what tae tell ye, old man, we've got nay choice." Braddock said with a shrug.

Just then, the other men came running onto the deck, shouting their alarm as they watched the dock move away.

"Keir is no' aboard! What are ye doing?" Rorik boomed, rushing to the rail to peer out at the dock.

Andrew went running up to the starboard rail and shaded his eyes against the sun. "There he is! Stop the boat!" Andrew shouted, pointing out toward the pier where Keir, burdened with his pack bags and an armful of bundles, was running at top speed toward them shouting profanities in Gaelic.

"Swing toward the far pier," Braddock called out to his steersman and the man eased the rudder right, banking the vessel toward the pier.

Keir, noting the boats bank toward the dock, picked up speed and as it neared the end of the quay he began tossing his bundles and bags onto the deck and took one long leap, just missing the deck. As the vessel banked away from the jetty, Keir flailed as he hung from the outer rail. The men leapt toward him, clasping him about the arms, yanking him bodily onto the deck where he slid into a heap on the far side of the craft.

"I should gut ye like the pig that ye are!" Rorik roared as he pointed his *sgian dubh* at the Captain, his eyes wide with rage.

"Stand down, lad, or I'll have ye put off!" Braddock shouted, two of his burly sailors coming to stand behind him. "Dinna forget whose vessel ye are on. I willna hesitate tae throw any of ye overboard if ye continue tae show signs of aggression."

"Rorik, lad," Caedmon urged from behind. "Put yer dirk away. 'Tis over now and Keir is here."

"I dinna like this man, no' one bit," Rorik seethed and sheathed his blade as he bent to help Keir to his feet.

"'Tis fine, cousin," Keir nodded as he brushed himself off. "Leave off the man."

"But he was going tae leave without ye after he gave his word that he would wait."

"I ken, Rorik, and I'm sure there was good reason for it." Keir said brusquely, offering a displeased look to the Captain.

"Aye, there is," Braddock groused as he came down the ladder and onto the deck. "There's a storm headed up the coast and if we stay here any longer we'll be tossed intae tinder afore we even get out of the harbor."

Keir nodded in agreement and gathered up his baggage.

"I apologize for holding ye here so long," he said, offering a handshake to the Captain. Braddock shook his hand graciously and apologized for the misunderstanding.

"We should get tae Ballycastle in two days, maybe three depending on the weather. Feel free tae walk about the deck, but stay clear of the men as they work." Braddock said as he looked out toward the water.

"We'll be sure tae stand aside," Keir said with a smile.

"All right then," the Captain smiled. "Let's get her underway, lads," he shouted to his men. "I hope ye have a pleasant journey aboard the Mawdelyn Blithe," he offered to Keir and his party and he tipped his cap to them as he went back to his duties.

"Let's get this baggage stowed away before the storm hits," Keir said to Caedmon and they went below deck to the hold where he dropped off his packages and larger bags.

After everyone was settled, they gathered in the room below the forecastle to sit and chat.

"How long until we reach Ballycastle?" Anwen asked as she rummaged through Morag's packet of herbs. She found a nice bit of ginger and she popped it in her mouth to chew it, hoping that its essence would help ease her stomach. She wasn't quite sure if her queasiness was due to the rough waters that were starting to toss the small boat or if her thoughts of home and what awaited her there were perhaps making her stomach uneasier than it truly was.

"'Tis a short trip," Keir said as he took the packet from her and pulled a twig of peppermint out for himself. "Braddock says it will be at least two days if we're lucky and miss the brunt of the storm."

"Aye, the skies were beginning tae darken when I was on deck last, but the waters dinna seem tae be churning too violently," Caedmon assured Anwen as he patted her leg.

Her blood was beginning to run cold as talk of the journey progressed into a more heated discussion of their remaining trek into Ireland. Keir had managed to sell the horses at a generous forty-nine pounds, adding an additional three when the ostler discovered the mare Andrew was riding was to foal. He was also able to sell off their saddles and tack for three pounds more and so they had added fifty-five pounds to their coin to help them on their way.

"I also picked up a few items at the market," he said with a grin. A small crock of crowdie brought a smile to Caedmon's elderly face. Bannock cakes and honey butter for the men and some smoked herring for any cravings got a rousing reception.

"I dinna ken what ye'd want for the trip," Keir said apologetically to Anwen. "So, I picked this up for ye."

He handed her the carefully wrapped package and she eyed it curiously. With cautious fingers, she untied the cord and opened the paper.

"Chrétien de Troyes," she said, astonished, as she ran her hand smoothly across the embossed leather cover of the small book.

"Have ye read him?" Keir asked as he took a seat next to her.

"No, I have not, though I have heard much about his works," she said as she flipped through its pages. "Have you read him?"

Keir grimaced as he looked around at the faces of the men at the table, who would undoubtedly tease him for his rather passive choice of entertainment.

"Aye," he nodded succinctly, "his tales of Lancelot and Yvain are brilliant."

"Och," Rorik rolled his eyes as he leaned back, "'twas rubbish! No knight would spend his days lazing about, coddling maids and reading poetry while his men, and the King, did the same. Ye'd be sure tae find a keep full of heavy-bellied, soft men who wouldna have the strength tae heave a sword should they have need tae do so."

"You've read his works as well?" Anwen asked Rorik, quite surprised by his statement.

"Och aye," he said, "a bit too romantic for my tastes, and a bit unrealistic, but easy enough tae digest if ye want something simple tae read on a rainy night."

Easy wasn't the word she would consider for this book as she skimmed through the yellowed pages filled with the old French text.

"I didn't realize you could read French." She cocked her head as she looked at Rorik, who chuckled aloud and glanced around the table at his kin.

"Oui, bien sûr," Rorik said with a grin. "Souhaitez-vous en attendre moins d'un Ecossais?"

Anwen nodded her head with a chuckle of her own because she didn't expect anything less of these men. They seemed to surprise her on a daily basis.

"Non, je suis agréablement étonné," she answered.

"Well done," Keir said, the smile spreading across his face.

"And I suppose, by Rorik's admission, that you and the rest of the men speak French as well?" she asked of him and he smiled genuinely.

"Oui, naturellement." He tilted his head with a grin. She could feel the heat rising in her cheeks.

Keir leaned closer and cooed in her ear, "approuvez-vous?"

"Aye," she giggled.

"Keir, lad," Caedmon said, smacking him on the leg. "Stop pestering the lass."

"So, tell me," Anwen asked as she gave Caedmon a wink of thanks for saving her from embarrassment, "Why is it you speak French so fluently?"

"Weel," Keir said with a sigh as he sat back, "France is a great ally and many of our families have taken refuge there from time tae time. When ye spend time in a foreign land, ye tend tae want tae blend in and learning the language seems a natural way tae do that."

"I suppose you're right," she said, taking the chewed bit of ginger out of her mouth. "But I'm surprised I hadn't learned more of your language while I was here. One would think I would have absorbed something."

"Weel, lass," Caedmon said. "Ye were only with us a short time."

"True," she nodded. "Though I'm surprised I was never taught to speak your tongue at home. My father comes from Scottish blood and has kin that still live there. As it is, I learned all I know of languages on my own by reading. I spent much of my time as a child in our library since there was no one my age to become friendly with and my brothers were often off on their own dealing with training."

"How could ye live like that?" Andrew nodded, his grimace echoed in the faces of the other men.

"I would have gone insane with the boredom and the silence." Cullen nodded.

"I learned to amuse myself. The books became my friends," she said with a bit of sorrow in her voice and the men at the table seemed to look away uneasily.

She realized, as she looked around at them and the kinship they shared, that she had very few friends in her life. Keir was one of the first and only people she considered a friend. How much had she lost in life being tucked away in a place so solitary for so many years? How much had she missed and not experienced being locked away from the world? Having no friends to account for was proof enough she had lost plenty and she wasn't sure she would ever forgive her father for it.

"I need to get some air," she said softly, feeling the sadness and anger compete within her, and she stood to leave the table.

"I'll go with ye," Keir offered, but she waved him off.

"I'll be fine on my own." She moved away from him quickly, catching the look of concern in his eyes. She needed to do for herself now. She could not allow herself to become accustomed to him being there when she needed comfort. She had been strong once, on her own. It was time she found that strength within herself again.

Once on deck, she was hit with the harsh, cold wind slapping her face, whipping her hair out of the loose braid she had plaited earlier. The sky was a churning mass of billowy grey clouds that seemed low enough to touch and though the rain had not started, the thickness of the air was overwhelming.

"Get back inside, lass!" Braddock shouted from atop his perch on the forecastle.

Anwen turned to go back when she caught a view of the sea. The water was churning furiously around the boat and the horizon was black as night though it was only midday. Her breath caught in her throat and she nearly dove through the door, entering the steerage with a clatter.

"It looks awful out there!" she said, catching her breath. "Braddock told me to get inside."

"I suppose those fishermen were wrong all along," Keir grimaced. "Fair seas my arse."

"We'll be safe enough in here," Caedmon said, noting her harried look. "Dinna ye fash, lass."

"I'm fine," she said, taking a seat next to Andrew, who was nonchalantly eating a bowl of pottage as if nothing were out of the ordinary. "'Tis only a squall."

"Fine enough," Caedmon said and stood from the table. "We should prepare for the storm then."

"Aye," Keir said as he stood as well. "I'll make sure our things are secure in the hold." He left the room and headed toward the cargo hold. Anwen sat watching Andrew continue with his meal, humored that he didn't seem aware of what was going on around him.

"How can you eat at a time like this?" she asked him with a smirk.

Andrew looked up from his bowl and smiled curiously. "Like what? The boat's hardly moving."

"You're serious?" she asked, looking over at Rorik, who just leaned back calmly and smiled.

"Aye, I am," Andrew answered. "This is nothing compared tae true rough weather at sea, aye, Rorik?" Andrew said as he nodded his head toward his friend.

"Aye, and what's a Scotsmen without his love for the sea?" Rorik grinned and leaned his head back with a yawn.

"I didn't realize you had such an admiration for seafaring," Anwen said, her stomach starting to churn.

"Oh aye," Caedmon added, "Seafaring has long since been a Celt tradition. We are an island people, after all, and we must work with what is at hand."

"I never thought of that." She cocked her head curiously. "My people are on an island as well, though I know no one who is a sailor."

"Aye, maybe no' sailors, but I can wager there are plenty of fisherman," Rorik said, his eyes closed as he enjoyed his brief nap.

"Well, none that I know of, though fishermen do come to my village with their catch to sell," she said reaching for the pouch of herbs that sat in the middle of the table. She dug through the contents until she found a nice stalk of peppermint and she stuck a piece in her mouth.

"Stomach bothering ye?" Andrew asked.

"Aye, a bit." She grimaced and sat back, closing her eyes to control her dizziness.

"Try some pottage," he offered as he slid the bowl toward her. "Sometimes it helps tae have something in yer stomach tae ease the sickness."

Anwen could only imagine how green her face turned when she caught a strong whiff of the mess that was in Andrew's bowl.

"No, thank you," she managed and then covered her mouth and nose with her hand.

Normally she liked pottage, and beef was her favorite, but right now the smell and the look of it nauseated her.

Suddenly, the small vessel lurched and pitched starboard, sending Anwen sprawling to the floor. Andrew's bowl of pottage came crashing down as well, flinging the mealy mixture everywhere. Caedmon stumbled to the door and caught himself on the doorjamb as Keir came stumbling back into the room.

"Looks like a bloody war out there," Keir gasped as he leaned down to help Anwen to her feet.

"Really?" Anwen asked exasperatedly as she came to her feet and struggled to get to a chair as the boat continued to pitch and sway.

"Aye, the men seem to be having quite a time getting the sail in," Keir mentioned as he handed Andrew his bowl. Andrew, noting its empty state, grimaced and slammed the bowl onto the table.

"Perhaps we should go on deck and help," Caedmon offered as he leaned his head out the door to see what was going on.

"Och, nay," Keir said, handing Andrew his spoon as well. "I dinna pay eight crown tae have tae work as weel."

"I suppose ye're aright," Caedmon said, shrugging his shoulders. "If they need us, they'll call."

"They better no'," Rorik groused as he stretched his arms overhead. "I've a mind tae wallop the Captain as it is. That would just give me more of a reason tae do so."

Caedmon laughed and winked at Anwen, who was sure she would not be able to make it through the entire trip without weaving her way to the rail to heave.

There was a tremendous scraping sound then and the cog stopped abruptly, throwing most everyone at the table against the port wall, piling them in a heap atop Rorik. They could hear the men on deck shouting and running about and the Captain's voiced bellowed commands above them.

Keir pulled himself off the pile and struggled to free Anwen from the tangle of bodies. "Are ye all right?" he asked, looking her over for damage.

"Aye." She nodded, "I seem to be in one piece."

"Is everyone all right?" Keir asked as he turned and began offering his hand to the men as they dismounted the pileup.

"Nay!" Rorik bellowed from beneath the stack. "I'm about crushed down here!"

"Och, ye big oaf," Keir laughed as the last man removed himself from the pile and Rorik blinked his eyes angrily. "Ye're screaming like a wee bairn. A hulking great man as yerself and ye canna take being squashed by a handful of yer kin?"

"Och aye," Rorik said as he stood and stretched his spine back into place. "I'd like tae see ye lying under a huge pile of yer men and then we'll see who screams like a bairn!"

"Will the two of ye just shut it for once." Caedmon scolded as he rolled his eyes heavenward. "Ye'll both be screaming like bairns if ye dinna hush yer mouths. God's teeth!"

Startled by Caedmon's harsh words, Rorik and Keir sat stunned for a moment while the other men chuckled under their breath. Anwen could not help but conceal a smile of her own behind her hand.

"Now, I'm going on deck tae see what's happened. Ye'll all just sit here until… until I tell ye tae no' sit here!" Caedmon said harshly and then turned and left the room.

"What's gotten intae his breeches?" Rorik asked, looking after Caedmon as he left.

Keir began to chuckle and then broke into absolute belly-splitting laughter that made the rest of them join in.

"I dinna ken, but it sure was funny!" he said, wiping his tearful eyes on his sleeve.

After a few moments, Caedmon returned and told them that they had run aground at the south coast of Islay to wait out the storm. He then gave them permission to leave the room, the lot of them chuckling as they passed him.

Anwen sat on a keg near the rail and watched as Caedmon filled his pipe for a smoke. Rorik and Keir wrestled jokingly behind him. They were a jovial bunch, she mused, trying to goad Caedmon into scolding them again and again. Cullen and Randal were quiet men, sitting on the steps of the forecastle chatting softly. Andrew seemed to always want to join in on Keir and Rorik's antics, though they often moved him aside as if they were older brothers not wanting him to intrude on their fun.

The boat crew hurriedly carried boxes and barrels from the deck, lowering them into the hold. She imagined what was inside the crates, perhaps foods from exotic countries or fabrics from beyond the east. Of course, they were probably full of fish and wool, but imagining their exotic nature made the trip seem more interesting.

Captain Braddock was standing at the far side of the deck arguing with a man who was bobbing up and down from his seat in his small currach next to the boat. Both men were gesturing wildly and pointing at the Captain's ship.

When the last crate was lowered into the hold, the crewman shouted to Braddock, who had lowered a ladder to the young man and had helped him onto deck. As her party began to make their way back to the steerage, Keir spun on his heels and went toward the man with a grin.

"Kestrel Weldon, ye old dog!" he said, clasping arms with the man and greeting him with a great hug.

"I never thought tae see you here, Keir," the man said. "I don't believe there are enough stews here tae suit yer needs." He laughed heartily and Keir, suddenly shocked by his words, glanced over at Anwen and winced with a shrug.

Stews, was it? She knew Keir wasn't an innocent when it came to women, but to think he spent his time in brothels all over Alba and that it was a known fact, at least to this man, made her question his integrity.

Keir was a man, of course, and men were known to be weak creatures, giving in to their carnal lusts as often as a child stumbles into a sweet shop, but she had no idea he was such a whore. What else would she learn about this man, whom she thought she knew and loved, before this journey was through?

Keir walked arm in arm with the man and they approached her.

"Lady Anwen," Keir said as he took a step toward her, obviously noting her angered expression. "This is Master Kestrel Weldon, a dear old friend of mine."

Kestrel bowed graciously and smiled just as kindly as he looked her over. "I am pleased tae make your acquaintance," he offered humbly.

"And I yours, Master Kestrel," she nodded in deference to him.

"Kestrel is quite the sea-faring man these days," Keir added, slapping his friend on the back soundly. "Last I saw him, no' five years past, he was a mere oarsman on the deck of a dilapidated longship. It seems he has advanced quite rapidly in his profession and is now the master of his own vessel."

"Truly?" Anwen asked with surprise. She surmised Kestrel was not much older than she was. "What a wonderful turn of events for you."

"Aye," Kestrel said as he motioned them onto the deck. "I spent countless months pulling away at an oar, shredding my hands on hemp riggings, even slopping the deck when the men lost their stomachs. I suppose it's the least good that could come of my efforts."

"Where is your vessel?" Anwen asked as the three of them entered the steerage and took a seat at the table.

Kestrel noted the rest of the men there and smiled with a nod, apparent that he knew each of them in turn.

"She's dry-docked at Donegal having her hull scraped and pitched." Kestrel answered, shaking hands with Rorik as he spoke.

"How did ye come by her?" Keir asked, offering him a mug of ale.

"Won her during a game of quekeboard, if ye can imagine that." Kestrel chuckled then took a drink of his ale.

"I dinna ken ye were the gambling sort. I would think that ye had learned yer lesson after ye had lost all but yer skin during the round of Nine Men's Morris we played the last time I saw ye."

"Aye, well," Kestrel sighed with a snicker. "I haven't always been lucky, but when I need to be, I am."

"Weel," Keir said as he took up a mug of his own, "Here's tae yer new rig."

Kestrel and the rest of the men toasted him and gave a great cheer.

"Did ye name her yet?" Rorik asked him as he wiped his mouth on his sleeve.

Kestrel blushed for a moment and then cleared his throat awkwardly.

"Aye, I have," he said with a crooked smile. "I named her Mo Siobhan."

The men snickered at this admission, but Keir seemed none too pleased with the moniker. Anwen just nodded and looked between the two of them blankly.

"What's Mo Siobhan?" she asked.

"It means My Jehanne..." Keir grimaced and took another sip of his ale.

"This Jehanne is someone you know?" she asked Kestrel curiously, and Keir grumbled under his breath.

"Aye." Rorik chuckled. "Mo Siobhan is what he calls Meara."

Anwen was beginning to understand. Apparently, Kestrel had something of an infatuation with Keir's sister. And a lucky girl she was to have such an admirer, she thought. Kestrel was a handsome man. Not in the same way she found Keir handsome, but Kestrel had definite striking features. His skin was deeply tanned and his body was lean and muscular from what she only assumed was a lifetime on the sea.

"I didn't realize you knew his family," she said.

"Aye," Kestrel said with a nod, "I've known them for many years and have served MacLochlainn many times."

"Your father has ships of his own?" she questioned Keir. "Why did we not utilize them?"

"Oh aye," Keir answered. "My father has a handful of small vessels at his disposal, but since the English have taken tae the inlets tae try tae keep us at port, he finds it necessary tae keep them docked.

He felt it was not only dangerous but foolish tae have ye aboard one of them. It would have been a huge risk."

"But how do you go about trading without the use of them?" she asked.

"We have currachs and other small boats which can navigate quite easily from port tae port and are still large enough to carry goods," Keir offered. "The English are no' as wary of them as they are the larger vessels."

"Aye, you'd be surprised how many men and military supplies have been transported that way, right under their noses, the fools." Kestrel chuckled.

"Aye, the English are a dim lot, every one of them." Rorik added and raised his mug with a smile.

"Your speech does not belie you as a man of Scottish decent, Kestrel," Anwen said off handedly. "May I ask where you hail from?"

"Here and there," he answered, sipping his ale quietly. "I was born in the west of England, near the Welsh borders, but I have not lived in one place long enough to call it home, except for the sea."

"You're English?" she said with surprise.

"Theoretically, aye, I am." Kestrel nodded. "But I was only born there. I have lived in numerous countries from Ireland to Spain and do not consider myself a subject of any crown."

"That's convenient," she said apathetically.

Keir balked at her comment and nodded his head. "Why convenient?"

"Well," she started, noting the disturbed looks from the men around her, "In times as these when one country is battling another for power, who do you support?"

"I support myself," Kestrel said plainly, "Myself and my friends," he added, patting Keir on the leg. "If the MacLochlainn were to have need of me, I would be at his side out of respect."

"But what of duty?" she asked.

"What's the difference?" Kestrel asked, a hint of cynicism in his voice. "My duty is to the sea and no crown truly owns her."

"I'm sure there are several kings who would disagree," she stated with a chuckle.

"Aye, but while they disagree, I go about my business and try to stay out of their way." Kestrel grinned.

"Speaking of duty," Keir said, "What were you arguing about with Braddock?"

"Ah," Kestrel smiled. "The old codger assumed I would want to work for my passage to Ireland. I told him he was misinformed and that I was more than happy to pay him for his troubles."

"Och, weel, they could probably use a pair of skilled hands as yours for this trip. The storm has the crew scrambling," Keir said, motioning to the deck.

"Storm, bah…" Kestrel chided. "These men wouldn't know a storm if it crawled up their arses." He smirked, then nodded in deference to Anwen.

Anwen raised her eyebrows.

"Think you this storm will not trouble our journey?"

"Nay, not at all," Kestrel answered knowingly. "Once we put to the sea the waves will die out. The water is choppier in the harbor because there is nowhere for its energy to go. I spoke to a mate of mine not an hour ago who came from Wales this morn and he said that though they rode with the storm nearly the entire voyage, there were clear, sunny skies behind them. This is nothing but a squall and we should be through it shortly."

And, like most seasoned seafarers, Kestrel's prediction was accurate. The storm blew past them in less than an hour and their passage across the channel and into open water was relatively uneventful. Once put to sea, the waves as well as the wind died away. They met with a handful of squalls, with one torrential downpour that had them huddling in the corner of the leaky steerage, but as a whole, the trip was swift and painless. Anwen had even become relaxed by the next day. Her stomach had returned to normal and she was able to eat the evening meal with the rest of them.

Now on deck watching the sun set before them, they marveled at the wondrous colors in the western sky. Its dusky purple and orange hues faded seamlessly, blending with the darkening sky overhead and the twinkle of the first evening stars guided them the rest of the way home.

Home, she thought solemnly, was now completely relative.

Chapter Twenty – One

As they drifted into the harbor of Ballycastle near dawn on the third day, Anwen couldn't help but sigh with despair. The only thing that separated her from her new life now was ninety miles of Irish countryside. They would be back at her father's keep in another two days and her nightmare would begin.

"Are ye comin', lass?" Caedmon called from the pier as they loaded the last of their baggage onto the wagon.

Anwen nodded and made her way down the gangplank and went to the wagon just as Keir was finishing securing everything in place.

"We'll take the wagon intae town and find some horses so we can get underway," Keir said as he helped her up and then leapt up into it himself, taking a seat on a pile of bags on the far end of the wagon.

As they bumped along the dirt covered road, she watched Keir gaze out behind them, his eyes distant. She heaved a great sigh and looked out across the land herself. This was her own soil now, but it no longer felt like home to her. No one recognized her, no one greeted her return. She felt so alone and so far removed from this place. She had only spent a short time in Scotland, but she felt more at home there than any other place on earth.

They came upon Donegal Town a few moments later and Keir hopped out and headed toward the stables across from where they had stopped. Anwen remained in the wagon, her body numb to everything that was going on around her. The men went about their business of securing supplies and saddling the new horses and she was bodily lifted from the wagon and placed on a horse of her own, as if she weren't even there.

She hadn't said a word all day, not that any of them were speaking much. The men had chattered on about this and that, but as they got further south, their banter died down. The remainder of the journey was a blur of scenery to her. They made it as far south as Ballintober before they decided to stop for the night and she wandered aimlessly into the room they secured for her at the inn, closing the door behind her in silence.

She sat on her small bed in a daze. She couldn't think, she could barely breathe. It was as if time had stood still and she was locked in a box that someone nailed shut.

She hadn't noticed the rise of the sun the next morn, and when a knock came at her door, she barely flinched at the sound. It echoed through her mind and then faded until she heard his voice.

"Anwen?" Keir's voice registered concern. "Anwen, are ye there, lass?"

Anwen's eyes looked slowly toward the door and even in the small room, it still seemed so far away. She wanted to go to the door. She wanted to throw it open and leap into Keir's arms, but her body remained still. She couldn't bear to make that step.

Everything in her mind told her that once she opened that door, the day would begin and her life would be over. Her father's keep was no more than a few hours away and once they arrived, Keir would be gone. He would have escorted her home as promised and then he would be on his way…out of her life.

Keir shuffled outside Anwen's door listening for a response, but when he heard none and sensed no movement from within, he began to worry. He knocked again, and when he received no response, he lifted the latch and entered.

Anwen was seated on the bed where he left her the night before. She was dressed and ready for travel, but he also noticed that the bed had not been slept in and that worried him even more.

"Anwen, are ye all right?" he asked as he knelt before her, taking her hands in his own. Her fingers were cold, her face pale and reflected no emotion. Keir's heart skipped a beat. Had she gone mad from another nightmare?

"Anwen, please, yer scaring me," he pleaded, squeezing her hands, trying to get some response. He was about to call to the others for help when her eyes, unfocused and distant, looked down at him.

"Keir," she whispered, her voice nearly inaudible.

"'Tis me, Anwen," he nodded, giving her hands another squeeze. "Are ye all right?"

Her eyes were like large pools of deep green ocean looking down upon him and then she bowed her head and he could feel the wetness of sudden tears falling upon his hands. He moved onto the bed and pulled her lifeless body into his arms and rocked her, kissing the top of her head.

"Did ye have another nightmare, lass? Why dinna ye call for me?"

Anwen fell against him heavily and her tears became sobs against the fabric of his shirt.

"I didn't have a nightmare," she said, looking up at him mournfully. "I don't need to, for I am living one."

"Och, lass," Keir cooed and pulled her back to his chest to comfort her. "Yer safe. I willna let anyone harm ye."

She pushed away from him and wiped her face in her hands.

"I'm safe now, but who will save me once I am wed?" she asked him, searching for an answer. "Will you be there when my husband is unhappy with me and decides punishment is his only recourse? Will you be there when he demands me to do something I do not wish to do? Will you be there..." she looked away from him, her tears flowing freely once more.

"I ken I canna be with ye at all times, but yer faither will and he willna allow this man to hurt ye, ye ken that."

"My father?" she laughed incredulously. "My father is the one who sold me to the enemy. Think you he will care what this man does to me? Besides, I have yet to meet my husband and he has already managed to hurt me by removing you from my life. He could beat me, I could die a thousand deaths at his hands, but nothing is more agonizing than being without you. Nothing."

Keir ran his hand through his already disheveled hair and stood from the bed. He was at his wits end with this whole situation and stopping himself short of doing something insanely drastic, his hands were tied. He understood her torment, for he was living it himself. It was bad enough this woman he loved was brutally attacked and returned to him, hanging by a shred of her life, but now she was being forced into a life she did not choose or accept and neither of them could change that.

Suddenly, his own life seemed miniscule in contrast. He had spent so much time complaining about his own fate and the indecencies he was made to withstand that he didn't realize how selfish he was acting. Reconsidering his life now, he was deeply ashamed of having been so inconsiderate.

"I ken ye dinna want tae hear this, but perhaps yer marriage tae this man willna be as awful as ye believe it will. Who's tae say he willna be a kind and generous man?" Making that assumption aloud was enough to turn his stomach. The man could be a saint and he'd still want to see him dead.

"Aye, I've been praying for as much," she said with a sniffle. "I pray that like some husbands he treats me as though I am invisible. Only then will I be able to breathe."

Me too, Keir thought to himself. Me too.

Roísíndubh Castle was relatively quiet when they arrived at the gates. As opposed to the MacLochlainn Keep, there were no boisterous greetings or informal recognitions here. The guard merely opened the gate at the acknowledgment of Anwen's arrival and the travel-weary group made their way into the courtyard and dismounted uneventfully.

Anwen turned and looked toward the main hall and took a deep breath. She had only been gone a few weeks but it seemed as though she had been gone a lifetime. Shielding her eyes in the sunshine, she looked up at the aging structure she once called home, how the pitted stone of the façade seemed duller, grayer than she remembered.

Everything changed for her in those few short weeks. Spending her life within these quiet, dark halls all her life made her an academic, but traveling the Scottish countryside and seeing the life of its familial people made her see the world as it truly was… full of color, light and love. Now, coming back to this place, she could not feel more like a prisoner. Once she was married, that feeling would only perpetuate itself.

"Anwen!" Galen's voice was a welcomed one and she turned to sprint toward him, catching him in a great hug. "Welcome home." He grinned, holding her away from him to look her over.

"How have you been?" she asked, smiling up at him happily.

"Och, you know me, always the same," he smirked and then gave her another hug. "But look at you. You've only been gone a short while and you've blossomed like a flower. Look how beautiful you are."

Anwen looked away from him embarrassed and caught the expression on Keir's face as he watched her conversation with Galen. He was smiling warmly, perhaps with pride, and he gave her a nod before going back to unloading the horses.

"Where's my father?" she asked, turning back toward Galen.

"He's in his council room going over preparations with Cedric."

"Cedric?" she asked, unfamiliar with the name.

"Your betrothed..." he offered with a hint of resentment in his voice.

"His name is Cedric?" It seemed odd. The name was so foreign. It sounded strange coming from her own lips.

"Cedric Banyon, to be exact, Duke of Coventry."

"What kind of man is he?" she asked as she took his arm and followed him into the great hall.

"He's English," he rolled his eyes. "High strung, temperamental, vain... English."

"Is he old? Young? Beastly? Please, tell me." She wandered into the expanse of the great hall and took a seat at one of the tables there.

Galen motioned to one of the servants to bring drinks in from the kitchen and then he took a seat opposite her.

"He's relatively young, perhaps eight or nine years older than you. Tall, rather good looking, well-built and deceptively smart."

His description painted an altogether different picture of her husband-to-be than she expected. It pleased her that he was young and attractive, but Galen's comment about him being deceptive caught her attention.

"And how do you find him?" she asked, her eyebrow raised questioningly.

Galen looked over at her with a smirk and nodded his head.

"I don't want to spoil your wedding, Anwen," he said. "My judgment is harshly impaired since he has come to take you from us. I would rather you formed your own opinion of him, lest I tarnish it before you meet."

"I understand," she said with a sigh. He was hiding something from her. She knew, somehow, that he did not like this man very much. If he did, he would have been speaking his praises from the moment she arrived. She could feel that tense knot returning, filling the pit of her stomach with an awful dread.

She saw Keir enter the great hall then, and she motioned for him to join them at the table while at the same time the servant arrived with a pitcher of cider and some empty glasses on a tray.

"You remember Keir?" she motioned to him as he approached and Galen smiled.

"Of course, well met Keir," he offered a handshake as Keir took his seat. "And thank you again for escorting Anwen back to us."

"It was my pleasure, really," he said with a smile and gave Anwen a nudge. "She was hardly any trouble at all."

"Thank you ever so much…" she said with a smirk as she filled a mug for each of them.

"We were just talking about Anwen's betrothed," Galen said as he took up one of the mugs and sipped.

The words fell hard upon Keir, she could tell by the expression he gave and the fact that his whole posture tensed at the mention of him.

"Aye, weel," he mumbled disparagingly, taking a sip of his own cider. "Here's tae the happy couple."

Anwen couldn't look at him. She knew this was more than they were both willing to deal with, more than they could handle in good faith.

"I'm sure you're eager to meet him," Galen said hopefully. "Why don't we go to your father's chambers then, he's there now."

"Yes," Anwen smiled awkwardly as she noted Keir's dissention. "I would like to meet him."

"I have tae go tend tae the baggage," Keir offered brusquely as he stood from the table. "Excuse me."

Anwen watched as he stalked out of the great hall, then she looked up to see Galen eyeing her with a troubled expression.

"Is everything all right?" he asked, taking her hand across the table.

"Aye," she answered a bit despondently. She wanted to share what she was feeling with him, but she couldn't bring herself to do it. It was bad enough she and Keir had to move past this awful moment, she didn't want to drag Galen into it as well.

"Well then, let us go to your father's chamber, shall we?" he smiled, lifting her hand to raise her from her seat. He came around to her side of the table and tucked her hand in his elbow. "Everything will be fine, lass."

"Aye, I hope you are right."

Chapter Twenty - Two

The short walk to her father's chamber was possibly one of the most distressing times of her life. She had a hundred different visions of what her betrothed would look like in her mind, she had even more visions of how horrid married life with him would be. Her thoughts must have been speaking volumes, for Galen stopped outside her father's door and gave her a hug.

"All will be well, lass, all will be well."

As she held her breath, Galen opened the door and allowed her entry, following her inside. Her father was seated across the room near the hearth, talking to the man who was to be her husband.

"Hello Father," she said nervously as her father noted her arrival and stood to greet her.

"Anwen, you've returned," he said drawing her into a stiff hug and then pushed her away from him, hesitant. "I'd like you to meet your betrothed, Cedric Banyon, Duke of Coventry."

His name reverberated in her head so loudly she almost lost her footing and collapsed at his feet.

He immediately stood to face her and she was pleasantly surprised by what she saw.

He was no short, rotund, slovenly beast. He was tall, muscular and mysteriously handsome. His hair, as black as night, was casually brushed back off his shoulders. She noted the surprise in his gray eyes as he looked her over and then he dropped into a deep bow before her.

"It is my utmost pleasure to make your acquaintance, m'lady." His voice was smooth and confident, sending an odd tremor of both intrigue and trepidation through her blood.

"'Tis a pleasure to meet you as well, m'lord," she offered, her words a bit unsure.

"Perhaps you two would like to sit and talk, get to know one another?" her father asked and gestured them toward the sitting area.

Anwen took a seat on the cushioned bench near the fire and Cedric sat across from her. Her father and Galen left them to their conversation, moving to his work area across the room in a vestibule.

"Tell me about yourself, m'lord," Anwen started, trying to keep herself at ease. "Where do you hail from?"

"First and foremost, please, call me Cedric," he said with a warm smile. "I couldn't have my wife treating me like a stranger now, could I?" He chuckled, but his words rang of irony.

Whether it was intended or not, she did not know.

"Of course not, I apologize… Cedric."

"I hail from Coventry, obviously, though I was raised in Northampton," he offered a bit pompously as he picked at the cuff at the end of his sleeve. "I spent quite a lot of my youth in the company of the royals at Windsor, in London, as well."

"That sounds exciting," she said with a genuine smile. "Other than my recent voyage to Scotland I haven't much been away from this keep for the whole of my life."

"Pity, that," he said looking over at her, his gaze expressionless. "You miss out on some of life's greatest pleasures in not traveling."

If only he knew, she thought cheerlessly. Some of her greatest joys, her brightest moments, were found on her sole voyage to Scotland in the arms of another man. A man who lingered nearby, whose arms she so desperately wanted to run to now, but could not.

"Is there anything you wish to ask of me?" she asked.

"Not particularly," he nodded, "Your father has answered all of my questions adequately and I am sure he knows you well enough."

"Aye, I'm sure he does," she looked back over her shoulder and caught her father's eye.

He hesitated, then stood and made his way to where they were seated.

"Now that you've had the chance to speak, I believe we should discuss arrangements," her father said as he took a seat next to her.

"Aye," Cedric said, sitting up in his seat, "I'm needed back at court and cannot be detained very much longer."

"Aye, and I thank you for taking the time that you had to wait for my daughter to arrive." Her father gave her an apologetic look and settled back into his seat. "We've arranged for the priest to hold the ceremony in chapel tomorrow morn. After that you are free to go."

"Free to go?" Anwen balked. "Where are we going?"

"Back to Coventry," Cedric smiled amusedly, "'Tis where my estate is and I have much work awaiting me there."

"England? But my home is here, in Ireland." The tears were immediate and uncontrollable. "Father, you are allowing this?"

"Anwen," her father offered with consolation, "A wife must go where her husband leads and Cedric resides in Coventry. That's where you are to live once you are wed."

"I cannot believe you are doing this to me." She stood from her seat and looked down at him incredulously. "First Scotland and now England? Why not just put me out of my misery now and be done with it?"

Her father stood immediately and grasped her by the arms.

"You will apologize at once to the Duke and you will march right down to your chambers and prepare for your wedding on the morrow, do you hear me?"

Anwen's heart was lying in a shattered heap at her feet. Her father was abandoning her to this stranger and she had no choice but to obey.

"I do beg pardon, m'lord," she curtsied shakily, "I shall be ready for you on the morrow."

"I do look forward to our next meeting," he said, taking her hand and kissing it lightly.

Anwen could do nothing but nod, then dazedly left the room. Once outside her father's chamber doors, she broke into a sob and quickly ran to her chambers.

Her chambers were filled with Cedric's baggage and clothing. The room reeked of his scent, his very essence, and it repulsed her. Distraught, she ran to her bed and threw herself upon it, sobbing. A few moments later, there came a knock at her door.

"Go away, I beg you," she cried, but the door creaked open a crack.

"M'lady? Are you all right?" Máiréad stuck her head in the open doorway.

"Máiréad, oh Máiréad, how happy I am to see you," she said as she sat up weakly. "This is so awful."

Her maid entered the room and closed the door behind her. She was carrying a rather large bundled package, which she placed at the foot of the bed as she came to sit next to her.

"I am pleased to see you as well," the maid said, soothing her mistress, stroking the damp hair from her face.

"Oh Máiréad, what am I to do? I am to marry this Englishman and then he is to take me to England where I must live out the rest of my days."

"It does sound awful," she said with a sigh as she offered her a dry cloth for her face. "But your father has given me leave to attend you at your new home, so that should be of some comfort."

"Aye, it is," she said as she wiped her face. "I can't imagine living with this man, let alone being holed up in some dreadful place in England. Have you had chance to meet him while I was away?"

"Aye," Máiréad said as she bowed her head.

"What is he like, do you know?"

"I couldn't say, m'lady," Máiréad shrugged. "Our meeting was rather brief."

"He is rather handsome," she sniffled hopefully, trying to take her mind off the situation.

"If you like that sort of thing, I suppose he is," Máiréad said insipidly.

"You don't find him attractive?"

"He's handsome enough," she smiled and then stood from the bed, reaching for the package she had brought with her. "He's sent this package up for you, 'tis a wedding gift."

Anwen smiled at that. As much as she wanted to hate the man, she was rather intrigued and he seemed cordial enough. The gift was unexpected and she opened it quickly on her lap. The unfolded paper revealed a beautiful violet gown made of raw silk, its length decorated with crystal beading and a delicate embroidery of gold and silver.

"'Tis beautiful," she said, holding it up in front of her.

"Aye, it is, and you will look radiant wearing it on the morrow." Máiréad said as she trailed her hand along the elegant embroidery.

Anwen's heart sank at her words. On the morrow… she would be marrying this man on the morrow. If she had any nerve at all she would find a way to dispose of herself before then, perhaps swallow poison or find a sharp dagger to plunge into her already broken heart, but she knew she could not do such a thing.

"I'll leave you to your peace now, m'lady. You'll need your rest to prepare for the day ahead." She moved away from the bed and opened the door. "I'll bring you some food later if you wish it."

"That is very kind of you, Máiréad, and I thank you."

"My pleasure," Máiréad smiled and left the room, closing the door soundly behind her.

Anwen had fallen asleep sometime that afternoon, her dreams drifting from the horrific visions of torture and despair to the mollifying feel of Keir's hands on her face and in her hair. She roused with a smile on her lips, but it quickly faded when she glanced down and saw the gown at her feet.

It was beautiful, there was no doubt there, and expensively made, but it did not warm her to her betrothed at all. She could picture his face in her mind, his dark hair and menacing gray eyes, but her mind would always return to Keir.

There was no comparing the two of them. Cedric was handsome in his own right, statuesque and proud, but Keir bore a more regal air. His every movement and gesture was laced with the confidence of his being who he was. What Keir bore naturally, Cedric seemed to have to work to achieve. His fancy clothing and overconfident words did nothing but make him seem more ostentatious, and for no reason.

She stood wearily from the bed and noted a tray of food near the door, bless Máiréad's heart. She retrieved the tray and brought it to her bed, then with a glance back at the door, went to it and bolted it shut. The thought of any visitors, namely Cedric, would have ruined her night completely.

Cedric paced near the window of the small guest chambers angrily. Things could not be going more terribly than he had planned. One simple task, that's all he asked of his men and still they failed him. There would be punishments, he would see to it personally.

A knock came at his door then and William entered solemnly.

"You asked to see me?" he asked from the doorway.

"Come in and take a seat." Cedric clenched his jaw trying to control his rage. He poured himself a mug of ale and took a seat opposite his lieutenant, his face tight with anger. "You said she was dead, Will," Cedric seethed, taking a sip of his ale.

"Aye, I did." William reached for a mug of his own and drank deeply.

"Then why, pray you, did I have a meeting with her in her father's chambers this morn?"

"I... I don't know what to say," he balked, choking on his drink. "She had been badly beaten by the men and I saw her fall into that pit. I swear no man could have lived through that."

"Apparently, she did, she was found by MacLochlainn's men and was coddled back to health at their keep."

"Damn Scots..." William growled into his mug.

"No, damn you," Cedric groused. "I sent you with one simple order and you couldn't even complete it as I commanded. How hard could it be to find her and kill her?"

"I thought we had, and I apologize, but there was no way to know if she had died in that fall and I was not willing to risk the lives of my men to be sure."

"Your men?" Cedric boomed. "My men! And you are one of them. Directly or no, you should have seen to her death or have dealt it to her yourself. Why did you not just kill her while you had the chance?"

William looked away from Cedric and sipped his ale somberly.

"I couldn't," he finally said, looking back at Cedric.

"Why not? You haven't gone soft on me, have you?"

"Aye, perhaps I have," he mumbled. "I couldn't bring myself to the task. If she were an awful person, someone I had some undying need to bring to justice, then I would not have thought twice, but she's actually a lovely girl, Cedric. I don't see why you don't just go through with the marriage and find that out for yourself."

"Marriage? Do you even hear yourself speaking, Will?" Cedric fumed, standing from his seat to begin his pacing again. "Think you I would make a good husband, with all the women that already hold me in such high esteem at court?"

"Perhaps it's time you settle for a wife and act with more propriety, more in keeping with the peerage of your station."

"As if I am the only peer to act thusly," Cedric smirked and took another sip of his ale. "I suppose I have no choice but to marry the wench now. The wedding is on the morrow."

"Then I believe congratulations are in order, my lord," William said, raising his mug to Cedric smugly. "To your new wife."

"And to her quick demise…" Cedric smirked and took a hearty drink, much to William's dismay.

Chapter Twenty - Three

Keir wandered the expanse of the courtyard, pacing its width and breadth more times than he could count. He spent his morning at the list, burning off his aggravation by hacking at the pell with his claymore until there was nothing but a whittled bit of wood left to the freestanding post. He had no stomach for the morning meals, he could barely sleep the night before. Rorik could do nothing to calm or humor him, so he left him alone with his angst.

Now, as he stood in the center of the courtyard and watched as the servants readied for the festivities of the day, he could do nothing but think of her and what he was losing. He hadn't even noticed that Galen had wandered out to greet him until his voice startled him from behind.

"Good morn, Keir," Galen smiled. "Glad to see you enjoying the day."

"I wouldna call it enjoyable," he mumbled as he turned to face him.

"Aye? Are you not glad for the lady Anwen? She is to be wed today."

"Aye, I ken," he nodded, walking away from him. "And nay, I'm no' glad for it."

Galen followed him as he made his way to the great hall.

"You've taken a fancy to the lass, haven't you?" Galen asked, reaching out to stop him.

Keir turned then and let out a strangled sigh.

"Is it that obvious?" he asked as he took a seat on the steps before the door.

"Obvious, no," he chuckled and then his cheerfulness faded. "I could sense a connection between the two of you when you met, there in the stables. I had just hoped that her betrothal would have dissuaded you against growing too attached."

"Betrothed or no', I couldna help but like the lass." He said, bowing his head.

"I know," Galen offered solemnly, putting a hand to Keir's shoulder. "She is a very special lady and I daresay I hate to see her being married off to that man."

"I as well," he nodded, looking back at him. "Could it no' have been stopped somehow?"

"No, I'm afraid not. We've done all we could to withdraw the contract, but Edward will not hear of it. It seems he is set on the match."

"Set on what the match has tae offer, more like," Keir chuckled half-heartedly.

"Aye, I suppose you are right. What's done is done, nothing we can do for it now, I'm afraid."

"Aye," Keir said, gazing out across the courtyard blankly.

"The ceremony is to start shortly," Galen said as he stood and offered Keir an arm up. "Anwen was asleep in her chambers the last I heard. Perhaps you would like to fetch her for me and escort her to the chapel?"

"Nay, I couldna," Keir shook his head. He couldn't even bring himself to see her now.

"Keir, you can't just leave here without offering her a parting word. She'll want to see you, speak to you. Go on, fetch her, spend some time with her before the ceremony."

"I canna," he said angrily. "I canna bear tae see her again, knowing it will be the last time that I…"

"I know, lad," Galen grasped him by the arms to settle him. "Think you I do not agonize over the moment I watch her leave with him? I have known her since she was a babe, much longer than you, and it is all I can do to keep myself from pummeling the bastard for taking her away from us." Galen shook him bodily and gave him a harsh look. "Go to her. Be the man she knows you are and give her that much."

Keir struggled with his indecision and decided he would do as he was asked. If only to see her once more.

What a sight she was… a heavenly creature lying amongst a mound of billowy lilac waves. Her hair was arrayed about her like a red-gold halo setting off her angelic face in a cloud of autumnal hues. She looked so frail, so tiny and delicate lying there, nothing like the woman with whom he had argued and conversed with in the past several days.

He moved closer to the bed and gazed down upon her as if she were lying in state. Her face, though touched with sadness, was peaceful and relaxed. He loathed waking her, bringing her into this reality that was to become her life, but the time had come and his men awaited his departure even as he stood vigil next to her bed as he had done not so long before.

He placed a hand upon her face and smoothed a roughened thumb over her graceful cheek. Her lashes fluttered but she did not rouse from her sleep.

"M'lady," he said softly, "Ye must wake now."

Her lashes fluttered once more and slowly her eyelids opened to reveal the deep green eyes he had grown to love. The instant recognition of his face was apparent as a smile crept onto her lovely lips and she sleepily gazed up at him.

"They are awaiting ye in the chapel," he said blankly. "And the men are waiting for me in the courtyard, I must depart."

"Depart?" she asked, her brows furrowed confusedly. "You're leaving?"

"Aye, we must return tae Argyllshire afore the weather changes."

"Will you not stay for the ceremony?"

Keir bowed his head and turned his face away from her.

"I canna," he said desolately. "I canna bear tae see it, but I will go as far as escorting ye tae the chapel. 'Tis the least I could do and it would be an honor."

She took his hand and swung her legs off the side of the bed and came groggily to her feet. The look on her face reflected his own, fraught with grief and remorse. His heart ached in his chest as he stood there helpless.

"How do I look?" she asked, smoothing out the wrinkles in her gown.

"Like an angel," he said with a sad smile. "Sent down from heaven tae steal the hearts of mortal men."

"You jest," she chuckled weakly, running a hand absently through her unruly locks. "Nay, I wouldna jest about something so beautiful," he said brushing the hair from her face and then he took her into his arms and kissed her deeply.

She fell against him willingly, her knees going limp as his arms closed around her. She wanted to stay there forever, in her chambers, in his arms. She wanted things to remain the way they were, but she knew they could not. She wanted to keep him here with her, but that was impossible as well.

Anwen pulled away from his kiss then, turning her face away from him.

"I cannot do this," she said, putting a hand to her lips. "Please, no more…." She wiped her lips in her fingers to somehow remove the feel of him, but it remained no matter what she did.

"We should get ourselves tae the chapel," he said softly. "Everyone is waiting for ye."

Anwen dislodged herself from his arms, her hand lingering upon his arm until she finally pulled it away with a sigh and turned away from him entirely. She went to the bedstand and took up the thin veil that lay there along with the circlet Galen had made for the occasion. It was a simple bronze band of delicate vines and leaves, dotted with pearls and emeralds, nothing like the formal circlet she had given to Christiona.

She lifted the veil into the air and let it fall down around her like the despair that was already settling there. Placing the circlet atop the veil to secure it, she nodded and let out a shaky breath.

Keir watched silently, taking in the very sight of her. There was nothing more for him to do here. He had to leave before he lost his mind. He went to the door without a word and opened it for her, nodding as she passed by and exited the room, following her in silence down the stairs, down the long, echoing hallways, and through the great hall to the door that led to the chapel. When Anwen reached for the latch, he stopped her hand.

"Anwen," he said as he pulled her hand away from the door, his voice cracking as he fought to keep his emotions at bay, "When ye walk through that door and intae his arms, ken that ye take my heart with ye... I willna give it tae another," he said sadly as he looked deeply into her eyes. "If ye ever need of me, call for me and I will be there. Ye will never be more than a moment from my thoughts. Still, I would have ye happy, even if it canna be in my arms.

For your sake, I hope ye find happiness with this man." speaking those words made his heart clench painfully and his mind raced with anger and disgust. He knew she was on the verge of tears and he needed to be away from her as soon as he could manage it. The parting was more painful than he had imagined it ever would be.

He lifted her veil and stroked her delicate face as he smiled.

"Whenever ye look up at the stars at night, think of the one who loves ye more than life itself," he said and kissed her again, this time with every ounce of love he had for her, down to his soul. Then he released her and turned to leave, offering a whispered "I will love ye til my dying breath," as he headed back through the great hall to the main doors, where he turned and then he was gone.

She could feel him leave as though some mystical bond had been shorn between them. She could feel the absence of him as if he were a severed limb and yet, it was her duty to carry on as if she had lost nothing. For King and country.

She took a deep, shaky breath and cleared her throat of the knot that was gathering there and then took the latch in her hand once more and opened the door to the chapel.

The room was veritably empty. For the wedding of a King's daughter, she would have thought there would have been more of a crowd gathered. Then again, the plans were hastily made and she didn't expect anyone to have been privy to an invitation. Still, she was happy to see the few familiar faces that were there: Galen and Máiréad, and Cook and Mrs. Ferguson from the kitchen. There were other men dressed in formal military attire, which she expected were friends or companions of Cedric's. The look of them in uniform filled her with immediate terror. The sight of them brought her back to that awful night she was abducted and she nearly collapsed at the thought. She clasped onto the back of one sturdy pew to steady herself.

At the front of the chapel, near the small stone altar where the priest stood, were her father and Cedric. Her father seemed distant, his face holding no expression at all as she approached them. In fact, at one point he looked away, his mind seemingly wandering. It was as if he refused to look her in the eye and rightly so. She no longer trusted him and he would find no solace or love in her gaze.

Cedric was more responsive. He gave her an easy smile as she walked toward them and nodded his head to show his appreciation for her gown as he looked her over. His attire was impeccable; all velvets, satins, shine and sparkle, down to his boots and spurs. He looked more like royalty than her own father, who hadn't even changed out of the tunic he had donned the day before.

When she was finally standing beside them, the priest started his sermon and began speaking of unions and alliances. His words began to drone on as he spoke of history and heritage, vows, commitments and honor… and she couldn't help but think of Keir. Here she was at the altar, before her family and God, her betrothed to her right, and she was thinking of another man. She was sure this constituted a new sin in the eyes of the church and wondered off-handedly if this perhaps cursed the marriage.

She cleared her throat and her mind, trying to pay heed to the priest's words.

"I require and charge you both, as you will answer at the dreadful day of judgment when the secrets of all hearts shall be disclosed, that if either of you know any impediment why you may not be lawfully joined together in matrimony, you must now confess it." The priest's words fell like boulders from his lips. She was quite sure he knew exactly what was going on in her mind.

"For be you well assured," he continued in ominous tones, "That so many as are coupled without God's blessing are not joined together by God and so are not considered lawfully bound by this church."

Anwen glanced over at Cedric, who looked more bored than concerned at this point.

She wasn't sure whether she should save her mortal soul and confess her true feelings or keep quiet and face the wrath later.

"Yes, yes…" Cedric finally said to the priest with a wave of his hand, his voice more than a bit agitated. "Continue."

The priest fumbled through his well-worn holy book and cleared his throat once more before addressing the couple.

"Do you, Cedric Gryffud Rhys Banyan, Duke of Coventry, take this woman, Anwen Tamsyn Ní Connor, daughter to the High King, Morgunn of Connacht, as your lawful, wedded wife upon whose blood your swear your troth and sword?"

Cedric shifted a moment, looking down at her quite perplexedly, and then he looked back to the priest to answer.

"Nay!" a voice came from the back of the chapel. "Nay, he doesna!"

Anwen spun on her heel and found Keir marching down the center aisle toward them with his men close behind.

"You shall be hanged for this, MacLochlainn, I swear it!" Cedric seethed as he strode forth to meet him halfway.

"Like ye swear yer sword on the life of yer new wife, even though your previous plans tae have her killed have failed ye?" Keir boomed pushing past Cedric to the altar where Anwen stood. "Ye should be sae lucky tae find yerself in the company of such a fine woman. Ye'd do better justice tae her tae throw yerself off a cliff in her honor."

"What?" Anwen asked breathlessly. "Have me killed? What are you talking about, Keir?"

"This whoreson requested his men hunt ye down like vermin and dispatch ye on sight," he raged, moving her behind him to shield her. "Lucky for ye, his men aren't as treacherous and soulless as he is, and had sense enough tae come forth and warn me of his misdeeds."

"Coventry! How dare you?" Morgunn boomed, striding forth with ill-intent. "I should have known... from the day I met you, I knew you were a worthless bastard. Edward will hear of this, mark you, he will hear of this straight away!"

"Think you Edward had no bloody idea what I was at here?" Cedric chuckled arrogantly. "You Irish are as dim-witted as your Scots counterparts... Edward all but gave his blessing in the carrying out of this deed. I'm sure he was probably quite displeased that he wasn't able to finish her off himself."

His words were met with great fury and Keir met him in two long strides, punching him hard in the face, knocking him to the ground.

"I'm going tae slaughter ye, Banyon," he fumed, standing over him with clenched fists. "And I'm going tae enjoy every moment of it until ye breathe yer last." He bent down and bodily brought Cedric to his feet and knocked him again across the face, sending Cedric sprawling into the surrounding pews.

"William!" Cedric shouted as he searched across the room. "My sword!"

William stepped forward and looking down at Cedric, nodding his head disagreeably. "I don't think so, Coventry," he said as he looked to Keir. "Not this time."

"Will, damn you, get me my sword!" Cedric bellowed as he struggled to get to his feet.

"Get it yourself, I will no longer be a part of this." William said and, spitting at Cedric's feet, then walked away from him to stand behind Keir.

"I'll have you sent down, do you hear me? You'll never be able to show your face in England again!" Cedric yelled, coming again to his feet, wiping the blood from him mouth with the back of his hand.

"You'll do no such thing," William chuckled. "And if I were you, I'd pack up and leave before you find yourself worse off than you already are."

"I should never have trusted you. I should have known you would fall to dissension."

"You talk boldly for one guilty of the same crime you accuse me of." William crossed his arms before him casually.

"It was you!" Anwen's words broke through the shouting of the men as she stepped forward, dragging the layers of gown with her to stand before William. In an instant she slapped him soundly, the rage more than evident in her eyes. "You were the one, that night at the soldier's camp!"

"Aye, m'lady," William offered shamefully, bowing his head. "And had I known that I was in the employ of such a deceitful bastard, I would not have done what I had. I am most humbly ashamed for my actions and beg your forgiveness."

"You left me there to die! You are no better than he is!" she shouted, but Kier grasped her by the arm and pulled her away.

William shook his head regretfully and looked up at Keir.

"I cannot take back the things that were done to her, but I am truly sorry for having been witness to them."

"Only God can forgive you in this and I daresay you will be hard pressed to receive as much kindness from him," he said, taking Anwen's hand and pulling her to his side. "Anwen, get yer things, we're leaving this place."

"Where will you go, MacLochlainn?" Cedric sneered, moving toward them. "I'll find you no matter where you run."

"How will ye find me if you're dead?" Keir growled through his teeth as he stepped forward, meeting him nose to nose.

"You'll never get away with it, you know that. Once Edward has found that you've interrupted our plans, he'll have your head on a pig pole."

"You'll have tae catch me first, ye evil whoreson."

"Well then," Cedric offered haughtily as he straightened his surcoat. "I hope you run faster than your kin."

"And what is that supposed tae mean?"

"Your father and brother are in battle now, are they not, fighting the English?"

"Aye, and God willing, they'll send your King's army back tae London with their tails between their legs."

"They should be so lucky," Cedric guffawed haughtily. "Last word I received, the King's army had express order to single them out and run them through on sight."

Nothing could have been more of a sting to Keir's pride. He had faith that his kin would fight bravely and come away unscathed, but the gravity of the situation left him with a most ominous feeling of dread.

"Ye'd better pray they return unharmed, Coventry," Keir pointed a finger into his chest. "If otherwise, ye will see yer end."

"Not if you see yours first!" Cedric shouted, shoving Keir away, knocking him into the scattered pews with a clatter. In an instant, Cedric dove across the room and took a sword from one of his men's scabbards. Jumping across the row of pews, he was upon Keir with a vengeance.

Keir scrambled to his feet and unsheathed his own, drawing the length of the massive six-foot claymore in one slick motion from its scabbard strapped across his back.

"Rorik, get her out of here!" he shouted and watched as his cousin struggled to pull Anwen out of the room, but Anwen fought her escort and pulled away.

"Keir, no!" she shouted as Cedric's sword came down.

Keir rolled away from the attack, catching the blow with his own sword, the blades clashing in a deafening ring.

Raging, Keir drew back and slashed at Cedric, the sharp bite of his blade catching him across the shoulder, leaving a trail of crimson to grow on his slashed sleeve.

Cedric roared at the strike and lunged forward, his own blade slashing a trail of blood across Keir's thigh. Keir reacted immediately, racing forward with strike after strike of his own.

"Keir, I beg you, stop!" Anwen's voice pleaded and he turned an angry glare on Rorik.

"Rorik, damn you, get her out of here!" he shouted as another lunge came at him and he dodged nimbly to the side, knocking Cedric's sword away from him, slashing him across the arm again.

Rorik lifted Anwen bodily and carried her out of the room as the clashing of their swords rang through the small chapel. Her father and the rest of the men moved back to allow them space, dodging them as they crashed about the room.

The quarrel continued at a heightened pace with Keir and Cedric vying for the upper hand, their swings becoming more aggressive with every step.

"I'm going to enjoy running you through," Cedric barked as he swung at Keir, his blade nicking his face. Keir jumped at him then and knocked him bodily across the pews, Cedric's body crashing in a heap in the aisle.

"Not as much as I'm going tae revel in the joy of sinking my claymore intae yer gullet. I'd aim for yer heart, but it's such a small target," he said through his teeth, taking a swing of his own. His claymore whistled through the air and came down hard, gouging a huge gash across Cedric's leg.

Cedric cried out in pain, roiling in agony at Keir's feet.

Keir caught him up by his collar and hoisted him to his feet, holding the blade of his claymore against his neck.

"It seems I have the advantage," Keir growled, huffing into his face. "Do ye yield?"

"I wouldn't yield to a whoremongering Scot if it meant my life," Cedric spat angrily, and as Keir drew back to finish him off, Cedric pulled a dagger from his boot and stabbed Keir, hard and deep.

Keir reeled, stumbling back against the pews once more, grasping the wound at his side.

His men dashed forward to help him, but he crawled to his knees and waved them off.

"Nay!" he seethed hoarsely, his voice harsh and malevolent. "He's mine."

With a violent roar, Keir came to his feet and in one swift motion, plunged his sword deep into Cedric's chest. Cedric's face registered shock as Keir grasped the hilt and with a boot to his chest, kicked him away and withdrew his blade. A sputter of blood, hot and free-flowing, burst forth from the wound.

Cedric staggered back a few paces, his hands coming to his wound with disbelief as he looked up at Keir incredulously.

"May you rot in hell, MacLochlainn," he gasped, blood spurting from his mouth.

"After ye…" Keir hissed, smashing him in the face with his bloodied hilt.

Cedric was sent sprawling, his limp body coming to rest awkwardly atop one of the toppled pews.

The priest rushed forward then and bent to Cedric momentarily.

"He's dead." His words rang out like the bells of a cathedral through the small room. There were hushed words mumbled around him and Keir turned to find William behind him.

"Good show," William said with a smirk.

"This willna bode well at court," he grumbled, taking a seat on one of the pews. "This willna bode well at all. They'll hang me for sure."

"No worries," William said as he sat next to him. "The men won't say a word, they were at their wits end with the Duke. His death will be a cause for celebration amongst them."

"I pray ye are right," he said, wincing as he put a hand to the bleeding wound at his side.

"We need to get you to a healer," William offered, glancing down as Keir pulled a bloodied hand away from his wound.

"Nay, I'll be fine," he said breathlessly, coming to his feet. "I want tae thank ye for telling me what ye did. I fear if I hadna stepped in, he would have killed her."

"Aye," William nodded. "I'm sure that he would have."

Keir looked about the room, searching the faces surrounding him. "Where's Anwen? Is she all right?"

"Aye," Rorik's deep voice echoed from across the room. "She's right here."

Anwen disengaged from Rorik's grasp and ran to Keir's side. Throwing her arms around his neck, she let out a deep, ragged breath.

"Oh Keir, you're all right, thank God."

"Aye, I'm fine, just a few scratches," he winced and the let out a ragged cough.

Anwen backed away from him and noted the deep gash at his side.

"No you're not, you're hurt," she exclaimed, putting a hand to the wound. "Someone fetch the healer!"

"He's on his way," her father said as he stepped forward. "I want to thank you, Keir, for saving my daughter."

"'Twas the least I could do for her, my lord," he smiled, offering him a handshake graciously.

"Morgunn, if you please," her father smiled. "I can't have my son addressing me so formally."

"Son?" Keir balked.

"Son?" Anwen repeated, looking back at her father.

"Aye, 'tis plain to see you belong together. Who am I to tell you who you should marry." Morgunn chuckled.

"Oh father!" Anwen beamed, rushing into her father's arms. "Do you mean it?"

"Aye," he said with a nod. "That is if Keir requests your hand."

Keir bowed his head and offered a silent prayer of thanks.

"Aye, I do indeed request yer daughter's hand in marriage."

"Well, then, why not do the deed now while we have the priest at hand?"

Anwen squealed with delight and hugged her father once more, kissing him soundly on the cheek.

"If Anwen agrees, I would be most humbled if she would have me," Keir offered, smiling warmly at her.

"Aye, I will have you," she beamed, rushing to his side. "I will have you for the rest of my life."

Chapter Twenty - Four

Their return to the Lachlan lands was a joyous one. Kestrel had offered his newly acquired vessel to give them free passage across the channel, gifting them with the use of it if ever Anwen had the desire to return home. But upon returning to the keep, they found his kin in disarray, the courtyard in a flurry of commotion.

"What is it?" Keir shouted as he dismounted and grasped one of the guard by the arm. "Where is my faither?"

"Dead, my lord," the guard said as he shook his head. "Fallen to an English sword."

"No!" Keir cried aloud, his throat burning, holding back the nausea that hit him full force. "What of Bowdyn, where is he?"

"Dead as well," the guard mumbled, pulling away from him. "He died trying tae save yer faither."

"No! This canna be happening!" He strode angrily and purposefully to the great hall where he found Caedmon, severely wounded, being tended to by the women.

"Grandy! What happened?" Keir fell to his knees beside his grandfather, taking a mug that was handed him, offering him a sip.

"We were outnumbered, lad. Their heavy cavalry treaded upon us unmercifully," he said, sputtering into the mug as the women sewed his wounds. "We were able tae gain ground on them, but they had called in fresh conscriptions and we were already so tired. There was nay escaping them at that point."

"And what of the battle, does it continue still?"

"Nay, it doesna," Caedmon said as he took another drink. "The Bruce arrived with more men and we were able tae quell their advance, though they made it as far north as Galloway."

"Galloway, God's teeth, but they were at Dumfries no' a fortnight ago."

"Aye, weel, it doesna take an army long tae travel when they are supplied with fresh horses and men. MacDougall's forces renewed their strength against us in the north, but The Bruce would have none of it. The pass was filled tae the hills with Campbell's and The Bruce's own army and afore long, they held the pass and MacDougall had tae forfeit. It is said that The Bruce gifted the Campbell's with MacDougall's beloved Dunollie Castle and the heathen MacDougall's ran back across the loch tae hide."

"Aye, then I am glad of our victory," he said, falling back onto his haunches.

"I am mightily sorry about yer faither and brother, Keir, mightily sorry," Caedmon offered, putting a hand to his shoulder.

"Aye, but they fought bravely and died thusly, no warrior could ask otherwise." Keir said, fighting back the tears that welled in his eyes.

"Nay, ye are aright in that," he nodded. "And I suppose ye will be needing tae get to council afore long yerself."

"Me? Why?" Keir asked, his tear stricken face glancing up at his grandfather.

"Yer next in line, lad," his grandfather said matter of factly. "Yer the new Laird."

"I'm what?"

"Aye, ye were the clans second choice after Bowdyn, and so ye are his successor."

"Successor? I'm tae be chief?" he repeated, the sound of it so odd in his ears. "Nay, lad, no' tae be... ye already are, save the ceremony tae swear ye in."

"I..." he stuttered, his mind racing. "I dinna ken what tae say."

"There is nothing tae say, Keir, it just is and I ken ye will do well."

"So many changes, so many..." Keir mumbled, looking back over his shoulder as Anwen entered the hall.

"Anwen, lass, what are ye doin here? I thought ye were tae be married..." Caedmon asked questioningly as Anwen approached.

"Aye, I was," she smiled warmly.

"And where is yer husband then?" Caedmon asked of her, looking behind her for the Englishman she was to marry.

"He's right here," she said as she placed an arm lovingly about Keir's shoulders.

Caedmon balked at her statement.

"Aye?"

"Aye Grandy, we were married at her keep." Keir chuckled as Caedmon looked to one then the other with some surprise.

"And what of the contract with Edward?"

"Let us just say it was incontestably broken."

"Sure enough then? Aye, weel, God bless ye both. Too bad ye couldna had the ceremony here, your Gran would have wanted tae see her favorite grandson finally wed."

Keir smiled as he came to his feet and took Anwen into his arms.

"Weel, we did have a ceremony in Ireland, but we decided no' tae get on with our married lives until we could have a ceremony here as well." He smiled, kissing the top of Anwen's head.

"Aye, we think of this marriage as a two-part process and won't consider ourselves legally married until it is done on your soil as well," she said, smiling up at Keir fondly.

"Weel then," Caedmon said, shoeing away the women hovering about him and getting to his feet shakily, "In light of the shadows that have befallen this clan of late, a wedding will be just the thing tae cheer everyone. I will see tae it that ye be wed proper and quick on the morrow." He clapped Keir on the shoulder and, despite his injury, gingerly made his way to the kitchens with a dance in his step.

"Shadows?" Anwen questioned. "Is something amiss, Keir?"

"Aye," he said, bowing his head to her. "My father and brother, they were killed in battle."

"Oh, Keir," she cried, pulling him into an embrace. "I am so sorry. How dreadful."

"'Tis no' the half of it." He grimaced tearfully.

"Aye?"

"It seems ye are tae marry the clan chief, m'lady."

"The…" she staggered, looking up at him. "What on earth do you mean?"

"It seems I am the successor tae my brother," he smiled with a touch of sorrow in his eyes. "So ye willna be marrying a mere merchant from Scotland after all. Ye'll need tae act with a bit more decorum now that ye are the MacLochlainn Lairdess."

"Aye," she smirked, nudging him playfully. "I suppose I will."

The wedding was a wondrous event. Even on such short notice, the great hall was filled with every allied clan member that could make their way to the keep.

Keir looked resplendent in his formal garb. His broad shoulders clad in a soft, green, velvet surcoat and his muscled thighs bedecked in the most remarkably soft doeskin trews that Anwen had ever seen. A plaid of MacLochlainn tartan was draped across his shoulder, pinned in placed with a large, bejeweled clan brooch. She smiled at him fondly as she entered the room, but as she made her way to the head of the hall dressed in her wedding best, the voices fell away around her. Had the faces of the crowd not been visible, she would have thought she stood alone.

Keir had purchased her gown the day before and had it beaded and worked through with golden threads by the ladies in his clan. The soft silk underdress, in the lightest shade of cream, was embroidered at the hem. Its collar was topped with a cowled hood that draped gracefully over her hair, which Meara had braided delicately into an elegant design, threaded through with golden thread and silk ribbon. Her surcoat, made of the same soft velvet as Keir's, was trimmed with fox fur and intricately inlaid crystals that sparkled majestically.

The priest was an elder from a nearby clan and unlike the wedding she had experience while she stood by Cedric, the words that this priest spoke were of love and honor, not of guilt or accusation.

Anwen wept through the vows, which were blessed, heartfelt words concluding with the traditional blood bond between them. The words Keir spoke to her were so strong and earnest, she could barely speak her reply through her joy.

After the ceremony, they feasted in grand style. Endless platters of food were passed about in royal fashion and drink was flowing freely amongst them. Kin and clan alike greeted them with boisterous cheers and toasts, and they laughed and danced for hours on end. As the merriment continued well into the evening, Rorik stooped to Keir's ear and he let out a hearty laugh.

"What did he say?" Anwen asked of Keir, who sipped wine from a delicate goblet and then rose to his feet.

"I have been charge with a great deed, my wife, a great deed tae be sure."

"Well, as their chieftain it is your duty to handle such matters," she said with a smile. "I will be fine here. Go, do your bidding."

"Aye," he said and offered her his hand. "M'lady."

"What do you need of me?" she asked, coming to her feet.

"I have been charged with taking ye tae bed, tae finish this bonding rite we have started, as tradition would have it be so."

Anwen's eyebrows rose as she followed beside him, stepping off the dais to great applause.

Keir walked her to the edge of the stairway and with a wink to his kin, whisked her into his arms and took to the stairs two and three at a time, trudging down the long corridor until he came to the master's chambers.

He kicked the door open and carried her to the massive oaken bed that had been decorated with garlands of roses and ivy. The fire had already been stoked and there was a tray of food and wine nearby, if they should have need of it.

Anwen lay still as Keir went to bolt the door and returned to her, crawling up onto the bed to sit beside her. She was nervous, as well she should be, but her body was near starved for his attentions. It was obvious by the look on Keir's face that his mind was in the same place.

"Are ye happy, my wife?" he asked, his voice soft and reassuring to her ears.

"Aye," she smiled warmly, reaching up to touch his face. "I daresay I am the happiest woman on these lands. And what of you, my husband, are you happy as well?"

Keir looked down upon her, his eyes sparkling in the firelight. He could do nothing but nod his head as he bowed to her, taking her lips with his own. They were so warm, so deliberate as the kiss deepened and his arms went around her. His hands went to her shoulder, prying away the layers of fabric to reveal her skin beneath and his mouth followed in turn, leaving a trail of heat searing through her as his mouth found her shoulder, his tongue dancing languidly along her collarbone to her cleavage, where he left a hot, wet kiss.

She fumbled with the ties of his shirt as he doffed his surcoat and her hands found the expanse of his chest, his skin hot to the touch, sending shivers of anticipation through her fingers to the depths of her very soul.

"Och lass," he whispered into her ear. "How I've longed for this night. How I've longed tae have ye in my bed."

Anwen could not speak, for the knot that had wedged itself in her throat grew larger at every movement he made.

He quickly removed his shirt and then bent to her lips once more, taking them passionately, hungrily. His fingers moved to the ties of her gown. Slowly and with great care he undid them and with utter delicacy, pushed the fabric off her shoulders. His hands moved over her softly, pushing the fabric down until she was bared to the waist before him.

His eyes drank in the sight of her and, suddenly embarrassed, she brought her hands up to cover herself.

"Nay, lass," he cooed, moving her hands away, kissing her palms with his warm lips. "Ye are a sight tae behold. Modesty has no claim on ye, for ye are the Goddess Creiddylad incarnate."

Anwen could feel the spread of her ever-growing blush as its heat crept down her neck to the flesh that had been exposed. She knew she shouldn't be embarrassed. Keir was her husband now and she had dreamed of this very moment so many times before, but now that she was faced with it, she didn't know where to begin. The more she thought about it, the more embarrassed she became.

Keir moved toward her then and she backed away, moving off the bed in retreat, pulling her bodice up to cover herself. His face spoke of concern, but his lips broke into a smile and he began to chuckle softly.

"There's nay need tae be afraid, lass, I'm no' going tae hurt ye at all."

"I know, Keir, it's just that I've never..."

"Hush now," he whispered as he stood from the bed and placed a finger gently to her lips. "I dinna expect ye tae have any knowledge of this. How could ye?"

"But you're skillful in such things. I fear I shall suffer by comparison to the many ladies that you've..."

"Lass," he stopped her words with a kiss. "Those ladies, few that there were, couldna hold a candle tae yer beauty. Look at ye," he took her hands and lifted them, allowing her bodice to slip back down, her gown now pooling at her feet. "'Tis all I can do tae no' take ye right here, right now."

Anwen bowed her head. She had never stood naked before a man. She had never stood naked before anyone that she could recall, not even her maid.

Keir's eyes seemed to glaze over as his glance grazed every last inch of her with hunger.

"If it'd make ye more comfortable," he started and then, releasing her hands, undid his trews and stepped out of them so that he was now naked as well.

Anwen stood aghast at the sight of him. He was so strong and well-built, but she had absolutely no idea just how well-built he was until he disrobed. His body was miraculous. Every muscle, every curve was as though it had been chiseled by the skilled hands of a craftsman. His skin was smooth and tanned, the firelight touching him gently as it flickered before them.

By the look of him, he was a virile man, and he wasn't at all ashamed to stand proudly before her as her eyes crept over every part of him.

He moved toward her then, his hands so slow and deliberate that she almost didn't notice their touch. When he stepped closer and their bodies came together, she thought she would faint, the feel of him was so implausible, the hot touch of his body melting against her own.

His mouth was on her then, creating a wave of heat that coursed through her so quickly it took her breath. His hands were in her hair, his lips searing every inch of skin they touched as they traveled over her face and down her neck.

"Keir," she sighed, her hands caressing the deep crevice of his back.

"It's all right, love," he whispered against her skin, his tongue tasting her, tantalizing her.

His hands stroked the smoothness of her shoulders, his fingers tracing a passionate trail along her neck and she nearly lost her knees when his hand gently cupped her breast. Her head fell back languorously at the sensation. When he bent and took one taut nipple in his mouth, her knees did buckle and he caught her up and placed her gently on the bed, his mouth never leaving her.

"Och, lass, yer like honey," he whispered gruffly, his tongue circling her there slowly. "Yer skin is so sweet, so soft…" His other hand cupped her breast again and he suckled intensely and she began to squirm on the bed beneath him. His teeth grazed the sensitive skin there and she cried out in pleasure, grasping his hair, entangling her fingers in its silkiness.

His kisses roamed then, traveling over her body like a lost explorer searching for a home and she could do nothing but moan against the aching need that was growing deep inside her.

She clutched at him, the feel of his flesh scorching her body. She could feel his passions rising, the hardness of him pressing against her thigh. She wanted to touch him, every part of him. She wanted to get so close that she crawled into his skin.

"Oh Keir," she moaned softly as the feel of his mouth on her skin sent torrents of fire through her. "I love you, so so much."

"And I ye, love," he whispered, "How I have ached for this moment. I would die for yer love."

"Nay," she said, shocked at his words. "Never say that, for I could not bear to live without you."

"I will always be with ye, love," he said, moving to kiss her lips. "No matter where I am, I will be with ye. I carry yer blood in my veins and ye will live forever in my heart."

"A warrior's heart you have, my Keir. So brave and passionate. How strongly it beats within your chest." She placed a hand to his heart and splayed her fingers there, feeling the heat of him.

He looked down on her then and took her lips as though he had never kissed her before. His kisses were hungry, ravenous, searching.

She returned the kisses in turn, her tongue hesitant, but as he reacted to its touch, the kiss deepened. Her hands clutched at him, as did his and he rolled and pulled her atop him. His hands caressed her buttocks, smoothed over the skin of her back, grasping at her long hair as it trailed like an autumn veil to skim his fingers.

"Och, lass…" Keir groaned. "I must have ye."

He sat up then, facing her, and laid her back against the foot of the bed. His hand slid across her belly leaving a trail of tormenting heat where they moved.

She was senseless with desire now and she wanted him more than she had wanted anything in her life. But the thought of the act itself terrified her and she tensed as he leaned forward and took her lips in a demanding kiss.

His mouth devoured hers and his hands roamed her body, his fingertips finding the responsive pink buds that longed for his touch. Then his mouth traveled down the length of her neck and when he took one swollen peak into his mouth once more, she cried out and clasped him by the hair, unable to move against the explosion of pleasure she felt. The slow boiling current that spread through her belly was now flickering in the most intimate of places.

His lips and tongue teased each taut, rosy peak until she was writhing beneath him, undone by this overwhelming sensation. His tongue made a wet path down her ribs to the trembling flesh of her stomach, his hands searching to grasp the soft swell of her hips. When she felt his hot, erratic breath ripple through the hair at the cleft of her thighs, she backed away from him suddenly.

"'Tis all right," he cooed, stroking her leg lightly. "I'm no' going tae hurt ye."

"I know," she offered, sitting up to kiss his face, his eyes. She took his mouth eagerly and twined her fingers in his hair, pulling him down on top of her. "I am yours. I will always be yours."

327

When he bent to taste the soft skin of her breasts once more, she arched toward him, offering herself to him completely and without the fear she had felt before. She was losing her senses, her nipple hardening against his tongue as he flicked at it teasingly.

Her hands groped at the corded muscles in his back, her fingers digging into his skin as she pulled him closer. When her hand grasped at the tight, clenched muscles of his buttocks, he let out a sound so primitive she thought the entire keep would hear him.

His hands began an arousing exploration of her body, caressing every curve. He kissed her neck, her breasts, her arms, her belly, and when his searching hands brushed against the downy curls below, she felt a shudder wash through her and she trembled against him. She could feel her arousal there, moist and hot, and he slowly urged her thighs apart with a nudge of his knee. She hesitated for a moment, looking up at him, searching his eyes for assurance, but when he kissed her again, gently teasing her lips, she opened to him and entwined her leg around his in a move of such affection that he nearly lost control.

"Slowly lass," he said in a gruff, low voice against her lips.

His hand moved gently up the length of her thigh and he fanned his fingers through the curly mass of hair at the cleft of her legs. She moved beneath him, raising her hips against him.

"I feel like I'm going to explode," she whispered against his ear as she kissed and nibbled at him there.

"No' the now, lass," he whispered as he licked at her nipple, flicking it with his tongue. "Savor it, let yerself float on the feeling."

Anwen closed her eyes and the sensation that washed over her was like none other that she had ever experienced before in her life. It was as if she stood beneath a waterfall of icy water washing over her naked body, yet she stood in the coals of a slow burning fire that leisurely flickered up her legs, pooling like hot lava in the core of her body.

He continued to tease her nipples with his tongue, bringing them to painfully taut peaks as he nibbled and bit at them while his hands roved her body hungrily, kneading her flesh into a mass of tingling nerves. He caressed the soft skin of her thighs, ever so slowly working his way back to the patch of curls above the folds of soft moistness that ached for his touch. When he finally eased his hand lower she shuddered and bit into his shoulder.

"Are ye sure ye're ready for this lass?" he asked and she nodded, the fear and anticipation creeping back into her veins.

"Aye," she whispered. "I want to be part of you."

Keir smiled warmly and kissed her.

"All right, I'll move slow as tae no' hurt ye."

"I understand," she said softly and then he lowered himself to lie atop her.

He took her lips and kissed her gently, stroking her face tenderly.

"I love ye, Anwen," he said and biting his lip, he slowly worked himself into her tight, warm world.

"Oh, Dear Christ…" he moaned aloud, squeezing his eyes shut.

She gasped then, clutching at him, digging her fingers into his back, and then with a deep breath, he pushed on and in a moment of hesitation, sunk himself into her.

She gave a low whimper and a tear came to her eye.

"I know it hurts ye lass, I'm sorry," he said as he slowly withdrew, watching her face.

"No, please don't stop," she said, grasping him by the buttocks to cease his withdrawal. "I'm not crying for the pain, I'm crying for the joy, for the love that I feel for you at this moment."

"It doesna pain ye?"

"No," she sighed against him. "There is only a delicious warm feeling spreading through my stomach."

He smiled then, withdrew, then slid in once more, this time more deeply, nearly to the hilt. She was heaven, the warm walls of her clenching and squeezing him mercilessly.

She gasped again, but then groaned and her hips started to move in time with him.

He withdrew once more, this time more quickly and he thrust into her more deeply, each time getting closer and closer to burying the complete length of himself into her warm depths. He leaned up now and bent to take her hard, rosy nipple into his mouth.

She moaned and clenched against him, her breath quickening with her heartbeat. Finally, he buried himself full deep, filling her with sublime and utter ecstasy. She flinched then and cried out. The mere sensation more than she thought she could bear.

"Keir…" she moaned his name, throwing her head back.

"Och, lass," he groaned as he thrust harder and more swiftly into her, his face fraught with concentration.

It was more than either could handle and as they ground against one another passionately, his release came to him in one flaming explosion, one last thrust throwing her into a frenzy of release herself.

"Ye are now indelibly and honorably bound tae my very soul… my wife," he whispered as he kissed her tenderly.

"And I am forever yours," she offered breathlessly.

As their heartbeats slowed and their panting quieted to steady breaths, he rolled away from her and they lay spent and lasciviously drunken with pleasure. She curled up into the comforting safety of his arms, laying her head atop his chest.

He stroked her hair, sending shivers through her still.

"How I have longed for that moment," he sighed, his fingers tangling in her hair.

"And I as well," she said softly, her fingers smoothing themselves over the skin of his chest.

"From the moment I laid eyes on ye, I knew I had tae have ye tae myself."

"And now I am yours," she sighed, looking up at him lovingly.

"Aye, ye are, as I am yours with all my heart and soul."

They fell into a deep sleep then, safe and contented in one another's arms, and for the first time since her awful abduction, Anwen passed through the night without nightmares.

She dreamed of Keir and their life together, of beautiful nights and healthy children. She dreamed of travel to distant lands, with her husband at her side, and of lazy days in their bed, whiling away the hours, basking in the passion she felt for him.

And for the first time in her life, she dreamed of her father holding her children... and she smiled.

About the Author

Bestselling historical author, Victoria Oliveri, is a lifelong history buff and reenactor, whose travels abroad have added to her wealth of knowledge and her love of all things historical. Touring and researching the castles of England, Scotland and Ireland have instilled in her the love of castle life and all that their antiquity holds. The majestic stone halls and spiraling staircases she has tread have only added to the myriad ideas swimming in her story-filled mind.

Visit her website: VictoriaOliveri.com for information on other novels available and upcoming works and events available to you, her beloved readers.

Mòran Taing